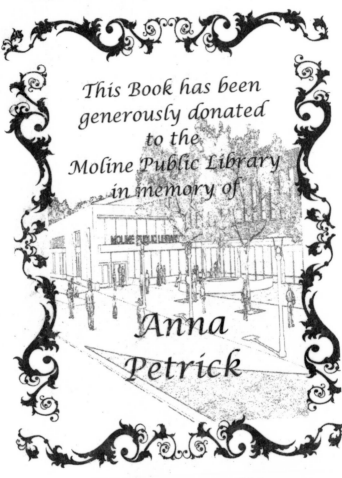

This Book has been
generously donated
to the
Moline Public Library
in memory of

Anna Petrick

TOO HOT TO HANDEL

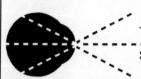

This Large Print Book carries the
Seal of Approval of N.A.V.H.

ANOTHER JOHN PICKETT MYSTERY

TOO HOT TO HANDEL

SHERI COBB SOUTH

THORNDIKE PRESS

A part of Gale, Cengage Learning

GALE
CENGAGE Learning·

Farmington Hills, Mich • San Francisco • New York • Waterville, Maine
Meriden, Conn • Mason, Ohio • Chicago

GALE
CENGAGE Learning

LIBRARY OF CONGRESS CATALOGING-IN-PUBLICATION DATA

Names: South, Sheri Cobb, author.
Title: Too hot to Handel : another John Pickett mystery / by Sheri Cobb South.
Description: Large print edition. | Waterville, Maine : Thorndike Press, a part of Gale, Cengage Learning, 2017. | Series: Thorndike Press large print clean reads
Identifiers: LCCN 2016041440| ISBN 9781410496027 (hardcover) | ISBN 1410496023 (hardcover)
Subjects: LCSH: Police—England—London—Fiction. | Aristocracy (Social class)—Fiction. | Jewelry theft—Fiction. | Large type books. | BISAC: FICTION / Mystery & Detective / General. | GSAFD: Mystery fiction. | Regency fiction.
Classification: LCC PS3569.O755 T66 2017 | DDC 813/.54—dc23
LC record available at https://lccn.loc.gov/2016041440

Published in 2017 by arrangement with Sheri Cobb South

Printed in Mexico
1 2 3 4 5 6 7 21 20 19 18 17

To Kathy and the gang at Thompson Valley Starbucks in Loveland, Colorado, who kept me supplied with mocha frappuccinos (nonfat, with whip) during the writing of this and other books.

CHAPTER 1

WHICH FINDS TROUBLE BREWING AT THE THEATRE ROYAL IN DRURY LANE

As an evening of amusement it was a disappointment on all fronts, reflected Julia, Lady Fieldhurst, widow of the sixth Viscount Fieldhurst. For one thing, the theatre offerings were of necessity sober during this Lenten season of 1809 — although as George, seventh Viscount Fieldhurst and cousin of her late husband, pointed out (several times), it was the very sobriety of Milton's *Samson Agonistes* that made the Theatre Royal in Drury Lane an acceptable diversion for a woman still in mourning for her husband. Quite aside from Samson's tragic fate being played out on the stage below, there was also the matter of Julia's present company: In addition to the current Lord Fieldhurst, the party included her mother-in-law, the Dowager Viscountess. Neither of these two would have been her choice for companionship, but as her dearest friend, Lady Dunnington, had recently reconciled with her long-estranged husband and was now wintering with him on the Dunnington estate in Sussex, Julia's options were limited. Heartily sick of her own company, she had accepted George's invitation with gratitude, if not eagerness.

If she were honest with herself, there was another reason for her disappointment in the evening's entertainment, one that had little to do with her present company, and still less with the actors onstage. In between acts, she found herself scanning the pit below for the familiar figure of a tall young man with curling brown hair worn unfashionably long and tied back in an outmoded queue. She had seen no sign of him — which, she told herself sternly, was probably a good thing. The last time she had spotted him in the pit, she'd had him summoned to her box — an impulsive action which had so scandalized Lord Fieldhurst and the dowager that they had exiled her to Scotland for her sins. As an act of penance, it hardly had the desired result: Through a series of circumstances she could only ascribe to the workings of a mischievous Providence, she had found herself joined in a Scottish irregular marriage to the very young man for whom she now searched the pit.

What she needed, she decided, was a

murder. Samson and his fair betrayer forgotten, she trained her opera glasses on the boxes across the theatre, scanning their occupants to decide whom among her various acquaintances she could best afford to spare. She was still engaged in this rather bloodthirsty pastime when the final curtain fell. The orchestra struck up the overture once more, and the Dowager Lady Fieldhurst awakened with a snort.

"Well, that's that," declared Lord Fieldhurst as he stood up and stretched. "If you're ready, Aunt Fieldhurst, Cousin Julia, we'll go."

"Yes, George."

Julia made no effort to comply, however, for at that moment she caught a glimpse of a man sitting on one of the benches below, a rather tall man with brown hair tied back at the nape of his neck. To be sure, his hair was darker and not so curly as she recalled, but the mind could play tricks on one, could it not? *Look up,* she thought urgently, as if she could somehow communicate with him through sheer force of will. *Look up.*

"Cousin Julia?" repeated George.

As if in answer to her silent plea, the man in the pit chose that moment to look up, revealing an unfamiliar face fully a decade older than the one she had hoped to see.

Yes, the mind could indeed play tricks. Heaving a sigh, she tucked her opera glasses into her reticule and rose from her chair with the air of one abandoning a forlorn hope.

She allowed George to lead her by the elbow while he offered his other arm to her mother-in-law, and the threesome exited the box and joined the throng of fashionables descending the stairs to the main floor. Here they were obliged to wait while cloaks were fetched and carriages summoned. Lord Fieldhurst placed the dowager's evening cloak about her shoulders, but as he turned to Julia to perform this same office, she became aware of a commotion near the door. She moved toward the sound, scarcely noticing as the cloak slipped from her shoulders and landed on the floor in a pool of black velvet.

"They are gone, I tell you," insisted an elegantly dressed woman of advanced years, pressing gnarled fingers to her bare throat. "They have been stolen!"

"There, there, your ladyship," the theatre's majordomo said soothingly. "Perhaps they were merely misplaced. A faulty catch, perhaps —"

"There is nothing 'faulty' about the Oversley emeralds," she informed him frostily.

"No, no, of course not," he amended hastily. "Still, I have sent a servant to look in your box, just in case —"

"What is the matter, Lady Oversley?" Julia interrupted.

"The Oversley emeralds are missing, and this fool insists the fault is mine!" said the older woman indignantly, waving one contemptuous hand at the offending party.

"I'm sure I never said —" the majordomo protested, then brightened as he saw the footman returning. "Ah, here he comes now! Did you find them, Edward?"

Edward shook his head. "No sign of them in her ladyship's box, sir."

"No, for I was wearing them when I exited the box," put in Lady Oversley. "I tell you, they were stolen! And that is not the first time it has happened here, is it? It was only two weeks ago, was it not, that the Duchess of Mallen's rubies disappeared from this very theatre?"

"Sadly true, my lady," conceded the majordomo, "but I assure you, we are doing all we can —"

"Which doesn't appear to be nearly enough," Lady Oversley pointed out.

"Maybe you should send to Bow Street," Lady Fieldhurst suggested with perhaps undue eagerness.

"Engage a Runner?" Lady Oversley scowled at the very idea. "One hates to bring outsiders into one's private affairs. The scandal, you know." She shook her head in disapproval, and her earrings — apparently part of the same set as the missing necklace — flashed green fire.

"But you do want the emeralds back, do you not?" insisted Julia. "If I remember correctly, Her Grace's rubies were recovered by the Bow Street force."

"That is true," Lady Oversley admitted, clearly wavering. "Well, I —"

"Cousin Julia, come away at once!" George, Lord Fieldhurst, pushed his way through the crowd that had begun to gather about the distressed Lady Oversley. "Our carriage is waiting, and your mother-in-law is growing impatient."

"In a minute, George." She turned back to the dowager marchioness. "If you want to have a message sent to Bow Street, my lady, I would be happy to wait with you until the Runner arrives. I have had dealings with them before, you know."

"Yes, for there was that unpleasant business with your husband, was there not, and a young man who was able to clear you of any wrongdoing?" Lady Oversley regarded her steadily for a long moment, then nodded. "Very well, Lady Fieldhurst. I shall take you up on the offer."

Julia was hardly aware of what followed, although she supposed the majordomo must have dispatched Edward or some other servant with a message to Bow Street. Nor was she more than vaguely conscious of George's grumbling or Mother Fieldhurst's scowling disapproval. All she could think was that she was about to see *him* again, the Bow Street Runner who had proven her innocence in her husband's murder, and who had played an increasingly important rôle in her life in the months since. And to whom she was, at least so far as the law was concerned, legally wed. She had not seen him in three long months, but she would never forget his last words to her. *I am in love with you . . . I know there is no hope for me . . . I will not see you again . . .* His voice floated at the edges of her consciousness during the day, and haunted her dreams at night. Of her own sentiments, she was not certain; she shied away from examining too closely feelings for which there appeared to be no outlet. After all, what future could there possibly be for a viscountess and a Bow Street Runner, no matter how irresistible the attraction between them?

She could hardly speak of these things to

Lady Oversley, however, so she restricted herself to describing for the dowager marchioness Mr. Pickett's competence, intelligence, and discretion. In spite of these reassurances — or perhaps because of them — Lady Oversley (as she later confided to friends) confessed herself taken aback when, some twenty minutes later, Edward announced the arrival of the Runner from Bow Street. The elder of the two ladies turned to thank the younger for staying with her, and found Lady Fieldhurst watching the door with an expression of such joyful anticipation that it could only be described as, well, *bridal.*

In the next instant a stranger entered the room, a man in his mid-thirties with straw-colored hair, a prominent nose, and rather cold blue eyes. This individual approached Lady Oversley and executed a deep bow that seemed somehow more insolent than respectful.

"Lady Oversley? William Foote of the Bow Street Public Office, at your service."

"Mr. Foote." The dowager marchioness inclined her head regally. "It was good of you to come so promptly. I fear a rather valuable set of emeralds has been stolen."

Her radiance abruptly extinguished, Julia could only stare dumbly at this stranger who should have been John Pickett. At last she became aware of George tugging at her arm.

"Come along, Cousin Julia," he said impatiently. "There is nothing more for you to do here."

Numb with disappointment, she nodded wordlessly and allowed him to lead her away.

"I hope you are happy, for you made quite a scene in there," he scolded, once they were settled in the carriage and headed westward toward the fashionable district of Mayfair. "Really, Julia, how can you expect Society to forget about the scandal of Cousin Frederick's death when you persist in reminding everyone of your friendship with that Bow Street fellow? A friendship, I might add, of which your late husband would no doubt have heartily disapproved."

Julia was scarcely conscious of his harangue, for she was hearing quite another voice. *I will not see you again . . . I am in love with you . . . I will not see you again . . .* It appeared he had meant it. What sort of man declared his love for a woman and then walked out of her life forever? Her brain had scarcely formed the question when the answer presented itself: a man who believed himself unworthy of her. No, she amended, a man who *knew* himself unworthy, according to every standard of the world in which they both lived.

"The evening post, my lady."

She blinked at the sight of her butler offering a silver tray bearing a couple of letters; she could not recall taking her leave of George and Mother Fieldhurst, let alone descending the carriage and entering her own domicile, so lost was she in her own misery.

She summoned a feeble smile. "Thank you, Rogers."

She took the two letters and, recognizing Lady Dunnington's spidery script on one, tore it open eagerly. The crossed lines were full of "Dunnington this" and "Dunnington that," but even the knowledge of her friend's newfound happiness was bittersweet, since it was Mr. Pickett who was indirectly responsible for their reconciliation.

The handwriting on the front of the other letter was unfamiliar. She broke the seal and spread the single sheet. The missive proved to be from Walter Crumpton, Esquire, of Crumpton and Crumpton, Lincoln's Inn Fields, solicitors to the Fieldhurst family for generations. He was (he wrote) happy to inform her that the annulment of her marriage to Mr. John Pickett would come before the Ecclesiastical Court on Wednesday, the

16

fifteenth of March, at which time she might put this unpleasant chapter of her life behind her. It was, he reminded her, unnecessary for her to appear personally before the court. Furthermore, he had taken the liberty of informing Mr. Pickett of the court date by the same evening's post, so she need have no further contact with that young man at all.

"Bad news, my lady?" asked Rogers solicitously, upon hearing his mistress make a small whimpering sound.

"Oh, no!" she said a bit too brightly. "Very good news indeed! Just — just unexpected."

Of course it was good news, she reminded herself firmly. It was the news she had been waiting for since November, when she'd first learned that they had accidentally contracted an irregular Scottish marriage. On the fifteenth of March, in only three weeks' time, John Pickett would be as completely erased from her life as if he had never entered it. There was no reason, no reason at all, for her to feel as if the ground were suddenly crumbling beneath her feet, and still less for the solicitor's words to blur on the paper, for all the world as if her eyes were filling with tears.

Chapter 2

IN WHICH MR. COLQUHOUN
HATCHES A SCHEME

Mr. Patrick Colquhoun, magistrate, surveyed from beneath beetling white brows the group of men gathered in the Bow Street Public Office. All six of the Bow Street Runners were there, as well as most of the more numerous but less prestigious foot patrol. He had summoned them himself for this meeting after learning late the previous night of the newest development in the most recent crime wave to strike his adopted city.

"I daresay most of you have heard by now that it happened again last night," he said sternly. "The Dowager Marchioness of Oversley lost a valuable emerald necklace at the Theatre Royal in Drury Lane."

A tall young man, his curly brown hair tied at the nape of his neck with a narrow black ribbon, looked up from the notes he was taking. " 'Lost,' sir?"

Mr. Colquhoun acknowledged the young

Runner with a nod. "So says the theatre's majordomo. Well, he would, wouldn't he? Can't blame the man for not wanting to admit his theatre has become a favorite haunt of jewel thieves. We, however, need have no such scruples. Like Lady Oversley, I believe it was a case of theft, and am treating it as such." He pounded his desk with one fist. "It will not do, men! This is the second case in as many weeks, and the fourth since Christmas."

"But all the jewels that have been stolen up to now have been recovered, have they not?" pointed out another Runner, this one considerably older than the first.

"They have indeed, but that is hardly the point. I am fed to the back teeth with paying out finders' fees — although I realize you have profited handsomely by them, Mr. Foote," he added, to a smattering of envious chuckles.

"I can't understand how this thief is snatching the jewels right off the ladies' necks," marveled Mr. Maxwell, a new Runner recently invalided out of His Majesty's First Foot Guards.

"It's not that difficult, really," put in the young Runner with the queue. "All it takes is a momentary distraction."

"You should know," Mr. Foote said with a smirk.

The younger man stiffened. "Yes, I should."

"And I, for one, am glad to have the benefit of Mr. Pickett's unique perspective," Mr. Colquhoun said, scowling at the senior Runner. "But as I was saying, I believe it is time we put a stop to the thefts once and for all."

"But how, sir?" asked Mr. Pickett, his brow creased in a thoughtful frown.

"We are going to set a trap," the magistrate announced. "On Friday there is to be a special performance of Handel's oratorio *Esther.* Several of the royals will be present, and among the guests in their box will be the Russian Princess Olga Fyodorovna. She is the proud possessor of a set of diamonds reputed to be the size of birds' eggs — an irresistible target for any jewel thief, as I am sure you will agree."

"Why not send Mr. Pickett to guard her?" suggested Mr. Foote with a grin. "He has a well-known partiality for women above his station."

A good deal of ribald laughter greeted this recommendation, and Pickett, flushing, slid lower in his chair.

"As the Princess Olga has almost thrice

Mr. Pickett's years in her dish, Her Royal Highness is a good deal nearer your age than his," answered Mr. Colquhoun, frowning. "No, all jesting aside, this is a task that will require the cooperation of the entire force. You will all be positioned at different points about the theatre. The Princess Olga and her party will be under observation at all times and from every angle. If anyone makes an attempt to steal her diamonds, he will not get far."

"And what of the princess herself?" asked Mr. Pickett. "Surely it can't be right to put her in danger, even to apprehend a thief."

One member of the foot patrol leaned over to whisper something in the ear of one of his fellows, and both men snickered. Pickett sighed. He did not know exactly what had been said, but he could hazard a guess. At such times as this, it was tempting to inform his colleagues that he was actually married to the Viscountess Fieldhurst, just for the satisfaction of seeing their jaws hit the floor. But no, it would only make the annulment three weeks hence that much more painful. The fewer people who knew of his irregular marriage to her ladyship, the better it would be in the end.

"There will be no danger to the princess, Mr. Pickett," the magistrate assured him.

"In fact, the lady wearing the diamonds will not be Princess Olga at all, but one of her ladies in waiting. The princess will be there, but among the other attendants. She and her lady in waiting will change places for the evening."

"And — forgive me, sir, but are you sure the princess will agree to this?"

"Agree to it? It was her idea! Quite delighted with her own ingenuity, is Her Royal Highness. Of course, I need not point out that she is placing a great deal of trust in the lot of you — and that I expect her confidence will not be misplaced."

A murmur of agreement answered this thinly veiled threat.

"Now," continued Mr. Colquhoun, "I have tickets for each of you for Friday night's performance. Members of the foot patrol, you will not wear your red waistcoats on this occasion, but plain clothes, so as not to call attention to your presence. Mr. Dixon, you will be in the pit, stationed as near to the exit as you can contrive. I'm afraid you will not have an uninterrupted view of the royal box, but more importantly, you will be the last line of defense should our jewel thief succeed and attempt to escape the theatre. Mr. Marshall, you will be seated in the gallery, directly beneath the royal box. Should the Princess Olga have need of you, she will thump the floor of her box three times with her cane. Mr. Pickett, you will be in the third tier of boxes, directly opposite that occupied by the royals. You should have an excellent view of the princess, or rather, her surrogate. Mr. Griffin —"

One by one, each member of the Bow Street force received his instructions for the evening, along with a theatre ticket.

"What, no ticket for me?" asked Pickett's tormentor when the last ticket had been handed out and the last assignment made.

Mr. Colquhoun shook his head. "No, Mr. Foote. Since you were the one to answer Lady Oversley's summons last night, you might well be recognized by our quarry. You will be left in charge here — after all, someone must see that the rest of London remains on the straight and narrow. I hope for your sake it is a quiet night, for I can't spare many men to help you."

"I'm sure I'll manage, sir," said the senior Runner, although his sullen expression gave the magistrate to understand he was not best pleased with his assignment.

"Good. Now, if there are no further questions, you may consider yourselves dismissed," Mr. Colquhoun said to the group at large. "Not you, Mr. Pickett. I'd like a word with you, if you please."

Pickett hung back until the others had dispersed, racking his brain to recall if he had done anything to warrant the magistrate's displeasure. There was, of course, the ongoing conflict with Mr. Foote, but surely Mr. Colquhoun could see that he did nothing to provoke the man. There was, too, his connection with Lady Fieldhurst, of which Mr. Colquhoun heartily disapproved, but that, he reflected bleakly, would soon be a thing of the past. "Yes, sir?" he asked when they could be assured of relative privacy.

"You may have noticed, Mr. Pickett, that while most of your fellows will be stationed amongst the hoi polloi, you will be occupying a box. As the success of this operation depends upon each of you being as inconspicuous as possible, it is imperative that you look as if you belong there."

Pickett nodded. "I shall brush my black coat this evening, sir," he promised.

This plan, however, found no favor with the magistrate. "I've seen your black coat, Mr. Pickett, and while it may serve very well for court appearances at the Old Bailey, it won't do if you are to present the appearance of a gentleman."

"It's the best I have," protested Pickett.

"I don't doubt it. Fortunately, I have had a word with my tailor, and he has agreed to let you hire a suit of clothing for the night."

Pickett rapidly performed a few mental calculations involving the amount of money in his pocket and the number of days until he would next receive his wages. "Begging your pardon, sir, but how much — ?"

Mr. Colquhoun held up a hand to forestall him. "The cost will be paid out of the department, so it need not concern you. You will need to stop by Mr. Meyer's shop in Conduit Street this afternoon so that your measurements may be taken. The clothing will be delivered to my residence. You may join me for dinner Friday evening before the performance."

"Thank you, sir," Pickett said, rather taken aback by this unprecedented invitation. "I should be honored."

"Nonsense! My Janet is away visiting relatives, so I'm batching it for the next few weeks. No reason why you shouldn't take your mutton with me. After dinner you may don your borrowed plumes. My valet will assist you."

"That is kind of you, sir, but I've dressed myself without assistance all these years —"

"I'm aware of that, Mr. Pickett, but since the idea is to have you look as much like a gentleman as possible, I think it best if I oversee the transformation."

The twinkle in his eye robbed the words of any insult, and Pickett grinned back at him. "Very well, sir, I shall try not to disappoint."

The magistrate's expression grew serious. "There is one other thing —"

"Yes, sir? What is it?"

"Since it would be most unusual for a man to attend the theatre alone, your charade might be more convincing if a female were to accompany you. Not just any female, mind you, but a lady — one who would not look out of place in the box herself, and who could, if necessary, prevent you from committing any glaring breach of etiquette. Would you happen to know of such a female?"

Pickett listened to this speech with dawning incredulity and no small sense of elation. "Sir? You — you're instructing me to invite Lady Fieldhurst to accompany me?"

"I'm doing nothing of the kind! In fact, if you know of another female who would fit the bill, I would urge you to choose her instead. But as I suspect that is not the case, I suppose we shall have to make do with her ladyship."

"But sir, you agreed not to send me out

on cases where I might be obliged to see Lady Fieldhurst again," Pickett reminded him.

"If I remember correctly, I agreed — and that only reluctantly — not to send you to Mayfair," pointed out the magistrate. "The last time I consulted a map, Drury Lane was not in Mayfair."

"No, sir, but — but *why,* if I may ask?"

Mr. Colquhoun did not pretend to misunderstand him. "To be perfectly honest, Mr. Pickett, I have no idea," he grumbled. "I daresay I'm growing soft in my old age. Or perhaps I'm merely tired of seeing you moping about the place."

"Not for much longer, sir," Pickett assured him somewhat bleakly. "I had a letter from her ladyship's solicitor by yesterday's post. The annulment will come before the ecclesiastical court in three weeks."

"Hmm. I wonder if that will make things better, or worse? Ah well, if you're going to ask her ladyship to accompany you, I suggest you do so without further delay. Women like to have time to prepare for these things, you know — assuming, of course, that she accepts your invitation."

"Yes, sir, thank you, sir! I shall do so at once," promised Pickett, all but falling over his feet in his eagerness to carry out this task.

Not until he had left the magistrate did he recall that there was bound to be a certain awkwardness in approaching Lady Field-hurst. He had not spoken to her in three long months, but he had not forgotten the circumstances under which they'd parted, any more than he had forgotten his last words to her. *I am in love with you . . . I know there is no hope for me . . .* He never would have said such a thing had he not been quite certain that he would not see her again. He reminded himself that at least she had not laughed in his face, but this was small comfort; she was too well bred — and, more importantly, too kind — to do such a thing, whatever her own feelings in the matter. He consoled himself with the knowledge that at least he had not committed the crowning folly of begging her to drop the annulment proceedings and be his wife indeed.

No, it would be too humiliating to seek her out now. And yet the temptation to see her again, whatever the embarrassment to himself, was irresistible. One thing was certain: he would issue his invitation on paper. He would not call on her; in fact, given what had transpired the last time they'd met, he dared not look her in the face until he was sure she was willing to see him again.

To this end, he collected pen and paper and set about phrasing his request. Should he promise not to refer to that Other Matter, or would it be best to pretend it had never happened? He decided it was best not to acknowledge it at all; he did not flatter himself that he held the same place in her thoughts as she occupied in his, so it was quite possible she had already forgotten the declaration that still plagued him with the memory of his own stupidity. If that were indeed the case, it would be foolish in the extreme to remind her of it by promising not to mention it. In fact, it would probably be a good idea to make plain from the outset that it was at Mr. Colquhoun's behest he was writing to her in the first place. Yes, he decided, that was the ticket.

My Lady Fieldhurst, he wrote, *As part of an ongoing investigation, it is necessary that I attend the performance of Handel's* Esther *at the Theatre Royal in Drury Lane on Friday, the 24th of February. My magistrate, Mr. Colquhoun, has suggested that my presence there will appear less conspicuous if I am accompanied by a lady. Since my acquaintance amongst the better class of females is limited, I wonder if you would oblige me by accepting my escort on this occasion.* After some hesitation, he added with perhaps less than perfect truth, *Mr. Colquhoun adds his entreaties to mine.* He signed himself *Yours, John Pickett,* then added a post scriptum: *P.S. I promise not to make you sit in the pit.*

He read through this model of the epistolary arts several times, and then, deciding there was nothing he could do to improve it, folded it, sealed it, and surrendered it to a messenger, along with instructions that it be placed in the hands of Lady Fieldhurst at Number Twenty-two Curzon Street.

Lady Fieldhurst, reading this communication approximately an hour after it had been written, was not quite certain what to make of it. Upon first reading, it seemed almost as if he were inviting her under duress; certainly he appeared to be acting upon Mr. Colquhoun's instructions, rather than any inclination of his own. She reminded herself that three months had passed since his declaration, and that his sentiments might have undergone a change; he might even have met another woman, a woman who was not of the "better class of females" and therefore ineligible to accompany him on this particular occasion. Then she reached his post scriptum, and smiled. Here was the rather endearingly gauche Mr. Pickett she remembered. His distant, almost cold invitation was no doubt due to embarrassment at the prospect of seeing her again, given his words to her at their last meeting. Well, she would find it a little awkward, too, but surely a few minutes of discomfort would be no worse than three long months of loneliness and misery had been. However infelicitously worded, his invitation was the answer to prayers she had not even been aware of praying.

She instructed the messenger to wait, then took the missive to her writing desk and sat down to compose a reply. It was brief almost to the point of curtness, but when she read back over it, she made only a one-word addition to the end before giving it to the messenger.

The brass bell over the door jangled a cheerful greeting as Pickett entered Mr. Meyer's shop in Conduit Street. There, however, his welcome ended. He stood awkwardly just inside the door, unsure quite how to proceed. Had the purpose of this call been to make inquiries regarding an investigation, he would not have hesitated to request of the first employee he saw an audience with Mr. Meyer. But he had never had the means to purchase clothing tailored specifically to his own measurements, and he was not at all certain how the thing was done. Perhaps more to the point, the Princess Olga and her fabled diamonds had faded from his mind somewhere between Bow and Conduit streets, and his primary concern had become the transformation of himself into an acceptable escort for Lady Fieldhurst.

And never had he been more painfully aware of his shortcomings. There were some half-dozen gentlemen clients in the shop, only three of whom troubled themselves to look up when the bell announced Pickett's entrance. One of these, a silver-haired man of middle age standing before a looking glass and admiring the fit of a black evening coat and form-fitting pantaloons, paused long enough to regard the newcomer with a contemptuously curling lip before turning his attention back to the far more satisfying sight of his own reflection. Two younger blades, both of them very nearly Pickett's own age, interrupted their debate on the merits of bottle green wool as opposed to mulberry long enough to exchange murmured quips, the only words of which Pickett could make out were "gapeseed" and "up from the country."

After what seemed an eternity to Pickett

(although it was in fact no more than thirty seconds), a small, wiry man with a tape measure draped around his neck and a pencil tucked behind his ear separated himself from his noble clients and came forward to meet him.

"Yes, sir?" he asked. "How may I be of service to you?"

"Mr. Meyer?" Upon receiving an affirmative nod, Pickett continued with more confidence, finding himself at last on familiar ground. "John Pickett of Bow Street. My magistrate, Mr. Colquhoun, said you would be expecting me."

"Of course, Mr. Pickett. If you will follow me?"

Pickett did so, and was relieved when the tailor led him into a small antechamber, away from the mocking curiosity of Mr. Meyer's aristocratic patrons.

"If you will be so good as to disrobe, Mr. Pickett?"

Pickett shrugged off his brown coat, conscious as never before of how his meager wardrobe must appear to one who was charged with dressing England's wealthiest and most influential men. He had never thought of his linen as being particularly dingy, and he was sure Mrs. Catchpole, who laundered his garments for three shillings and sixpence in addition to what he paid her each month for rent, did her best. But when he compared his shirt and cravat to the snow-white linens of the men just outside the anteroom door, he could not deny that they bore a faint but unmistakably yellow hue.

Waistcoat, shirt, shoes, and breeches followed the brown coat, and soon Pickett stood before the tailor in nothing but his smallclothes. Mr. Meyer whipped the tape measure from his neck and set to with a will, taking measurements and jotting them down, pausing occasionally in his work to offer some comment on Pickett's breadth of shoulder or length of leg. Pickett, feeling rather like a horse up for auction, found the experience only slightly less embarrassing than the doctor's examination he had been forced to endure in order to provide Lady Fieldhurst with grounds for an annulment.

At last the tailor's work was done, and Mr. Meyer set Pickett free to dress himself, promising that, although the particular articles of clothing he had in mind were already made up (and, in fact, were sometimes shown to wealthy clients as samples of the tailor's art) he himself would make whatever minor alterations were necessary before having the garments delivered to Mr.

Colquhoun's house.

"Depend upon it," he assured Pickett, "they will fit as if they had been made for you. In fact, you will look every inch the gentleman."

Pickett rather doubted this, but as he left Mr. Meyer's establishment and headed back toward Bow Street, his mind was not on the coming Friday night's experiment, nor even of his sudden (if temporary) rise in the world. In fact, he could think of nothing but the progress of his own letter to Lady Fieldhurst. Had it reached Curzon Street yet? Surely it must have done by now. Assuming that were the case, what had been its reception there? Would her ladyship wish to give the matter some consideration before penning a reply? If so, he might not receive a response before morning. For that matter, he might not receive a response at all. He had just spent half an hour in close proximity to the sort of men to whom she was accustomed; however friendly she might be toward him when they were alone, appearing publicly with him would likely be quite another matter. Perhaps she would think it kinder to spare him a rejection by not replying to his invitation. Perhaps his communication, so agonizingly worded, had been promptly consigned to the fire, and was at this very moment curling to blackened ash. Yes, that was probably it, he thought miserably.

This bleak prospect took such strong possession of his mind that he was stunned upon his return to Bow Street to be met with the information that a letter had come for him in his absence. He recognized the handwriting at once, and broke the seal with trembling hands. It was quite short — almost terse, in fact — but when he reached the end, he could not suppress a rather fatuous smile.

Mr. Pickett, it read, *I would be honored. You may call for me at eight.* It was signed, *Julia Fieldhurst Pickett.*

CHAPTER 3

IN WHICH JOHN PICKETT MAKES HIS DEBUT AS A GENTLEMAN

"Thank you, McElwain, that will be all." As the valet gathered up the tools of his trade and left the room, Mr. Colquhoun bent a rather stern gaze on his protégé. "Well, John, let's have a look at you."

Pickett turned away from the looking-glass to face his mentor with a self-conscious smile. "I look a regular popinjay, don't I, sir?"

In fact, "popinjay" was not the word that sprang to the magistrate's mind as he regarded the young man he had plucked from the rookeries of London a decade earlier. Pickett's workaday brown serge was gone, replaced by a dark blue double-breasted tailcoat of Bath superfine, worn over a white waistcoat of silk brocade. Calf-length pantaloons of black stockinette clung to his long legs like a second skin, and kid leather pumps encased his feet. His hair needed no assistance from curling tongs, but was tied at the nape of his neck with a black velvet ribbon fully an inch wide. Mr. Colquhoun scowled all the more fiercely in order to hide the lump forming in his throat.

"You'll do, John, dashed if you won't," he said gruffly, making the tiniest adjustment to Pickett's snowy white cravat. "Remember, the clothes must be returned to Meyer by noon tomorrow, so for God's sake, don't spill anything on them. Any damage will come out of your wages."

"Yes, sir."

"Now, your box should afford an excellent view of the royal party. In order to avoid the crush at the end of the performance, the Prince of Wales and his guests will leave the theatre at the beginning of the last scene of the final act — don't know how many there are, but you can look it up in the printed program. When you see the royal party preparing to go, you are to slip out and follow them down the stairs — at a discreet distance, mind you, and with her ladyship on your arm for the sake of appearances. The Princess Olga might consider the whole thing a great lark, but I'm taking no chances. If those diamonds are stolen — or worse, if Her Royal Highness comes to any harm — it could spark an international incident at a time when good relations with Russia are crucial." He sighed. "We need all the help against Boney we can get."

"Yes, sir." Pickett was fully alive to the importance of his assignment, but the butterflies cavorting about in his stomach had less to do with the elderly princess than with the beautiful young widow who was to be his companion for the evening.

The magistrate made a shooing motion with his hands. "Be off with you, then. You may report back to me after you deliver her ladyship home, if you wish. I don't mind waiting up."

Pickett nodded, and turned to go.

"Oh, and John —"

He paused with one hand on the door. "Sir?"

"Anything that might happen between you and her ladyship afterward is your own affair, but while you are at the theatre, your time and your attention are mine. Is that understood?"

"Yes, sir. Perfectly, sir," said Pickett, flushing a little at having his thoughts so easily read.

Mr. Colquhoun nodded. "Good luck to you, then."

"Thank you, sir," Pickett said, and then set off to fetch his lady.

■ ■ ■ ■

Some distance to the north, in Mayfair, Lady Fieldhurst sat at her dressing table and held her head perfectly still as her lady's maid fixed an aigrette of dyed ostrich plumes amongst her golden curls.

"I can't pretend I approve, my lady," remarked the scowling, black-garbed female standing over her shoulder.

Mistress's blue eyes locked with maid's black ones in the looking glass. "Your disapproval has been noted, Smithers," said Lady Fieldhurst in frigid tones meant to dampen the woman's presumption.

Alas, subtlety was lost on Smithers. "It's not decent if you ask me, your wearing that dress scarcely ten months after his lordship's death."

"Perhaps not," Julia conceded. "But then, I *didn't* ask you, did I?"

"Why, your ladyship, I'm sure I never meant —" While her abigail sputtered in respectful indignation, Lady Fieldhurst rose from her seat before the mirror.

"That will be all, Smithers. You need not wait up for me."

"Very good, my lady." The lady's maid bobbed a stiff curtsy and left the room, her spine rigid with offended propriety.

Julia sighed, wondering why she had ever agreed to engage the sister of George's butler as her personal servant. More galling than the woman's impudence, however, was the knowledge that Smithers was right: she would no doubt provoke more than a few raised eyebrows amongst the *ton* by wearing colors two months before her year of mourning was complete.

But when she inspected her reflection in the looking glass, it was easy to dismiss all other concerns. She had ordered the dress, a celestial blue satin with an overskirt of Urling's net, two months earlier so that she might have something ready when she was at last free to wear colors again. She had not had any particular function in mind at the time — or so she had told herself, until she had received Mr. Pickett's invitation and realized that her new finery had been destined all along for the Theatre Royal in Drury Lane, in the hope that he would be seated in the pit below the Fieldhurst box, and would look up . . .

He had only ever seen her in mourning, and she desperately wanted to be seen at her best just once before their acquaintance was ended. It was probably foolish and perhaps even a little cruel, after hearing from his own lips how he felt about her, and knowing, just as he did, that nothing could ever come of it. But she could not help herself, any more than she could explain why it was so important that he should see her thus adorned. She leaned nearer the mirror to affix pearls at her ears and throat, then draped her black velvet evening cloak over her arm and descended the stairs to await her escort's arrival.

She had quite some time to wait, as she reached the drawing room a full twenty minutes before eight. The fire had not been lit in the room, since she had no plans to linger there, and she allowed the butler, Rogers, to place her cloak about her shoulders in order to ward off the chill. After a quarter-hour delay during which she paced a path in the carpet, she at last heard the knocker on the front door. Faint voices sounded in the hall, and a moment later the drawing room door was flung open to admit Rogers, a stately figure with a most unbutler-like twinkle in his eye.

"Mr. Pickett, my lady," he announced in his most grandiose manner.

Then John Pickett entered the room, and it was as if, for the first time in three long months, the sun had broken through the clouds.

■ ■ ■ ■

"Good evening, Mr. Pickett," she said, suddenly breathless. If she had thought to dazzle him, the joke was surely on her, for she had never seen him like this. If she had not known better, she would have taken him for an aristocrat — and, consequently, a suitable match for herself. The knowledge that it was only an illusion made her want to cry. But there would be time for tears later. For now, she would delight in his company, and if she allowed herself to indulge in a little make-believe, well, no one else would ever be the wiser. She crossed the room to meet him, smiling as she held out her hands in greeting. "I was pleased to receive your invitation."

"My lady." He took her hands and bowed over them. "It is good of you to accommodate me in this."

"It is my pleasure," she assured him. "Thank you for thinking of me."

I think of you every minute of every day . . . No, he would not say it. He'd said far too much on the subject already; he would not embarrass either of them further. "Not at all, my lady," he demurred.

"But how very fine you look, Mr. Pickett!

43

I am quite overcome!"

"The clothes are hired," he confessed, grinning sheepishly. "I don't know what hold Mr. Colquhoun has over his tailor, but he persuaded Mr. Meyer to allow me the use of them for the night. Mr. Colquhoun has promised me that if I spill anything on them, it will be taken from my wages."

"Then perhaps it is just as well we are going to the theatre, and not to dinner." She hesitated a moment, then added on a more serious note, "It is good to see you again, Mr. Pickett. I — I've missed you."

"And I you, my lady." It was a masterpiece of understatement, but it was as far as he was prepared to go; he could not trust himself to say more.

A discreet cough from Rogers served as a reminder that Mr. Colquhoun's horses were standing.

Pickett realized he still held his lady's hands, and dropped them abruptly. "If you are ready, my lady, shall we go?"

He offered his arm; she placed her hand on it and allowed him to lead her outside, where Mr. Colquhoun's carriage stood. The coachman waited to hand Lady Fieldhurst up the step and into the vehicle, but Pickett performed this task himself. Once they were both seated and the carriage had begun to move forward, she turned to regard him in the faint light from the carriage lamps.

"Now, Mr. Pickett, you must tell me about this investigation you are conducting. It sounds most mysterious."

"Not so mysterious, really, and the investigation is not mine alone. In fact, it involves most of the Bow Street force. You may have heard rumors of a series of jewel thefts taking place in and around the Drury Lane Theatre. The Dowager Lady Oversley was the latest victim —"

"Yes, I know!" exclaimed Lady Fieldhurst. "I was at the theatre that night."

"Now, why does that not surprise me?" Pickett wondered aloud.

"What do you mean?"

"Only that when there is trouble amongst the aristocracy, you always seem to be in the thick of it — not that I'm complaining, mind you."

"I wasn't 'in the thick of it,' precisely," protested Lady Fieldhurst. "I merely suggested to Lady Oversley that she send to Bow Street, and offered to stay with her until a Runner arrived. In fact, Mr. Pickett, I hoped —" She broke off abruptly. "But do you expect there to be another such theft tonight?"

Pickett hardly heard the question, so

distracted was he by the words she had not said. *I hoped* — what? Was it possible that she had wanted to see him again? In fact, he had not been on duty that night, but if he had been . . .

"Mr. Pickett?"

Realizing she was still awaiting an answer, Pickett came down from the clouds, albeit reluctantly. "Mr. Colquhoun thinks there might be an attempt made tonight. Princess Olga Fyodorovna will be there as a guest of the Prince of Wales, and according to Mr. Colquhoun, she'll be wearing a set of diamonds any jewel thief would be unable to resist. Most of the Bow Street force will be on hand to stop him and, if necessary, to protect Her Royal Highness."

"I should think so! I wonder the princess should want to wear them, under the circumstances."

He shrugged. "I suppose she wanted to dazzle all you English ladies with their magnificence. But the woman wearing the diamonds will be one of the princess's ladies in waiting. She and the Princess Olga are trading places for the evening."

"What fun for them!"

Pickett's lips twitched. "I suppose that's one way of looking at it."

"But what is your responsibility this

evening, and what can I do to help?"

"I'll be watching the royal box from a vantage point on the opposite side of the theatre. If anyone accosts the supposed princess, I'm to get over there as quickly as possible and help apprehend the thief; if not, I am to follow the royal party as they leave their box, in case any attempt should be made between the time the princess leaves the box and the time she enters the carriage."

"What about me?" Lady Fieldhurst asked eagerly. "What do you want me to do?"

"To tell you the truth, my lady, your biggest task is, well, to lend me consequence, and to prevent me from making any glaring errors. Mr. Colquhoun is persuaded I should be out of my element sitting in a box. I can't imagine why," he added, with tongue planted firmly in cheek.

"Nor can I, Mr. Pickett, for in your present guise, you would not disgrace the royal box yourself. But can you not give me some more active way to participate?"

Pickett could not agree to this. "No one admires your pluck more than I, my lady, but I would prefer to keep you well out of harm's way."

"What possible harm could come to me in a theatre filled with almost four thousand people?" she insisted.

"If there is one thing I have learned, it is that no one can predict how a criminal will react when faced with arrest. No one is more dangerous than a man with nothing to lose. I will take no chances with your safety, my lady." He shuddered at an unpleasant memory. "I can't forget that incident in Scotland."

She regarded him quizzically. "To which incident do you refer, Mr. Pickett? The episode on the cliff, or the irregular marriage?"

He had been determined not to mention it, but it was almost a relief to have it brought out in the open. "I meant the cliff. As for the marriage, that particular incident, at least, will be over in three more weeks."

"Indeed, it will."

This happy prospect had the effect of reducing them both to glum silence.

At last Lady Fieldhurst found her voice. "Mr. Pickett, about the annulment — I wish there had been some other alternative — I am so very sorry —"

Of its own volition, his hand covered hers, and he gave it a little squeeze. "Please, my lady, you need not apologize."

"I know it is rather embarrassing for both of us, but can we not meet as friends? It has

—" The words were scarcely more than a whisper. " — it has been a long winter, Mr. Pickett."

He sighed. "Yes, it has." Neither of them was talking about the cold weather, and they both knew it. "Friends, my lady," he said, and held out his hand.

Even as they shook on the deal, he knew it was a mistake. And yet, if she desired his friendship, he could not deny her. He was, God help him, putty in her hands.

It was perhaps fortunate that at that moment the carriage lurched to a stop before the theatre. Pickett would have risen to open the door, but Lady Fieldhurst clutched his sleeve.

"No, Mr. Pickett, let the footman do it." As he hesitated, she added, "If you are to appear at ease sitting in a box, you might as well begin by behaving as if you are accustomed to having servants to do for you."

Thus entreated, he sank back onto the seat beside her. Once the door was opened, however, he sprang down and turned to assist Lady Fieldhurst. He had no idea if this was correct, and he didn't really care; he had waited three long months to see her again, to touch her, if possible, in socially acceptable ways, and he did not intend to let an opportunity go to waste. Her ladyship having safely disembarked, he offered his arm to his "friend" and led her up the stairs and into the theatre.

Once inside, she excused herself to the cloak room, and when she emerged a few minutes later, having removed her cloak, Pickett beheld her for the first time in colors. The sight took his breath away. *Friends?* He must be insane. How could one be friends with a powder keg?

"Mr. Pickett?" If Julia had thought — feared? — that his sentiments had undergone a change over the past three months, she saw him standing there staring at her with his heart in his eyes, and had her answer. "Is something the matter?"

He opened his mouth, shut it again, and swallowed hard. There were no words. And even if there were, he would have no right to say them.

"I — I think —" he began, when he could speak at all, "I think I could have saved myself a great deal of trouble by letting you seek an annulment based on mental incompetence."

Whatever reaction she had expected from him, it was not that. "I beg your pardon?"

He gave her a sad little smile. "I must be insane to let you go."

What could she possibly say in answer to

that? Fortunately, he did not wait for a reply, but took her elbow and steered her through the crowd toward the stairs leading up to the boxes. As the common areas on the first floor gave way to the more rarified heights reserved for those who could afford to pay five shillings for a seat, the more imposing became the plastered ceilings, marble floors, and polished woodwork.

"You are gawking, Mr. Pickett," said Lady Fieldhurst, slanting a sideways look at him.

"I beg your pardon?"

"You are gawking," she said again, hiding a mischievous smile. "If you wish to appear at home in a box, you would do well to act as if you have been there before."

"I'm afraid it will have to be an act, then, for I've never been anywhere except the pit."

"Of course you have!" she scolded. "I know you have been in a box at least once before, for I summoned you there myself. Or have you forgotten?"

"No, but —" *But on that occasion, I was too busy thinking of seeing you again to spare a thought for my surroundings.*

"But what, Mr. Pickett?"

He shook his head. "Nothing, just — no."

She had a fair idea of how his thoughts were running, and gave his arm a little squeeze in understanding.

51

Their seats were in the third tier, directly opposite the royal box. After they were both settled in the velvet-upholstered chairs, Pickett scanned the theatre. As he lived only a stone's throw away from the Theatre Royal in Drury Lane, he had been there many times before, but on all those other occasions he had been seated in the pit, where one might purchase a spot on one of the backless benches for a shilling. As Lady Fieldhurst had reminded him, he had been in a box only once before, but while on that previous occasion he had been too overawed at being summoned by her ladyship to take much notice of his surroundings, tonight he hadn't the luxury of inattention. Recalling his magistrate's warning, he took a moment to survey the cavernous expanse of the theatre. The three rows of boxes were arranged in the shape of a horseshoe, each box adorned with red velvet curtains and separated from its neighbors by a wall on each side supporting a massive brass sconce holding at least two dozen candles.

The royal party had not arrived yet, for their box was still vacant, but the Bow Street force was already in place. Below the empty royal box, Mr. Marshall sat ready to respond to the thump of the Princess Olga's cane. In the last row of the pit, Mr. Dixon had staked out a seat at the end of the bench, prepared to make a hasty exit if necessary. Pickett knew there were several others present yet unseen, whose positions he could not recall at the moment.

Suddenly the door at the rear of the royal box opened, and Pickett rose along with the other theatre patrons as the Prince of Wales and his guests filed in and took their places. Pickett had no difficulty in identifying the portly Prince, his chest bristling with the various badges of his office, but of the identity of the others he was not quite certain. As they returned to their seats, Lady Fieldhurst opened her reticule and withdrew a small brass instrument inlaid with mother of pearl. She aimed it in the direction of the royal box and peered through it for a long moment before offering the instrument to Pickett.

"Opera glasses," she explained. "I know you favor a quizzing glass on occasion, but I thought you might find these more useful tonight."

He held them up to his eyes, and the royal party appeared near enough that he might have spoken to them without raising his voice.

"Very useful, my lady. I thank you."

While Pickett scanned the royals through

the glasses, Lady Fieldhurst put names to their faces, having been introduced to many of them at her Court presentation following her marriage. "I suppose you have already located the Prince of Wales. He is rather difficult to miss, in more ways than one. I daresay the lady in the position of honor on his right is the Princess Olga, or rather her surrogate — and I quite see what you mean about the diamonds! The lady on the prince's left is his sister-in-law, the Duchess of York. She much prefers the kennels at Oatlands to the amusements of Town, so her presence speaks volumes about the princess's importance. The gentleman on the princess's right is Prinny's brother, the Duke of York, and the gentleman on the Duchess's left is another of Prinny's brothers, the Duke of Cumberland. I was obliged to stand up with him once at a ball — not an experience I would care to repeat, for he is a most unpleasant person! I can't be certain of the people in the second row — various royal attendants and hangers-on, I daresay. Oh, look! I wonder if that woman — second from the left, beside the large gentleman with the black beard — is the real Princess Olga?"

"Very likely, my lady, but perhaps we'd best keep that information to ourselves," suggested Pickett in an undervoice.

Lady Fieldhurst clapped one gloved hand to her mouth. "I beg your pardon!"

"No need. I daresay no one could hear, but one never knows who might be listening."

"Very true, especially when everyone in the theatre seems to be agog to know your identity."

Pickett lowered the glasses abruptly. *"What?"*

"You once said yourself that the upper classes come to the theatre to watch one another, rather than the action on stage. I assure you, by breakfast tomorrow it will be all over Town that the scandalous Lady Fieldhurst has appeared publicly in colors scarcely ten months after her husband's death, and in the company of a gentleman, no less. I daresay I will be inundated with morning callers. Shall I be very coy and mysterious?"

"My lady, I hope you are jesting!"

"I assure you, I am quite serious. If you wished to be unobtrusive, you could not have chosen a worse female to escort. I heard someone on the stairs speculating that you might be related to the Yorkshire Manningtons, as they are a tall lot. What rubbish!"

Of course it was nonsense that he might be taken for a member of a noble family, but it stung to hear her say so, all the same. "Rubbish, indeed," muttered Pickett.

"Yes, for anyone can see that you are much handsomer than any of the Manningtons."

Pickett's spirits rose considerably at this observation, but he felt compelled to say, "I wish you had warned me how conspicuous we would be, my lady."

"So that you might have found a less notorious female to ask in my stead?" Her voice grew pensive. "Perhaps I should have, but I — I wanted to see you again, Mr. Pickett. I wanted it very much."

After that admission, a whole army of jewel thieves might have stripped the entire royal party bare, and Pickett would not have noticed. "My lady, about — about this 'friendship' of ours — I —"

At that moment the house lights dimmed, and a hush fell over the audience as the rich red velvet curtains opened and the soprano Esther began the arioso, "Breathe soft, ye gales."

As Pickett lacked Lady Fieldhurst's musical training, it was inevitable that he did not derive the same enjoyment from the performance as she obviously did. But his purpose was not to listen to the music in any case, and so while the bass singing the role of Haman commanded the chorus of Persian soldiers to "pluck root and branch from out the land," Pickett kept a weather eye on the royal box across the way, with only occasional glances at the lady seated beside him.

One did not, however, require a musical education to recognize passion when one heard it, and when, late in the second act, Esther and the tenor who played King Ahasuerus joined their voices in the ardent duet, "Awake My Soul, My Life, My Breath," Pickett would have been hard pressed to remember the Russian princess's name, so conscious was he of Lady Fieldhurst sitting so close to him that their shoulders almost touched. His gaze drawn like a magnet, he looked down at her, and when he found her looking up at him with eyes sparkling, cheeks becomingly flushed, and lips parted in anticipation, he was a lost man. It was a very good thing that they were in full view of almost four thousand other people, Pickett thought, or else he would have no choice but to kiss her. Again.

It was perhaps fortunate that thunderous applause greeted the end of the second act, breaking the spell and recalling Pickett's attention to the task at hand. As the third and final act progressed and the sopranos soared ever higher, anchored by the booming tones of the bass section, a man entered the royal box and exchanged a few words with the attendant stationed nearest the door.

"What is he — ? That's odd," said Pickett, frowning as he reached for her ladyship's opera glasses. "May I?"

She nodded wordlessly, her eyes fixed on the performers on the stage below. He raised the glasses to his eyes, and suffered a shock. The entire royal party had risen to its feet, and was now moving toward the door at the rear of the box.

"What are they doing?" Pickett snatched up his program and scanned the printed lines again to be sure he wasn't mistaken. "They aren't supposed to exit until the beginning of the third scene of this act! It's scarcely into the first!"

"Mr. Pickett?" Lady Fieldhurst tore her gaze from the stage. "What is wrong?"

He shoved both program and opera glasses at her and leaped to his feet. "The royal party is leaving early, and I'm nowhere near to being in position! Why wasn't I informed of the change?"

The music came to an abrupt and unmelodious halt as the musicians snatched up their instruments and hurried off the stage, while the patrons in the pit climbed benches and shoved each other in an effort to reach the doors. The air rang with screams, but these were soon drowned out by more ominous crackles and roars. Baffled, Pickett leaned over the low wall that fronted the box and looked down.

"Mr. Pickett? What is happening?"

He turned back to her with an expression of such horror that it made her blood run cold.

"Fire! My God, the theatre is on fire!"

CHAPTER 4

IN WHICH JOHN PICKETT PAYS
A HIGH PRICE FOR HEROICS

The sound of shattering glass filled the air as the window panes succumbed to the intense heat, and the ensuing rush of oxygen fanned the blaze. Lady Fieldhurst had abandoned her chair and joined Pickett at the front of the box, clinging to his arm as they watched the pandemonium below.

"What do we do now?" she asked, raising her voice to be heard above the roar of the flames and the screams of terrified theatre patrons.

"We get out of here any way we can," he said, heading for the door at the rear of the box. He remembered the Covent Garden Theatre fire the previous September well enough to know that, once alight, the cavernous structures went up like kindling.

"What about the Princess Olga?"

"The royal party escaped just ahead of the fire."

In fact, their timely departure was a puzzle

in itself, for the man who had warned them — but he could think about that later. For now, his first priority — his *only* priority — was getting Lady Fieldhurst out of the burning theatre alive. And after all his fine talk about keeping her out of harm's way! He grabbed the door knob and pulled, but the door would not give. He pushed, with as little result. He rattled it frantically, to no avail.

"It won't open!"

Lady Fieldhurst, coughing from the smoke rising from the lower levels, appeared at his elbow. "What? But how — ?"

"Have you a hairpin?" While she fumbled among her curls for a pin, he dug a handkerchief from the inside breast pocket of his borrowed coat. "Here, hold this over your nose and mouth to keep from breathing the smoke."

He gave her the handkerchief and took the hairpin she offered, then knelt before the door and inserted the hairpin into the lock. This useful talent, one of several skills of dubious legality learned at his father's knee, had never failed him — never until now, when his hands shook so violently he could not maintain contact with the locking mechanism long enough to release it.

"Damn, damn, damn," he muttered under

his breath.

He had been picking locks for more than half his life, but never before had the stakes been so high. Neither a tongue-lashing from the constable for successfully picking a lock, nor a thrashing from his father for failing to do so, held any terrors to compare with the prospect of allowing the woman he loved to die a particularly ghastly death.

Abandoning a strategy that was accomplishing nothing but the waste of precious time, he scrambled to his feet and snatched up one of the chairs. He raised it high over his head and brought it down on the door knob with all the strength he could muster. It hit the knob and splintered into pieces.

"Mr. Pickett!" exclaimed Lady Fieldhurst, aghast at this hitherto unsuspected penchant for violence. "Must you destroy the furniture?"

"You can report me to the management in the morning," he retorted, "if you can find them." He picked up another chair and repeated this act of vandalism with no visible signs of remorse. The second chair also splintered, but the door knob gave beneath the force of the blow. The entire locking mechanism clattered to the floor, leaving an empty round hole in the panel. Pickett thrust his hand through and jerked the door open.

And immediately stepped back as he was struck with a wall of heat. The corridor was alive with flame, and as they stood staring into the inferno, a burning beam from the ceiling fell almost at their feet. Pickett slammed the door shut.

"We won't be going out that way," he remarked, glancing wildly about the box for some other method of exit. He seized one of the heavy curtains flanking the box and pulled until it collapsed into his arms in a pile of red velvet. He located the edge and began ripping it into long strips.

"What are you doing?" asked her ladyship, her voice muffled by the folds of his handkerchief over her mouth.

Pickett jerked his head toward the sconce mounted on the wall between their box and its neighbor. Its many candles, so impressive only moments ago, now appeared pale and puny compared to the flames dancing all around them.

"I'm making a rope to tie to that candelabrum. You can climb down into the pit and escape from there. And don't wait for me. As soon as your feet reach the floor, I want you to forget everything you ever learned about being a lady — push, shove, do

63

whatever you have to do, but *get out,* do you understand?"

"And what about you, Mr. Pickett?"

He glanced at the brass fixture. "I'm not sure if it will bear my weight, my lady. I suppose I'll have to try — I don't much fancy my chances in the corridor — but I'll not make the attempt until I see you safely down."

She leaned over the balustrade and looked past the three tiers of boxes to the pit some forty feet below, then turned back to confront Pickett. "Setting aside the likelihood that I would lose my grip and plummet to my death, do you honestly think I would leave you alone up here, to make your escape — or not! — as best you might? No, Mr. Pickett, I will not have it! Either we go together, or we do not go at all!"

The crash of falling timbers punctuated this statement, and although there was nothing at all humorous in the situation, he gave her a quizzical little smile. " ' 'Til death do us part,' Mrs. Pickett?"

She lifted her chin. "Just so, Mr. Pickett."

He raked his fingers through his hair as he cast about for an acceptable alternative, and found only one. He could not like their chances, but they seemed to have no other option, and he had no time to waste in trying to persuade Lady Fieldhurst as to the wisdom of his original plan.

"All right, then, here's what we're going to do. I'll climb down the rope with you on my back."

She looked doubtfully at the wall sconce. "It seems to me that if it might not bear your weight alone, it would be even less likely to support the both of us. Are you sure, Mr. Pickett?"

"I'm not sure at all, my lady, but I see no other way and, as you say, at least we would go together. Do you think you can hold on?"

She stuffed his handkerchief into her bodice and began stripping off her long white kid gloves. "To be perfectly honest, Mr. Pickett, I don't see that I have a great deal of choice!"

He nodded. "Exactly."

Having finished tying the lengths of curtain together, he looped one end around the sconce where it met the wall. He tied it, then tugged on it with all his might to pull the knot taut.

"I'm going to sit on the balustrade and get a good grip on the rope. As soon as I'm ready, I want you to lock your arms around my neck and wrap your legs around my waist."

"But — my skirts —"

"You'll have to hike them up." Anticipating her objections, he added, "Modesty has no place here, my lady. Everyone is trying to save his own skin. No one is going to be looking up your skirts, least of all me."

Without waiting for her consent, he sat on the balustrade and swung his legs out so that they dangled in empty air. He wrapped one arm around his makeshift rope to strengthen his grip, then seized it with both hands. "All right, my lady, it's time."

She did not hesitate, but stepped up behind.

"John?"

Her anguished tone, as much as her almost unprecedented use of his Christian name, made him turn his head.

"Yes, my lady?"

"For luck," she said, and kissed him swift and hard on the mouth. Then she hitched her skirts up over her knees and wrapped her arms around his neck.

There would be time later, Pickett reflected, to savor the memory of bare arms about his neck, of warm breath in his ear, of slender silk-clad ankles locked about his waist. For now, there were more urgent matters at hand.

"Hold tight," he said, then strengthened his grip on the velvet rope and eased himself off the balustrade.

As they descended, Julia was overcome with a curious sense of detachment, as if their present danger were nothing more than a scene from a play being enacted on the burning stage below, or a dream from which she knew she would soon awaken. Perhaps she had no doubt of his ability to rescue her from any disaster; perhaps her traumatized brain could only seek refuge in numbness. Whatever the cause of her unnatural serenity, she drew strength from the realization that there were surely worse fates than dying with John Pickett in her arms.

At his residence in Westminster, Mr. Colquhoun sat reading in his study and trying not to watch the clock. It was more than half past ten; the musical program being performed at the Theatre Royal in Drury Lane would by now be drawing near to its conclusion. Had he been twenty years younger, he might have taken a more active rôle in the operation he himself had planned. But such plots were meant for younger men, and besides, the sort of music he would be obliged to listen to sounded to his untrained ear like so much caterwauling. No, he would spend a quiet evening reading before his own fireside, and hear a full report in Bow

Street the next morning.

Unless, of course, his young protégé brought him news tonight. A satisfied smile curved his lips as he thought of John Pickett, and wondered what that viscountess of his had thought of the boy in his finery. If she possessed the sense to see beyond the circumstances of a man's birth, she would fall into his arms. Indeed, thought Mr. Colquhoun, if his own daughters had been a few years younger and still unwed, he would not have hesitated to entrust any one of them to John Pickett's keeping. In fact, he might have welcomed the opportunity to formalize a connection that —

A scratching at the door made him look 'round, and he was surprised and disturbed to see his own coachman hovering on the threshold. The expression on the man's face was enough to tell him that something was wrong. If that confounded woman had insisted upon being taken home early, or done anything else to botch the operation, he would have something to say about it, something that would make her ladyship's ears burn.

"Jervis? Back so soon?"

"Bad news, sir," the coachman said. "The theatre's burning. I couldn't get closer than St. Martins Lane before being obliged to turn back."

"Burning, you say?" The magistrate stood abruptly, and the book in his lap fell to the carpet unnoticed. "How bad is it?"

Jervis shook his head. "It's bad, sir. There'll be nothing left by morning but ashes, mark my words."

Mr. Colquhoun brushed past the coachman into the hall, and thence out the door and onto the front stoop. Far away to the northeast, the sky glowed with an eerie orange light, and clouds of dark smoke rose up to obscure the gibbous moon.

"Nothing but ashes," murmured the magistrate, horrified. "And most of the Bow Street force trapped inside."

"I wouldn't say 'trapped,' sir," the coachman hastened to reassure him. "If the number of folks running about in the streets is anything to judge by, I'd say most of them got out safe enough."

Those sitting in the pit, perhaps, or near enough to the stairs to make their escape before the inevitable panic made an orderly evacuation impossible. But for those in the boxes, particularly those boxes located at some distance from the stairs —

"What of the Prince of Wales and his party?" he demanded.

Jervis shrugged an apology. "I wouldn't

know, sir. I suppose they might have held everyone else back until the royals had been got out," he added hopefully.

Mr. Colquhoun nodded distractedly. "Yes, of course."

But John Pickett was in the box opposite, about as far removed from the royal party as it was possible to be and still occupy the same building. Even if those in the pit and the gallery had been held back in order to allow the royals to escape safely, the lad would have been trapped on the other side of the theatre. In fact, Mr. Colquhoun reflected, he gladly would have sacrificed the entire useless, expensive lot of Hanovers to guarantee the safety of one former pickpocket.

"I'm going to Bow Street," he announced.

"The roads are choked with traffic, sir," Jervis protested. "Nothing can get through, not even a saddle horse."

"I'll go on foot," said Mr. Colquhoun, and set out without even going back inside for his greatcoat.

It was his own fault. If anything had happened to the boy, he would have no one but himself to blame. There had been Runners stationed all around the theatre, and several members of the foot patrol besides; surely they could have kept an eye on the Princess

Olga without having one positioned in the box directly opposite. But no, he had taken an almost fatherly pride in seeing the young man tricked out as a gentleman, in setting him down in the midst of the aristocracy, perhaps even in giving him one last chance to win the well-born lady he loved.

And in doing so, he'd sent Bow Street's best and brightest to his death.

Their descent was clumsier than Pickett had anticipated, due in large part to the awkward burden on his back; his sweaty palms did not help matters, either. They had maneuvered safely past their own box, and were now almost level with the one below it. Or at least Pickett thought they were; he dared not look down to ascertain their position. Instead, he kept his gaze fixed on the brass sconce that anchored his makeshift rope, as if he could keep it fixed firmly in the wall by sheer force of will. And then, just as the second-tier balustrade appeared in his peripheral vision, the sconce began, not to tear out of the wall as he had feared, but to bend under their combined weight. Weakened by the heat, it bowed lower and lower, until at last the candles kissed the velvet folds. The superheated fabric caught at once, the flames racing down the rope toward his white-knuckled hands.

"Hold fast, my lady!" Pickett cautioned his fair burden, and loosened his grip so that the rope slid easily through his fingers. Their descent accelerated rapidly, even as the friction shaved a layer of skin from the palms of his hands. They had not quite reached the last tier of boxes when the fabric burned completely through, and they fell the last few feet. Pickett managed not to land on top of Lady Fieldhurst, but the effort of cushioning her fall caused him to land awkwardly. Pain lanced through his left ankle.

With their abrupt landing, Julia's preternatural detachment was shattered, and the need for immediate action reasserted itself. She scrambled off Pickett and pulled down the skirts that had bunched around her waist. "Are you all right, Mr. Pickett?" she shouted over the crackle and roar of the flames.

He nodded, too short of breath to speak. He inhaled deeply, and fell into a paroxysm of coughing. "Are you?" he choked out.

"Yes." The smoke was much thicker here, nearer the source of the fire. She fumbled in her bodice for Pickett's handkerchief, and pressed it against her nose and mouth.

"We've got to get out of here." Pickett

clambered to his feet and took a few limping steps.

Lady Fieldhurst looked at him sharply. "You're *not* all right! You are injured, Mr. Pickett."

"I landed a bit heavily, that's all," he panted. "I'll be fine. Let's *go,* my lady."

He threw his arm around her, holding her tightly to his side as they raced up the aisle, Pickett favoring his left foot. As she ran, her net overskirt fanned out and brushed the end of a burning bench. Seeing the fabric ignite, Pickett grabbed a handful and pulled, ripping it free at the high waistline before it could set her whole dress aflame. She made no objection to this rough-and-ready treatment, but snatched up her skirts and held them close to her body to prevent another such occurrence. After several more seconds that seemed like hours, they reached the foyer, where the fire had not yet taken hold.

"My — my cloak is in there," she gasped, gesturing toward the cloakroom where the evening had begun with such promise.

There were as yet no flames in this part of the theatre, but black smoke poured from the cracks around the cloakroom door.

"Leave it!" Pickett commanded.

"It's cold outside," she protested.

"It won't be now," he predicted grimly.

Tightening his arm around her, he half-pulled, half-carried her out of the theatre and into the night.

The sight that met their eyes looked like a scene out of Danté's *Inferno.* Flames leaped high into the sky, and tiny glowing cinders danced in the air like nocturnal insects. Occasionally a burning timber broke free of the main structure and crashed to the ground, sending up its own plume of smoke and flame. The fire brigade had arrived and pumped water as vigorously as they could, and a line of men passed buckets from hand to hand, but their efforts were futile in the face of the conflagration. From a safe distance across the street, people screamed and sobbed as they searched for loved ones, their forms reduced to dark silhouettes moving against the flickering light. One woman fainted from either heat or terror, while another had to be held back to prevent her from rushing back into the theatre in search of something — or someone — she'd left behind.

Pickett did not hesitate, but dragged Lady Fieldhurst into the mêlée, intent on putting as much distance as possible between the pair of them and the doomed theatre. They had not yet reached the opposite side of the street when the roof collapsed with a crash, and the resulting blast of heat knocked him off his feet. He fell heavily forward, dragging her down with him.

His weight knocked the breath from her body. "Good heavens, Mr. Pickett," she panted as she edged out from underneath him. "You should warn me —"

She broke off abruptly. Without her beneath him to cushion his fall, he collapsed facedown and lay motionless on the ground.

"Mr. Pickett?" She shook him by the shoulder. Receiving no response, she withdrew her hand, and found it wet with blood. "Mr. Pickett! Mr. Pickett! *John!*"

And while the world burned around them, she knelt in the middle of the wet street, cradling his bleeding head in her arms and crying, "Help! Please, someone, help!"

Chapter 5

IN WHICH LADY FIELDHURST
EXPERIENCES A REVELATION

Mr. Colquhoun made the trek from his residence to Bow Street with a speed that might have been envied by many a younger man. He was in no mood to bask in this athletic achievement, however, as he strode into the Bow Street Public Office and glanced wildly about. Dixon was there, as was Marshall, both men mopping the sweat and soot from their brows as they pitched in to lend a hand with the petty burglaries and thefts that inevitably ensued as London's criminal element saw the opportunity to profit from a crisis.

"Mr. Dixon! Good man," said the magistrate, clapping him on the shoulder. "Mr. Marshall, glad to see you made it out safely. Any word from Mr. Pickett?"

Marshall shook his head. "I haven't seen anything of him, sir."

Dixon concurred. "He hasn't checked in yet."

One by one, the Bow Street men returned, most of them coughing smoke and a few nursing minor injuries. Their accounts of the evening varied slightly from man to man, but of one thing they were all agreed: In the confusion of the evacuation, no one had seen anything of Mr. Pickett.

"And Mr. Foote?" prompted Mr. Colquhoun, scanning the room. "He was supposed to be in charge here. Where the devil is he?"

"I expect he went to lend a hand when the fire broke out," Dixon speculated.

The magistrate nodded distractedly. "I suppose that's all right." He could not like the idea of the Bow Street office being left virtually empty, but he was experienced enough to know that even the best-laid schemes tended to go out the window in the face of a greater calamity.

Suddenly a crash shook the building, reverberating in the air for seconds after the initial impact.

"Good God, what was that?" demanded Mr. Colquhoun.

"The roof just collapsed," reported Mr. Griffin, entering the Bow Street office in a rush of smoky air. "The theatre's gone."

Gone. The theatre was gone, and with it his last hope that John Pickett might somehow be alive. Mr. Colquhoun groped for a chair and sat down heavily, feeling suddenly older than his sixty-four years.

"He might still turn up, sir," said Dixon, seeing the magistrate's ashen countenance. "Stranger things have happened."

Mr. Colquhoun nodded, but could not quite bring himself to believe it.

"Help!" screamed Lady Fieldhurst in between paroxysms of coughing. "Someone, please, help!"

"Beg pardon, ma'am, but may I be of assistance?"

Looking up, Julia saw a masculine silhouette standing in stark relief against the flames. "This man has been injured," she explained. "He needs a surgeon, but I can't move him alone."

"Where should he be taken?"

She was about to give her own Curzon Street address when a bit of long-forgotten conversation recalled his own much nearer residence to her memory. "He has lodgings in Drury Lane. I don't know the number, but he hires rooms above a chandler's shop. Can you fetch a sedan chair?"

The man glanced around, revealing the sharp outline of a beaky nose as he surveyed the chaos all around them. "Horse traffic still can't get through, so any sedan chair is likely to be besieged with people seeking transportation. If you will forgive the impertinence, it seems to me that an attractive female would stand a far better chance of getting a chair than a man."

Privately Lady Fieldhurst doubted that her present appearance would offer much of a temptation, but she did see the man's point. She was, however, extremely reluctant to leave Mr. Pickett alone.

"I'll stay with him until you return," the stranger offered, anticipating her objections.

She gently lowered Pickett's head to the ground. "Thank you. I'll return as soon as I can," she said, although whether this promise was made to the stranger or to Pickett himself, she was not quite certain.

She scrambled to her feet and darted through the crowd until she spied a sedan chair. Unfortunately, it had already been claimed by a portly gentleman who was even now climbing inside. She ran up behind him and grabbed his arm.

"Forgive me, Lord Lindlay," she said, breathless from exertion and smoke inhalation, "but there is an injured man whose need of this chair is greater than yours."

Lord Lindlay turned and beheld the late Lord Fieldhurst's slightly scandalous widow looking thoroughly disheveled in a torn and muddy gown, her hair coming down and the dyed ostrich plumes that had once adorned her coiffure now leaning drunkenly over her left ear.

"What's that?" he asked, raising his voice to be heard in the confusion. "Have you any idea how difficult it was for me to procure this chair?"

"I don't doubt it —"

"Well, then!" declared the affronted nobleman, and turned back to heave himself into the sedan chair.

"I am truly sorry to impose on you in such a way, my lord," insisted Lady Fieldhurst, retaining her grip on his arm, "but a man's life may be at stake!"

"What's that you say?" he asked, clearly wavering. "An injured gentleman, is it?"

"Yes," she lied without hesitation. "Would you please, *please* oblige me by surrendering your place to him, sir?"

"Well, I never —" he blustered. "Still, I suppose one must do what one can. I daresay I would want someone to do the same for me in similar circumstances. Very well, my lady, my chair is yours."

He executed a courtly bow that should have appeared ridiculous under the circumstances, but that inspired her to plant a quick kiss on his cheek.

"Thank you, Lord Lindlay! You are very kind."

"Not at all, not at all," he demurred, then turned to the chair bearers, who had watched this exchange with unconcealed interest. "You heard the lady. Get along with you, now."

The two men had to run to keep pace with her — no easy matter, with the boxy wooden chair balanced between them on its poles — but soon she arrived back at the place where she'd left Pickett lying in the street. Her guardian angel still stood over the motionless form, just as he'd promised, but by this time he had been joined by a knot of curious onlookers.

"There he is," she instructed the chair bearers, gesturing toward the place where Pickett lay. "If you will allow me to enter the chair first, you may lift him and hand him in to me. And you, sir, I never had a chance to get your name, or to express my gratitude to you for —"

But when she turned to thank him, her benefactor was gone. She had no time to wonder at his disappearance, for fear someone else might commandeer the sedan chair from her in the same way she'd seized it from the hapless Lord Lindlay. She climbed inside and held out her arms to receive Pickett's inert form.

"Gently now — be careful of his head."

As Pickett was quite tall and the sedan chair not overly roomy, the bearers were obliged to set him down on the floor of the chair, with his head resting on Lady Field- hurst's lap and his legs folded up so that the door might close. Once this operation was accomplished, they looked to Julia for further instructions.

"Drury Lane," she said, peering up at them through the window of the convey- ance. "I don't know the number, but there is a chandler's shop with a hired flat above."

One of the bearers merely gave her a blank look, but the other nodded. "I think I know the shop. Come on, then," he told his fel- low, and they lifted the chair by its poles and set off down the street.

Lady Fieldhurst tried her best to cradle Pickett's head, but it was a lurching, bumpy trek nonetheless. At length they reached the chandler's shop, which blazed with lights in spite of the lateness of the hour. Nor was it alone in its uncharacteristic illumination; every shopkeeper in Drury Lane was awake and alert, each one guarding his property lest it fall prey to fire, or looters, or both.

The chair bearers stopped before this

edifice and lowered their burden to the ground, then opened the door and stepped back for their passengers to exit.

"Can you help me get him up the steps?" Lady Fieldhurst asked. Seeing unpromising expressions on both faces, she stamped her foot. "Surely you cannot expect me to drag him upstairs on my own! You will be well recompensed for your efforts, I can assure you."

But even as the words left her mouth, she remembered the reticule lying beside her chair in the box. There would be nothing left of it now but ashes. Fortunately, help arrived in the form of a stout woman rushing from the shop, twisting her hands in her apron.

"Good heavens! Johnny, is that you? I've been beside myself with worry — bless my soul!" she exclaimed at the sight of Pickett unconscious in the arms of a disheveled woman whose demeanor nevertheless suggested a lady of genteel birth.

"As you can see, Mr. Pickett has suffered an injury."

The two chairmen removed Pickett, albeit grudgingly, and Lady Fieldhurst, her arms feeling strangely empty, disembarked stiffly in his wake.

"When I saw the smoke and heard the

theatre was burning, I feared the worst," confessed the woman. "I knew he would be there tonight."

"And you are Mrs. — ?" prompted Lady Fieldhurst.

"Mrs. Catchpole, Johnny's landlady."

"Mrs. Catchpole, I would be much obliged to you if you could pay these good men for their services. I will be happy to repay you at any rate of interest you care to name."

"That's kind of you, ma'am, but there's no need for no interest. Why, Johnny's almost like family," she added, having long entertained hopes of a match between her handsome young tenant and her unmarried niece.

"Thank you." Having settled the matter of payment, Lady Fieldhurst turned back to the chair bearers. "Now, if you will carry him, please, Mrs. Catchpole will show you the way."

The landlady, quick to take her cue, lost no time in taking up a candle and lighting the way up the stairs and into Pickett's rooms, where Lady Fieldhurst directed them to lay him on the bed.

"I shall need you to fetch a surgeon without delay."

The bearers, having by this time realized that they were dealing with a Personage, tugged at their forelocks and set out at once. Now that the immediate crisis was past, Lady Fieldhurst shivered; it was very odd, but she had not noticed before how cold the room was.

"I'll just light the fire, ma'am, shall I?" offered Mrs. Catchpole, already moving toward the fireplace.

"Yes, please."

While the landlady set about building the fire, Lady Fieldhurst turned to examine Mr. Pickett by the light of the single candle. His face was as black as a chimney sweep's — she suspected her own was not much cleaner — but save for the blood still seeping from the back of his head, there appeared to be no other signs of injury. Gently, so as not to jar him, she untied the cravat from about his neck and wrapped it around his wounded head, sacrificing two of her hairpins to anchor it in place. Spying a bowl and pitcher on a washstand, she located a cloth and poured water from the pitcher into the bowl. It had no doubt been warm that morning, but by now it was almost frigid. She could not feel this to be entirely a bad thing; perhaps the shock of the cold water would recall him to consciousness. She plunged the cloth into the cold water, wrung out the excess, then

85

returned to the bedside and began to bathe his face. Alas, he showed no signs of waking up.

Having cleaned the dried blood and soot from his face, she set about the awkward task of removing his dirty, blood-soaked clothing. By rolling him carefully onto first one shoulder and then the other, she was able to divest him of his coat and waistcoat, but the shirt presented a problem, as she dared not attempt to pull it over his head.

"Mrs. Catchpole," she addressed the woman still kneeling before the fire, "have you any idea where I might find a scissors, or perhaps a knife?"

The landlady turned and beheld her tenant being undressed with surprisingly gentle efficiency. "Here, ma'am, there's no task for a lady! You'd best let me do that."

"Nonsense! I was married for six years. I've seen a naked man before," Julia insisted, blushing nevertheless as she spoke the words.

"Oh!" Mrs. Catchpole's eyes widened in sudden recognition. "You must be Johnny's widow!"

"He's not dead!" Lady Fieldhurst cried hotly. "You are not to speak of him in that manner!"

"No, of course not," the older woman

hastened to reassure her, even as she recognized that her own hopes of a match between her niece and her handsome young boarder were doomed, whether he recovered his health or not. "I only meant that — that is, Johnny told me once that he'd met —"

Lady Fieldhurst dashed a hand over her eyes. "I beg your pardon. Of course you did not mean anything of the kind! It has been a most trying evening, and I fear my nerves are on edge."

"Well, and how could they not be?" Mrs. Catchpole asked soothingly. "Perhaps you'd care for a nice cup of tea? If you're sure you don't need my help, that is."

In fact, Lady Fieldhurst was more than a bit daunted by the prospect of undressing Mr. Pickett's lower half, but she would allow no one else to touch him, and did not particularly desire an audience while she did so herself. "Tea would be lovely, Mrs. Catchpole."

After the landlady had gone, Lady Fieldhurst turned back to the still figure on the bed. She took a deep breath. "I'm sorry, Mr. Pickett. I know you would not like it, but your clothes are shockingly wet from the fire hoses, and you will feel much more the thing once you are warm and dry," she said, then set to work unbuttoning the fall of his breeches.

Soon, having stripped Mr. Pickett to his smallclothes (further than that she refused to go, no matter how damp his drawers), she covered him with a blanket. She glanced over her shoulder at the fire, burning brightly now although it had yet to dispel the chill in the room. She shuddered at the sight, and wondered if she would ever be able to look at even the most innocuous candle flame in quite the same way.

"Here we are," announced Mrs. Catchpole, entering the room bearing a steaming cup and a knife with a short blade. She set both on the bedside table, then stood regarding Lady Fieldhurst expectantly.

"Thank you, Mrs. Catchpole," said Julia, nodding a dismissal.

Alas, the landlady was not to be so easily dismissed. "I don't know what the world's coming to, ma'am, honest I don't! The theatre at Covent Garden last September, and now the one at Drury Lane! It's a good thing I don't hold no truck with make-believe acting on stage, for it's plain as a pikestaff those places aren't safe. And to think that only a week ago I was telling my niece —"

"You've been most helpful, Mrs. Catchpole," said Julia, interrupting what promised to be quite a lengthy reminiscence, "but I'm sure you will want to go back downstairs and keep an eye on your shop. I feel certain I can manage quite well on my own from here. Pray do not let me keep you from your own concerns."

Mrs. Catchpole wavered between resentment at being so summarily dismissed, and knowledge that her boarder's aristocratic companion was quite right: In addition to the possibility that the fire might spread, there was the ever-present threat of thieves, who were quick to take advantage of chaos and confusion in order to enrich themselves.

"Very well, ma'am," she said with obvious reluctance. "If you're sure you don't need me no more, I'll leave you. I'll be up in the morning with fresh water and more coal for the fire, shall I?"

"Yes, thank you, Mrs. Catchpole," said Julia with real gratitude. "I would be most appreciative."

Alone with the man who was and yet was not her husband, Julia fortified herself with a sip of tea, grimacing at the taste; Mrs. Catchpole's tea leaves were clearly inferior to the blend found in her own kitchen in Curzon Street. Setting aside the cup, she unbuttoned the neck of Pickett's shirt, then took up the knife. She slit the garment open from placket to hem, then eased it off with the same side-to-side motion she'd used in removing his coat and waistcoat.

The light in the room was somewhat brighter now, thanks to the fire, and when she slipped his arm through the sleeve, she could see clearly what she not noticed before. The palms of his hands were red and raw, with blood blisters forming on the tender flesh. She recalled their swift descent down the makeshift rope, and cradled his hand against her cheek.

"I don't know if you can hear me, Mr. Pickett," she whispered against his abused palm, "but I wish I could tell you how wonderful — how brave —"

Her throat closed, and she could say no more. As her eyes blurred with tears, she knew with blinding certainty that if he were to die, everything good and beautiful in her life would go with him. She should have realized the truth weeks ago. After all the loneliness and misery of the last three months, it seemed the cruelest of ironies that she should not know her own heart until now, when he lay as still and quiet as if under some malicious spell.

"Please wake up," she begged. "Please come back to me. I couldn't bear it if you should — I — I —"

She might never have another opportunity to say what was in her heart, what she should have said long before now. Sitting on the edge of the bed, she leaned over his motionless form.

"I love you, John Pickett," she whispered, and pressed her lips to his unresponsive mouth.

To Pickett, dimly aware of the pain in his head, it seemed as if he were floating weightlessly in some viscous liquid he could not identify. Not the waters of the Thames, surely; he'd done his share of mudlarking along its banks in his formative years, and its waters had never been so clear. He supposed he could swim for the surface and look about to ascertain his location, but he found himself extremely reluctant to do so. Above was fire and pain and something else, something important that he had to tell someone. Below, on the other hand . . . Below, all was velvety darkness and gentle caresses and a familiar, beloved voice saying things he knew he would never hear it speak Above.

It was the easiest decision he'd ever made. He relaxed and gave himself up to the darkness.

CHAPTER 6

IN WHICH LADY FIELDHURST
ROUTS A CHARLATAN AND
MAKES A DISTURBING DISCOVERY

Lady Fieldhurst had no idea how much time had passed before the surgeon finally arrived. Certainly it seemed like hours, but then again, time had ceased to exist on this, the longest night of her life. At last there was a knock on the door, and she opened it to admit a grizzled man wearing spectacles and carrying a worn black leather bag.

"Oh, thank God!" she exclaimed.

"Willard Portman, surgeon," he said by way of introduction. "I believe you have a patient for me?"

"Yes, Mr. Portman. Right this way, if you please."

She led him through the outer room, which served as both sitting and dining room, into the small bedroom, where Pickett lay exactly as she had left him.

"Mm-hmm." The surgeon studied him for a long moment, then began carefully unwrapping the makeshift bandage she had fashioned from his cravat. "Mm-hmm," he said again when the blood-encrusted wound was revealed.

He turned to the bedside table, opened his bag, and began laying out a number of ominous-looking instruments.

"What — what are you going to do?" Lady Fieldhurst asked, eyeing this collection with growing unease.

"In cases where the head has suffered an injury, ma'am, the greatest danger is the possibility of brain fever. In my opinion, the best way to prevent this is to alleviate any swelling of the brain. I myself have developed a procedure that I believe will accomplish this." He glanced down at the instruments lined up on the bedside table and picked up a straight razor. "I will begin by shaving the patient's head. This will allow me to drill a hole in the skull, which will reduce pressure on the brain, thus allowing for —"

"And you've done this before?" asked Lady Fieldhurst, aghast.

He nodded. "On two occasions, yes."

"And — and your other patients? They eventually recovered?"

"Alas, they both died. But," he added quickly, "they undoubtedly would have done so much sooner had not a cure been attempted."

"Get out," breathed Lady Fieldhurst, moving to position herself between surgeon and patient.

"I beg your pardon?"

"You heard me," she said, more strongly this time. "Get out."

"May I remind you, ma'am, that it was *you* who sent for *me*? If you do not allow me to treat him —"

She snatched up the knife she'd used to cut open Pickett's shirt, and pointed it at the surgeon's throat. "I said, get out."

He gave a nervous little laugh. "There, there, ma'am, I'm sure there's no need for —"

"If you touch him," she said with great deliberation, "I will kill you."

Eyes wide behind his spectacles, the surgeon stuffed his instruments back into his leather bag and began to back away slowly. "Very well, ma'am, but if he dies, then on your own head be it!"

Having delivered himself of this Parthian shot, he turned and took to his heels. Lady Fieldhurst slammed the door and locked it behind him, as if fearful he might return and attempt to perform his hideous operation without her permission. Then she buried her face in her trembling hands and surrendered to the tears she could no longer hold back.

As dawn broke over the City, Mr. Colquhoun left the Bow Street office and walked to the intersection of Russell and Brydges streets, where the Theatre Royal had once dominated the landscape. The air was still thick with smoke, but through the haze he could see one broken and blackened wall rising above the ruins, the two large holes that had once housed its windows gaping over the wreckage like sightless eyes. The deep crater beyond, he supposed, had been the orchestra pit, which meant the piles of smoldering beams on either side must be all that was left of the boxes that had once risen on each side, flanking the pit. The royal box would have been to the right of the stage, so directly opposite, on the left . . .

A curl of smoke rose from the ashes as from a funeral pyre. God only knew what the boy must have suffered, thought the magistrate. He found himself hoping the lad had succumbed to the smoke long before the flames reached the box. Asphyxiation was a nasty enough way to die, but surely less horrific than the alternative. He supposed Lady Fieldhurst must have been among the fallen as well, and hoped Pickett

95

had derived some comfort from the fact that she was with him at the end.

It occurred to him that he had made many friends in high places over the course of his magisterial career; perhaps he could pull a few strings and obtain permission to claim the — the remains — once the wreckage was cleared away. God knew John Pickett had no one else, aside from a ne'er-do-well father in Botany Bay. He refused to allow the boy to be buried namelessly in a pauper's grave.

"Damned smoke," he muttered, dragging a handkerchief from his pocket and mopping his stinging eyes.

Then, turning away from the ruined site that was John Pickett's grave, he made his way slowly back toward Bow Street. Here life went on, for in addition to the usual petty crimes, there were now a host of other issues related to the fire. A man described a horse that had been either lost or stolen in all the confusion; an elderly woman complained loudly that she was not allowed to search the wreckage for the walking stick she was quite certain she had left behind when the blaze broke out. Nearer the magistrate's bench, a grizzled man wearing spectacles waved his arms in agitation.

"A madwoman, I tell you!" he insisted, to

Mr. Foote's skeptical amusement. "She threatened me with a knife!"

Mr. Colquhoun heaved a sigh and stepped nearer. "What's all this?"

Having received little encouragement from his previous audience, the man turned eagerly to the magistrate. "I'm trying to tell this fellow there's a madwoman on the loose with a knife! She threatened to kill me if I didn't leave the premises!"

"I see." Mr. Colquhoun scowled. "Where was this?"

"Shabby little flat in Drury Lane. Number eighty-four, I believe, although I don't mind admitting I didn't stick around to make sure."

Mr. Colquhoun recognized the number, and scowled all the more fiercely. "Over a chandler's shop, was it?"

"Aye, I believe it was, at that."

Mr. Colquhoun addressed himself to the Runner. "I'll look into it, Mr. Foote, you need not trouble yourself."

Suiting the word to the deed, he left the Bow Street office without a backward glance. He knew there were unscrupulous persons amongst the criminal classes who stole the possessions of the dead in order to sell them, but he would be damned if he would let someone else profit from everything John Pickett had worked for over the course of his short life. The magistrate sighed. He did not look forward to the grim task of shipping the boy's meager belongings halfway around the world to the scoundrel who had sired him, but he supposed he owed the man that much; after all, he'd killed his son.

Drying her tears, Lady Fieldhurst returned to the bedroom, where she found Mr. Pickett lying exactly as she had left him. Surely it was not natural for him to be so still and, yes, so *lifeless*. Surely he had not . . .

Fearing the worst, she moved quickly to his bedside. She folded down the blanket enough to expose his smooth, bare chest, and laid her hand over his heart. She felt it then, the faintest flutter of his heartbeat, the slightest rise and fall of his breathing. Letting out a long sigh of relief, she pulled the blanket back up to his chin, replaced the bandages that the surgeon had removed, then straightened up — and got a good look at herself in the spotted mirror above the washstand.

It was perhaps a good thing he could not see her, for the hideous sight she presented would have surely been enough to frighten him to death. Her face, at least that part of it that had not been covered with his handkerchief, was grimy with soot, and her hair was coming down from its few remaining pins. Her dress — her beautiful blue dress, for which she'd had such high hopes — was nothing more than a rag, its hem scorched, its skirts sodden and bloodstained, and most of its net overdress ripped away. And yet in her imagination it would always remain just as it had appeared at that moment when she had emerged from the cloakroom, and Mr. Pickett had seen her in it . . .

She smiled a little at the memory, then began to strip off what was left of the gown. She glanced uncertainly at the still figure on the bed before allowing the dress to fall from her shoulders, but she need not have worried; he was utterly oblivious to her presence. Or perhaps, if she were to be honest with herself, she was not worrying at all, but rather indulging the wild hope that the prospect of seeing her *en déshabillé* might rouse him when nothing else would. If so, it was a wasted effort, for he did not stir.

Although the fire was beginning to heat the room quite nicely, it was still rather chilly to be wearing nothing but one's chemise, stays, and petticoats. Unfortunately, she had no other dress to put on.

She rubbed her arms for warmth, wondering whether to ask Mrs. Catchpole for the loan of a shawl when she caught sight of Pickett's two coats, one black and one brown, hanging on a peg beside the door. She recalled that the black one was his best, so she chose the brown (her favorite of the two in any case, since she had seen him wearing it much more frequently than the other) and shrugged it on over her undergarments. The sleeves were much too long — in fact, they covered her hands — but this problem was easily resolved by rolling them up. Having completed this simple alteration, she turned up one lapel and buried her nose in it, inhaling deeply of the scent that was uniquely John Pickett.

She washed her face with cold water from the basin, then took down what was left of her coiffure and twisted her hair into a simple knot at the nape of her neck. She had just finished securing it with her few remaining hairpins when a knock sounded on the door. Mrs. Catchpole, she thought, come to deliver the promised coal and water and to inquire, no doubt, after her boarder's health. Julia regretted that she had nothing more encouraging to report. She crossed the drawing room and opened the door — and found herself face to face with Mr.

Pickett's magistrate, Mr. Colquhoun. For a long moment they stared at one another with identical expressions of incredulity, until Julia recalled that she was wearing nothing but her undergarments and Mr. Pickett's coat.

She clutched it tightly closed at her throat. "This — this is not what it looks like —"

So overwhelming was the magistrate's grief over the loss of his young protégé, he might have discovered the pair of them *in flagrante delicto* and felt nothing but the most profound relief. "He — he's alive?" he managed, almost afraid to hope.

She nodded. "Barely, but yes."

He closed his eyes. "Thank God! Where is he? May I see him?"

"Of course. Come in."

She stepped back and allowed him to enter, then led the way to the bedroom where Pickett lay motionless, his head swathed in bandages. Mr. Colquhoun drew up short on the threshold.

"Good God!"

"He was struck on the head when the roof collapsed." Her gaze fell on the pile of bloodied clothing on the floor, and she remembered it had been hired for the evening. "He was bleeding heavily. I'm afraid I had to use his cravat to fashion a bandage, and I cut his shirt off rather than try to pull it over his head."

Mr. Colquhoun followed her gaze to the blood-soaked garments, but his tailor's wrath was not uppermost in his mind. "And I told him not to spill anything on them," he said unsteadily. "I never dreamed the only thing 'spilled' would be his own blood!"

"Mr. Colquhoun, I hope you will allow me to square things with your tailor."

He shook his head. "No, my lady, there's no need for that. Mr. Pickett was injured in the performance of his duty. The department will cover the expenses — although I may be obliged to place a large order with my tailor, if I am ever to be restored to his good graces."

She smiled a little at this not entirely successful attempt at humor. "If it will help, you may tell your tailor from me that he outdid himself. Mr. Pickett looked quite splendid."

"Aye, he did at that, didn't he?" His smile faded as he regarded the still figure in the bed. "He's a good lad. I would hate to lose him."

"So would I," she said softly.

"It was kind of you to stay with him," Mr. Colquhoun said. "I'll arrange for someone to relieve you as soon as may be, and you can return home. I'll send a hackney for you, shall I?"

"No!" The word came out more forcefully than she had intended. "That is, I thank you for your generous offer, Mr. Colquhoun, but it is unnecessary. I won't leave him. Nor will I entrust him to anyone else's care," she added, thinking of the surgeon she had so recently routed.

He opened his mouth as if prepared to argue the point, but apparently thought better of it. "Very well, then, if you insist." He paused for a moment before adding uncomfortably, "Look here, my lady, I hate to ask, but there's some fellow at Bow Street claiming a madwoman at this address threatened him with a knife."

"Oh." She gave a shaky little laugh that held more of hysteria than humor. "I'm afraid that would be me. It was the surgeon, you see. He — he was going to shave Mr. Pickett's head and — and drill a hole — a hole in his skull and — and —"

They came again, the tears that were never far away. Mr. Colquhoun put his arms around her and patted her awkwardly on the back while she sobbed onto his shoulder. "There, there, my lady, he's young and strong. He may pull through yet."

At length she extricated herself from his

embrace and looked up at him, her expression tortured. "Mr. Colquhoun, that surgeon — Mr. Portman — he said if I refused to let him operate, Mr. Pickett's death would be on my head. Tell me, did I do the wrong thing in sending him away?"

"I think it much more likely that you saved the boy's life — although for how long is anyone's guess." He hesitated a moment, then added in gruff tones, "I believe I owe you an apology, my lady. I once accused you of toying with Mr. Pickett's affections."

She shook her head and dabbed at her eyes. "No, you were quite right to speak to me as you did. At the time, I had no thought of — I should have scoffed at the notion that —" She broke off and looked down at Pickett's slumbering form, then bent to brush a brown curl away from his forehead. "He has a way of slipping past one's defenses."

The magistrate followed her gaze to his youngest Runner, and nodded. "He does, I'll not deny it."

There seemed to be nothing to say to this observation, so Lady Fieldhurst reached for the torn and blood-stained gown lying on the floor. "You may sit with him, if you wish. I'll just go into the other room and make myself presentable." She wrinkled her nose.

"If this garment can be so described."

"Pshaw! I've daughters older than you, so you need not put that thing back on for my sake. I would like to sit with him awhile, if you've no objection, and when I leave I should be happy to deliver a message to your servants with a list of your requirements, if you wish."

"I should be most grateful, Mr. Colquhoun. I shall make out a list at once."

The magistrate returned to the outer room to fetch a chair, while Lady Fieldhurst cast about in her mind for where in the small flat she might find paper and pencil for writing out a list of her immediate needs. She recalled that Pickett carried a small notebook — an occurrence book, he called it — in the inside breast pocket of his coat, and she picked up the ruined blue coat he had worn the previous night and reached into its pocket. Her fingers located both notebook and pencil, as well as something else that her mind immediately rejected as impossible. She drew it out, and found herself staring at a necklace set with the largest diamonds she had ever seen.

"Oh, John," she breathed, glancing from the diamonds to the still figure on the bed. "What have you done?"

CHAPTER 7

WHICH INTRODUCES
MR. THOMAS GILROY, PHYSICIAN

A moment's reflection was sufficient to convince Julia that, appearances to the contrary, Mr. Pickett had done nothing at all, at least insofar as the Princess Olga's diamonds were concerned. Granted, she knew all about his past as a juvenile pickpocket; Mr. Colquhoun had told her some months earlier, while practically in the same breath accusing her of amusing herself at Mr. Pickett's expense. But whatever Mr. Pickett had been forced to do in his younger days, whether to keep food in his belly or to please a father who was apparently a habitual ne'er-do-well, she knew what sort of man he was. And she knew — she *knew* — he never would have resorted to theft now, not even to make himself a wealthy man and, therefore, a more acceptable husband to a woman above his station . . .

Stop it, she told herself firmly. Mr. Pickett had not stolen the diamonds, and that was the end of it. Unfortunately, there remained the question of how they had come to be in his pocket. Had they been stolen already and had he, perhaps, already recovered them? She dismissed this hopeful notion at once. They had been together the entire time, except for the few minutes she had been in the cloak room, and that hadn't been nearly long enough; to be sure, John Pickett was good at his work — as she had reason to know — but no one was *that* good.

There was only one thing to do. She would give the diamonds to Mr. Colquhoun, and let him sort it out. She let the ruined blue coat fall to the floor and rose to her feet with the diamonds in her hand, then turned to the magistrate.

She froze where she stood. Mr. Colquhoun had drawn up a chair next to the side of the bed and sat there holding Mr. Pickett's limp hand in his. The magistrate's shoulders were slumped, and it seemed to Julia that he had aged years since she had seen him in Scotland the previous October. It seemed almost indecent to witness the man's silent grief. Feeling like a voyeur, she began to back quietly from the room.

But apparently not quietly enough.

"In my profession," Mr. Colquhoun said, his gaze never leaving the unconscious young man in the bed, "you learn very quickly that you can't save them all. Still, if I could save only one, I'm glad it was this one."

She could not add to his burden by introducing the possibility that his reformed pickpocket was perhaps not quite so reformed, after all. She slipped the diamonds into the inside breast pocket of the brown coat she still wore, and crossed the room to stand beside him.

"You are much attached to Mr. Pickett, are you not?"

"I could not love the boy more if he were my own son."

She laid her hand on his shoulder and gave it a little squeeze of silent sympathy. If he noticed the gesture, he gave no sign.

"He looks so very young," the magistrate continued. "Scarcely older than when I sent his father to Botany Bay."

Lady Fieldhurst could not agree. Yes, he was young, but it had been no boy who had carried her down a makeshift rope on his back while fire raged all around them. Nor, for that matter, had it been a boy whom she had stripped and bathed, but she could hardly make such an observation to Mr. Colquhoun.

Almost as if he had read her thoughts, the

magistrate turned away from Pickett to ask, "If I may be so bold, my lady, who undressed him and put him to bed?"

She lifted her chin and said with a hint of defiance, "I did."

To her surprise, Mr. Colquhoun smiled. "He's going to hate that, you know, when he wakes up and finds out."

She could have kissed him for saying "when" and not "if."

"I wonder," she said, answering the magistrate's smile with a mischievous one of her own, "would it make things better or worse if I were to assure him that I saw nothing to give me a disgust of his person?"

"Oh, decidedly worse," he said, chuckling. He heaved himself up from the chair. "I'd best be getting back to Bow Street. It promises to be a busy day, but I'll look in on him again as soon as I'm able."

She nodded. She hated letting the Bow Street force labor in ignorance, but she dared not reveal John Pickett's possession of the diamonds until she'd had time to consider the matter more carefully.

Mr. Colquhoun glanced down at the still figure on the bed. "I'll have my own physician stop by to take a look at him, shall I? Besides being an old friend, Thomas Gilroy trained in Edinburgh in both medicine and surgery." Seeing rejection writ large on her expressive countenance, he added, "He needs medical care, my lady, and I promise you he could not be placed in better hands."

She considered the offer with obvious reluctance before reaching a conclusion almost against her will. "Yes, please."

"You will not regret it, I assure you. Now, if you've finished with that list, I'll see that it's delivered."

It took her a moment to remember that she was supposed to be making a list of anything she needed her servants to send. The discovery of the diamonds in Mr. Pickett's coat had driven everything else out of her mind. "I'm afraid I haven't even started it," she confessed. "I haven't any paper, and don't know where he might keep it."

"Pray allow me."

Mr. Colquhoun reached into the pocket of his coat and withdrew a notebook similar to the one Mr. Pickett carried. He offered it to her, and she detached the tiny pencil and jotted down her immediate needs. Clean clothes, of course, and a toothbrush. A brush for her hair, as well as hairpins to replace the ones she'd lost. Decent tea would be nice, along with something to eat. Last but by no means least, a warming pan for Mr. Pickett's bed.

Having completed her inventory, she handed the list back to the magistrate. "Thank you, sir. It is good of you to take the trouble."

He waved away her thanks. "Not at all. The least I can do, under the circumstances." He looked down at Pickett, still unmoving. "You'll take care of him?"

"I will." The two simple words carried the weight of a solemn vow.

He subjected her to a long, searching look, then, apparently satisfied with what he saw, gave a nod and took his leave.

Left alone to wait for the doctor, she decided the first order of business was finding something to do with the diamonds. It would not do for them to be found in Mr. Pickett's possession before she'd decided how to handle the situation. She glanced around the small room in search of a hiding place, and settled on a rickety chest of drawers in one corner. She pulled open the top drawer (grimacing at the screech of ill-fitting wood on wood) and found herself looking at Mr. Pickett's linens. Two folded shirts held pride of place in the center of the drawer, with as many cravats on the left and several pairs of stockings on the right. She slipped the diamonds underneath the pile of stockings, noting as she did so the hole in the toe of one and the ladder in another.

She bent a stern gaze upon the still figure in the bed. "Your stockings are in a deplorable state, Mr. Pickett," she scolded. "You need a woman to take care of you — and I *don't* mean Mrs. Catchpole!"

Nor, for that matter, did she mean the brazen creature in the bilious purple bonnet who had accompanied him to the theatre on that earlier occasion, while as for Emily Dunnington's former housemaid, Dulcie — well, the less said about her, the better. Really, thought Julia, the man had an absolute genius for attracting women who weren't good enough for him.

Having disposed of the diamonds, at least temporarily, there was nothing for her to do but await the doctor's arrival. She tugged Pickett's brown coat more closely around her, noting the early-morning chill in the room; the fire had died in the night. She instinctively looked 'round for a bell pull, then remembered that Mr. Pickett would not have the luxury of summoning a servant. If she wanted a fire, she would have to build it herself. She had seen her servants perform this task a thousand times, but never paid particularly close attention to how it was done. She knew how to light her own

112

bedside candle, however; how different could it be?

With this argument to give her confidence, she identified the coal scuttle next to the hearth, and was thankful to find it full; she would have had no idea how to obtain more, had it been empty. She dumped a pile of coals over the ashes of last night's blaze, sending up a cloud of dust that sent her into a fit of coughing. Having accomplished this small feat, she struck the flint, but by the time she set it to the coal, the spark was extinguished. A second attempt fared no better, nor did a third. Clearly, lighting a candle and starting a fire were not so similar as she had supposed.

Lighting a candle . . .

Inspiration dawned. She rose and lit the candle on Pickett's bedside table, then picked it up and, sheltering the tiny flame with her cupped hand, carried it across the room to the hearth. Here she knelt and held the candle to the coals, snatching her hand back as soon as the flame caught. Or such had been her intention. In her determination to avoid singed fingers, however, she had not held the flame to the coals long enough. Worse, her abrupt movement in withdrawing the candle had caused its flame to go out. Heaving a sigh, she relit the candle and repeated the process. Gingerly, she tried again, and again, and on the fourth attempt the coals finally ignited.

She stood up and dusted her hands, congratulating herself on achieving this minor victory, then glanced about the small flat. It was surprising to discover that, although she had no doubts about John Pickett's integrity — even to the point of exonerating him of jewel theft in the teeth of all evidence — she really knew very little of the minutiae of his life. She supposed he must do the same things any other man would do: there on the washstand, for instance, was the bowl and pitcher from which he must wash every day, and she supposed the spotted mirror that hung above it from a rusty nail would reflect back his face every morning as he shaved. She glanced back at him, and saw the faintest shadow on his jaw. His beard was not heavy — little more than peach fuzz, in fact — and for this she was grateful. The poor man had suffered enough without having his throat slit by her inexperienced attempts to shave him.

She wandered from the bedroom into the larger outer room, and here too she found fodder for her growing curiosity. The mismatched cups hanging from hooks above the table, for instance: Did he ever entertain visitors to tea? She rejected the mental image of the purple-bonneted girl from the theatre sitting at Mr. Pickett's table, sipping tea with her pinkie finger extended. Perhaps, Julia told herself hopefully, he owned three cups simply to spare himself the constant washing of one. To give her thoughts a happier direction, she turned her attention to the little collection of books over the mantel. Were they worn from repeated readings, or had they been purchased at secondhand? She took down a volume at random and opened it.

"*The History of Tom Jones, a Foundling,* by Henry Fielding," she read aloud. "Why, Mr. Pickett, you wicked man!"

She returned the scandalous tome to its shelf and chose another. *The Vicar of Wakefield,* one of her mother's favorites. Would he be able to hear her, she wondered, if she were to read aloud?

Her explorations were interrupted by a knock at the door. She opened it to discover a man with a black leather bag, a tall, lean man with a lined face and mild blue eyes behind wire-rimmed spectacles. "Mr. Thomas Gilroy, physician," he said, offering his card. "My longtime patient and friend, Mr. Patrick Colquhoun, sent me. I hope I have the right place, Mrs. — ?"

"Mrs. Pickett," Julia said without hesitation. "Mrs. John Pickett. Yes, you've come to the right place. Won't you come in?"

As she stepped aside, she recalled her unorthodox costume. If she were truly Mrs. Pickett, and lived here with him as his wife, she would surely have had other garments readily to hand. "I apologize for receiving you like this, Mr. Gilroy. The fire, you see — I've had no time to change —"

The physician nodded in understanding. "I have seen worse in my years of practice, Mrs. Pickett, I assure you. And the patient?"

"My husband." Strange, really, how easily the words came. "If you will come this way?"

She led him into the bedroom, wondering a little at the physician's easy acceptance of them as husband and wife. Had Mr. Colquhoun cautioned him to expect an unequally matched couple, or had the fire and its aftermath eradicated the most obvious indicators of their difference in station? Somehow this possibility was not as distressing as it should have been.

She watched as the physician deftly unwrapped the bloodied cravat from Pickett's head, frowning as he exposed the injury. "How — how bad is it, Doctor?"

"It is difficult to say, at least until I can have a better look." He opened the bag and began taking out instruments. Among the more easily identified of these were a scissors and a straight razor.

"What are you going to do?" asked Julia, wide-eyed with apprehension.

"First I am going to cut the hair away from the wound, then shave —"

She flung herself across Pickett's recumbent form. "No! I won't let you!"

"Mrs. Pickett —"

"Mr. Colquhoun said you would be different, but you're just like that other one! Now, get out!"

His brow puckered. "What 'other one,' ma'am, if I may ask?"

"Mr. Portman, the surgeon who saw him first. He wanted to shave his head and drill a hole in his skull, and — and — and I wouldn't let him, and I won't let you, either!"

"I should think not!" exclaimed the doctor, appalled. "It sounds barbaric! Mrs. Pickett, I have no intention of drilling any holes in anything, least of all your husband's head. I merely wish to get a good look at the injury, and to do this, I must cut away some of the hair covering it. It may need to be sutured, and I have found that if hair is caught inside, the wound is more likely to become infected, which is always the greatest danger in cases where the skin is broken. I assure you," he added, seeing her beginning to waver, "I will cut no more than is absolutely necessary."

She sat down on the edge of the bed and studied Pickett's expressionless face as if searching for answers there.

"All right," she said at last, brushing the long brown curls back from his forehead with gentle fingers. "But may I — may I have the lock of hair you cut?"

The physician smiled kindly and proffered the scissors. "Ma'am, you may wield them yourself, if you wish."

She thanked Mr. Gilroy but declined his offer, well aware that her hands were shaking far too badly to attempt so delicate an operation. Instead, she watched as the doctor snipped away a lock of Pickett's hair, leaving a shorn spot about the size of a shilling on his scalp. When he had finished, she accepted the lock of hair and tied it with one of the ribbons from her ruined blue dress. While the physician continued his work, she fetched a handkerchief from Pickett's linen drawer and folded the token inside, then tucked it into her bodice.

When she turned back toward the bed, the doctor was just straightening up, having cleaned Pickett's wound and wrapped his head in a smaller and rather neater bandage.

"Well, Mr. Gilroy?" she prompted him. "How — how is he?"

The physician did not answer at once, but gestured toward the door leading to the outer room. Julia followed him, and once they were out of the bedroom, the doctor closed the door.

"Can he hear us?" she asked.

"It is difficult to say. There have been cases where the patient awakened and was able to recount in great detail conversations that had taken place while he was apparently insensible. In other cases, the newly awakened patient seemed unaware of anything that had taken place, not even the passage of time." He hesitated a moment before continuing in quite a different tone of voice. "And in others, I fear, the patient never woke up at all or, perhaps worse, awoke only to live out the rest of his life in an infantile state, unable to speak or even to care for himself in the most basic ways."

Feeling suddenly ill, Julia groped for the nearest chair and sank down heavily upon it. "And — and is this what you believe will be the case with Mr. Pickett?"

"Not at all," he assured her hastily. "In fact, it is far too early for me to make any such prediction. But while we must certainly hope for the best, I must caution you to be prepared for the worst."

She made a little whimpering noise and, hugging Pickett's coat more tightly around her, began rocking back and forth.

"On a more positive note, I could introduce you to a colleague of mine who believes that in cases such as this, where the patient is apparently unresponsive, there is a great deal taking place inside the body that we cannot see. He claims the body is actually rallying its defenses to fight its way back to health, much as an army might beat a strategic retreat in order to regroup and go on the attack."

"Like our own army at Corunna a month ago?" asked Julia with a skeptical twist of her lips. "That retreat, as I recall, did not end so well."

"Alas, too true," he acknowledged with a sigh. "And in just the same way, the body may or may not be successful in its fight. I do not wish to distress you, Mrs. Pickett, but I wonder if you will tell me exactly what befell your husband. I believe he was injured in the fire last night?"

"Yes." She forced herself to speak, and found that the effort of framing a coherent reply served to calm her. "It was when the roof fell. Something struck him in the head.

I suppose a board or something must have been thrown from the burning building by the force of the crash."

The physician frowned thoughtfully. "How very odd! God knows I am no expert, but I should have thought that the force would have been directed inward, rather than outward."

Now that Julia thought of it, she did not recall any such charred plank or timber lying on the ground nearby. Surely any piece of wood capable of striking a man with sufficient force to render him unconscious must have been large enough to be easily seen and identified.

"In fact," the doctor continued, "if you had not told me otherwise, I would have assumed — but I must not speculate."

"You would have assumed what, Mr. Gilroy?" asked Lady Fieldhurst, her curiosity by now thoroughly engaged.

"Look here, Mrs. Pickett," he said reluctantly, as if the words were being dragged from his unwilling throat, "when I cleaned your husband's wound, I removed several black splinters embedded in the flesh."

She nodded. "I see. From the board, or whatever it was that struck him."

"That is just it, ma'am. The black color was not that of charred timber, but of wood, which at some time had been painted."

Julia, picturing the opulent interior of the doomed theatre, recalled a great deal of cream, crimson, and gilding, but little if any black. "What are you saying?"

"If I had not heard an accounting of your husband's injury from your own lips, Mrs. Pickett, I would have sworn that he had been deliberately struck in the head."

CHAPTER 8

IN WHICH LADY FIELDHURST CONFRONTS TWO VERY DIFFERENT ADVERSARIES

The doctor left her with instructions to try and get water or broth down Pickett's throat, should he awaken, along with a tall black bottle containing laudanum, which she might administer should he appear to be in great pain. And yet these were not the words that filled Julia's thoughts long after the physician had gone. *Had I not heard an accounting of your husband's injury from your own lips, Mrs. Pickett . . .* But what if her accounting had been inaccurate? It was true that she had been present when the accident — if accident it was — had taken place, but she had been tucked safely under Mr. Pickett's arm and had seen nothing. In fact, she had been unaware that anything untoward had occurred until he had fallen, bearing her to the pavement beneath his weight. Was it possible she had been mistaken, and the blow to Mr. Pickett's head had been the result of a deliberate attack? But who would have done such a thing?

The answer was obvious: The same person who had planted stolen diamonds in his pocket. Which raised another disturbing possibility: Mr. Pickett had said his presence at the theatre that night — had it really been only twelve hours ago? — was supposed to be inconspicuous. In fact, his entire reason for inviting her to accompany him was so that he might be less likely to attract attention, either by committing some *faux pas* or simply by occupying a box in solitary splendor. And yet it appeared that someone must have recognized him, someone who had reason to do him harm.

Who could it be? To be sure, Mr. Pickett had achieved a certain notoriety during his investigation into her husband's murder, but even the caricatures that had appeared in the windows of the Oxford Street print shops would not have been sufficiently accurate to allow a stranger to identify him in a crowd. The first examples of the caricaturists' art had been deliberately insulting, presenting Mr. Pickett as a lecherous buffoon in the familiar red waistcoat of the Bow Street foot patrol (from which he had been promoted almost a year earlier — an inaccuracy that, to her mind, spoke volumes about the artists' integrity); the later prints, published immediately after he had cleared her name, had depicted him as possessing all the more heroic physical characteristics of a Greek god. In fact, in the days following the trial she had donned a veiled bonnet and traveled incognito to Oxford Street to purchase one of these prints for herself, and it was even now discreetly tucked away in the bottom drawer of her writing desk. She had not been entirely certain at the time of her own reasons for making this clandestine purchase; looking back, she wondered if she had been rather more taken with her rescuer than she was willing to admit. Still, she doubted that anyone unacquainted with Mr. Pickett could have successfully identified him from a likeness that even she must admit was excessively flattering.

No, someone at the theatre that night had seen Mr. Pickett and had recognized not only the man himself, but also his purpose in being there, as evidenced by the appearance of the diamonds. Perhaps she had been wrong not to turn them over to Mr. Colquhoun at once; clearly there were forces at work here far beyond her power to understand.

She returned to the bedroom where Pickett lay, and sat down on the edge of the bed.

"Mr. Pickett?" She shook him by the

shoulder as firmly as she dared, not wishing to jostle or otherwise disturb his abused head. "Mr. Pickett! John, you must wake up. Something is happening here, something frightening, and I don't know what do. Please, darling, *please* wake up!"

There was no response. She rose from the bed with a sigh and turned away. As she reached the door, however, a slight sound caught her attention. She whirled back toward the bed. The blankets stirred with the movement of Pickett's legs beneath them.

"John!" She flew back to his bedside and perched on the edge of the mattress. "John, can you hear me?"

"Foot . . ." he rasped, shifting his shoulders from side to side. "Foot . . ."

"Which foot, darling?"

She knew he had landed heavily upon their descent from the box; in fact, she rather suspected she had landed on his ankle, and he had been too gallant to say so. But which foot was it? She remembered him limping heavily, but could not recall which side he had favored. She pulled up the blankets at the end of the bed to expose his bare feet. There was no obvious injury, nothing like the wound on his head, but was his left ankle perhaps just a bit swollen? She closed her fingers around it and began to massage it gently. There was something disturbingly intimate about the act, and it occurred to her that in six years of marriage she had rarely seen Lord Fieldhurst's bare feet; certainly she had never handled them in so familiar a manner.

"Foot . . ." Pickett breathed, and slipped back into whatever nether world from which he had come.

"John? *John!*"

She received no response, but she felt hope for the first time since the dreadful moment when he had fallen. Surely the doctor's worst fears, those of a man still living yet trapped in an infantile state, were proven groundless! While she would do much to spare Mr. Pickett pain, she was convinced the fact that he could feel it at all, much less express it, was reason to be encouraged.

A knock sounded on the door, and she went to answer it with a much lighter heart.

"Thomas! Thank heaven you've —"

It was not her footman at the door, however, but a sharp-faced young woman with dark curls beneath a ghastly purple bonnet. Both women stared at one another for a long moment before the newcomer demanded in far from refined accents, "Who

127

are you, and what are you doing in John Pickett's flat?"

Lady Fieldhurst recognized the caller at once, having seen her at Drury Lane Theatre on an earlier occasion — and in the company of Mr. Pickett, at that — but she refused to give the girl the satisfaction of knowing this. "I might ask you the same thing," she responded at her aristocratic best.

The visitor lifted her pointed chin. "I'm Lucy Higgins. You might say as how I'm his dolly-moppet."

"Indeed?" responded Julia in a voice that could have frozen water. "Julia Fieldhurst Pickett. You might say as how I'm his wife."

Lucy, however, was less than impressed with this revelation. "Oh, I know all about *that*," she said, dismissing the fact of Pickett's "marriage" with a wave of her hand as she brushed past the viscountess into the room. "Say, where is he? I wanted to know what he thought about the fire last — gorblimey!" She drew up short on the threshold of the bedroom door, staring within at the still form lying in the bed, his head swathed in bandages.

"I should have liked to know what he thought about it, too, but it appears our curiosity will go unsatisfied, at least for the nonce," said Lady Fieldhurst, joining her at the bedroom door.

"What — what happened to him?" Lucy asked softly, as if fearful of waking him.

"He was at the theatre last night when the blaze broke out. We both were. He was struck in the head during our escape." There was more, of course — much more — but she had no intention of confiding in the girl, no matter how sincere her attachment to Mr. Pickett.

"And you?" Lucy regarded her incredulously. "You're nursing him?"

"Can you think of anyone better entitled to do so? I am his wife, so far as the law is concerned."

"His wife!" Lucy gave a snort of derision. "Well, that's as may be, your ladyship, but I don't mind telling you, I don't think much of any woman who would make a fellow claim his little soldier won't stand to attention, so to speak, just for the sake of letting her wriggle off the hook!"

To Julia's mind, that was the worst part of the annulment procedure, but she was not about to discuss the matter with a girl of Lucy's stamp. In fact, she was surprised and more than a little disturbed to know that Mr. Pickett would confide in the girl on a matter of such intimacy.

"He — he told you?"

Lucy shrugged. "He had to unburden himself to someone, didn't he?"

Julia supposed she should be glad he'd apparently chosen to confide in Lucy rather than Mr. Colquhoun, who until quite recently had believed her to be amusing herself at Mr. Pickett's expense. If the magistrate had known what she was asking of his protégé in order to procure an annulment, he would never forgive her. And she wasn't sure she would blame him.

She sighed. "I don't like it either, Lucy, but there are no other grounds by which we might obtain an annulment." Seeing Lucy was not convinced, she added, "I don't make the laws, you know. I'm bound by them just like everyone else."

Lucy sniffed derisively, and Julia was annoyed at her own urge to defend her actions to this impertinent female.

"I should have thought you would be happy to see the marriage annulled by whatever means possible," she said tartly. "After all, that will leave him free for you."

Lucy gave a short, bitter laugh. "Oh, I couldn't have him, even if he was to be free tomorrow." She glanced back toward the bed, and her expression grew wistful. "Not that I blame him, mind you. He's too good for the likes of me."

Julia knew she should not ask. She had no right to discuss his most intimate affairs with a relative stranger. Still, it was the question on which the annulment hung, so it might be argued that she had some right to the information. Besides which, she might never have a better opportunity to hear the answer from someone who would have every reason to know. "Lucy, is it true that he's never — that is, that he — that he's —"

"That he's a virgin? It's true so far as I know — although I've tried my best to change that. I would've done it for free, too, but he wouldn't take me up on it, not even to put a stop to the annulment once and for all." She bent a sharp look upon Julia. "He said he was tempted, but that he didn't want to trap you."

Julia was conscious of a profound sense of relief, one that had little to do with the annulment. "Believe me, Lucy, if there were any other way to annul the marriage, I would be quick to seize upon it. I am fully aware of the debt I owe him."

"And yet you're too fine a lady to marry a man who thinks you hung the moon." Lucy's tone made it clear that the words were not a compliment to Julia's breeding.

"Who are you to judge me, you insolent girl? You know nothing about my life, nothing at all!"

After all, how could Lucy possibly understand? If *she* were to marry Mr. Pickett, her status in the world would take an enormous leap forward. Besides becoming a respectable woman, she would have a husband to support her, a husband whose twenty-five shillings a week must seem like vast riches compared to Lucy's own dubiously derived earnings.

Julia, on the other hand, would be ostracized from Society and given the cut direct by all her friends. Surely no one would expect her to make such a sacrifice; Mr. Pickett, at least, did not.

It was perhaps fortunate that a knock on the door interrupted a conversation that had become uncomfortably personal. Julia hurried to answer it, and found Thomas standing just outside with a wicker basket in one hand and a large paper-wrapped parcel under his arm.

"I beg your pardon, my lady," he began, looking over her shoulder at Lucy. "I can come back later —"

"Not at all," she said hastily. "Miss Higgins was just leaving."

Lucy tossed her head and swept from the

room, leaving Thomas to follow the sway of her hips with an appreciative gleam in his eye.

"Thank you, Thomas — *Thomas!*"

His mistress's voice recalled him to the task at hand, and he surrendered his burdens. "Mr. Rogers asked me to say on behalf of the staff that we're all glad you were unharmed by the fire, my lady, and we hope Mr. Pickett is soon restored to health," he said with the air of one reciting a prepared speech.

"Please convey my thanks to the staff," she responded. "I fear I may be asking a great deal from all of you over the next several days. I promise you will be well recompensed for the extra work."

Thomas left her with assurances that all the staff were willing, even eager, to do their bit. After he had gone, she tore into the parcel in search of something to wear. Great was her indignation when she discovered that every gown inside was the unrelieved black of deepest mourning; Smithers, it seemed, had not forgiven her lapse of the previous evening. Well, Julia thought, she would not have it! If — no, *when* — Mr. Pickett awoke, he would *not* imagine himself to be attending his own funeral!

"Thomas!" She was out the door and

halfway down the stairs before she remembered she was still wearing only Pickett's coat and her own undergarments. Fortunately, her footman had heard, sparing her the necessity of pursuing him further. "Thomas, wait. I must return with you, but I dare not leave Mr. Pickett alone. Can you find the young woman who was just here, and fetch her back?"

"Yes, ma'am!" agreed Thomas with enthusiasm, pleased and gratified at the rare intersection of duty with inclination. "Right away, my lady!"

Having dispatched Thomas on this errand, Julia carried the paper parcel into the small bedroom and shut the door. She divested herself of Pickett's coat and hung it back on its hook, then stripped off her undergarments and put on fresh ones, topping them off with one of the despised mourning gowns. She sat on the edge of the bed to put on the sturdy kid half-boots (the only item in the parcel of which she could wholeheartedly approve), then bent over Pickett's still form.

"I have business to attend to at home, my love, but I'll be back soon, I promise. I've sent for Lucy to sit with you in the meantime." She leaned nearer, and lowered her voice. "You know I want you to wake up, but if you prefer to wait until I return, you will hear no objection from me," she whispered, and pressed a kiss to his forehead.

When she returned to the outer room, she found Lucy had returned and now stood regarding her warily.

"What do you want with me?" the girl demanded.

"I must make a short visit to my own residence, and I do not wish to leave Mr. Pickett alone. I wonder if you would be willing to sit with him until I return? I will be happy to recompense you for your time," she added hastily, having a vague notion that she might be taking Lucy away from potential customers.

Lucy's suspicious gaze softened as she glanced toward the bedroom door. "You don't have to pay me to stay with him, your ladyship."

"Thank you. I am obliged to you." Julia bundled up the parcel of black gowns and headed for the door. She paused on the threshold, however, and turned back. "Oh, and Lucy —"

"Your ladyship?"

"If it makes you feel any better, he's too good for the likes of me, too," she said, and left the flat, closing the door softly behind her.

When she was set down before her own house some time later, Julia burst through the front door with the light of battle in her eyes.

"My lady!" exclaimed Rogers, startled by his mistress's unexpected arrival. "May I say how pleased I am —"

She lifted a hand to cut short his greetings. "Rogers, I must see Smithers at once. I am going up to my room. Please have her attend me there."

"About Smithers, my lady —" Her foot was already on the first step, but Rogers's voice held her back. "She is in the drawing room at present."

"The drawing room? What should a lady's maid be doing in the drawing room?"

Rogers gave a discreet cough. "I believe she is closeted with Lord Fieldhurst. The current viscount, that is, not his late lordship, obviously."

"George?" She did not wait to hear more. She crossed the hall and flung open the door to the drawing room. "George! I wasn't expecting you. How very accommodating of Smithers to offer you hospitality in my absence! Shall I ring for tea, or

has she already done so?"

"Begging your pardon, your ladyship —" began the abigail, her spine ramrod straight.

"Now, Cousin Julia," interrupted the viscount, wagging his finger at her. "If half of what Smithers has been telling me is true, it seems you have been making quite a spectacle of yourself!"

"As far as the truth of Smithers's assertions, I cannot say one way or the other, for I fear she does not confide in me; that privilege is apparently reserved for you."

The viscount ticked off her sins on his fingers. "Giving up mourning before the year is out, being seen publicly with that Bow Street fellow — really, Cousin Julia, I cannot allow you to blacken the Fieldhursts' good name!"

"I see." Her accusing gaze slewed from George to Smithers, and back again. "When you suggested that I hire your butler's sister as my lady's maid, George, I believed myself to be doing a kindness for a widow in need of a position. I didn't realize I was unwittingly installing a spy beneath my own roof."

"Begging your pardon, your ladyship, but I was persuaded your lack of a steadying male influence was leading you into indiscretion. I felt Lord Fieldhurst, as the head of the family, had a right to know."

"Really, Cousin Julia, going out in colors with two months of mourning yet to run — your appearance must have been quite shocking!"

"If you think my blue gown shocking, George, you should have seen my costume an hour ago," Julia put in sweetly.

"And now — *now* — I hear you are actually staying under that fellow's roof —"

Julia took a deep breath, controlling her temper with an effort. George might say anything he pleased about her — in fact, she was quite accustomed to it by now — but he would *not* say one word against a man who was even now lying insensible due in large part to his valiant efforts in her own behalf.

"That is quite enough, George. It may have escaped even Smithers's notice that Mr. Pickett was injured last night while escaping the fire. He is lying unconscious as we speak, so I believe my virtue is quite safe."

"Then what are you doing there?" demanded George.

"I am nursing him, and I intend to do so as long as he has need of me."

"Admirable of you, I'm sure, Cousin, but I hardly think it is your place —"

Julia fairly quivered with impotent rage.

"*Not my place?* I suppose I am too fine a lady," she sputtered, unconsciously echoing Lucy's words, "to sully my hands with caring for a man who was injured in trying to rescue me from a burning theatre. What's that, George? I daresay your sources neglected to mention that Mr. Pickett fashioned a rope from the curtains and carried me bodily all the way down from a third-tier box on his back. I cannot think of a single *gentleman* of my acquaintance, including my present company, with the intelligence and resourcefulness to concoct such a scheme, much less the physical courage to carry it out. If you know of one, George, by all means introduce me, and I will be more than happy to throw Mr. Pickett over for him!"

Lord Fieldhurst, she was pleased to see, had the grace to look ashamed. "I can see why you feel you owe the man something, Cousin Julia, and I will resist the temptation to point out that had you not offended propriety by accompanying him to the theatre, you would not find yourself thus indebted. But of course a Fieldhurst, even one by marriage, must fulfill her obligations. Still, there is no need for you to tend the fellow yourself. I will be happy to hire a competent nurse to stay with Mr. Pickett as long as is necessary."

Julia regarded her late husband's heir speculatively. "Thank you, George, but no. Setting aside the fact that I am Mr. Pickett's wife, at least in the eyes of the law, I fear I can have no very great confidence in any nurse acting under your direction. I will do you the justice to say I don't think you would instruct someone to cause deliberate harm to Mr. Pickett, but I suspect you would not shed any tears were he to succumb to his injuries."

From this stance Julia refused to be moved, and at last Lord Fieldhurst, still sputtering objections, had no choice but to concede defeat.

"And now, George," she concluded, with a nod toward the paper-wrapped parcel she still held, "if you will excuse me, I must provision myself for a stay that may prove to be quite lengthy."

"But your ladyship," bleated Smithers, "I prepared that parcel myself. Did I fail to include something you requested?"

"How could I forget? Thank you for reminding me, Smithers. I see you have taken it upon yourself to pitch me back into mourning whether I wish it or not. You seem to be laboring under some confusion as to which of us is the mistress and which is the maid."

"I'm sure I never meant to —"

"Oh, I think you did *exactly* what you meant to do. Having had time to consider the matter, I am persuaded you will be much happier in the employ of a lady whose notions of propriety are more closely aligned with your own."

"What — what are you saying, my lady?"

"I am giving you notice, Smithers. You shall have two weeks' wages, but as for a reference, I fear I cannot oblige you. Perhaps George would be willing to do so. Now, if you will both excuse me, I have a great deal to attend to before I return to Drury Lane."

Rogers, an unintentional witness to this scene, lost no time in bestowing Lord Fieldhurst's hat and gloves upon him and flinging open the door for him to escape with whatever dignity he might still possess. Julia likewise dispatched Smithers to the servants' hall to pack her bags. Alone with the butler who had served her since her marriage, she regarded him ruefully. Of Rogers's loyalty, at least, she had no doubts. He had been very patient and understanding with her when she had been a young bride thrust all unprepared into command of a noble household, and she believed she had repaid his kindness when, fearing himself under suspicion of murder, he had disappeared after the death of her husband.

"Well, Rogers, I'm afraid you were an unwilling audience to quite a scene," she observed with an apologetic smile.

He executed a little bow, but his eyes twinkled in a most unbutler-like manner. "And very well played, my lady, if I may say so."

"Thank you, Rogers, you may," she said, laughing aloud in elation at having held her ground against the Fieldhursts — and won! — for the first time in her life. On a more serious note, she added, "You may also inform the laundry maid that I will be sending Mr. Pickett's soiled garments along with my own for laundering. Mrs. Hughes will no doubt notice a difference in the quality of Mr. Pickett's linens compared to those of his late lordship, but I shall expect them to be treated with equal care, and so you may tell her."

"Yes, my lady." Rogers gave a discreet little cough. "Begging your pardon, but if your ladyship wishes to bring her young man home, I can assure you that the staff will treat him with all the respect due her ladyship's husband, or they will answer to me."

Her eyebrows rose. "Surely you cannot think Mr. Pickett and I are truly married! Good heavens, George would go off in an apoplexy! In fact, it was nothing but a dreadful misunderstanding, and the annulment proceedings have already begun. How could you possibly think otherwise?"

Rogers lowered his eyes deferentially. "I'm sorry if I have misspoken, my lady, but it was an honest mistake, under the circumstances."

"Was it?" asked Julia, taken aback. "And what 'circumstances' are those, pray?"

"You will recall that I announced young Mr. Pickett last night," he reminded her apologetically.

"Yes, what of it?"

He gave her an understanding smile. "From my vantage point by the door, my lady, I could see your face when first he entered the room."

CHAPTER 9
THE CURIOUS CASE OF
THE DISAPPEARING DIAMONDS

Alone with Pickett, Lucy planted her hands on her hips and heaved a sigh. "Well, John Pickett, I always knew I'd have you naked in bed someday, but this is *not* what I had in mind."

She received no response from him — nothing new there, she reflected — so she wandered listlessly about the flat, searching for something to do to pass the time until Lady Fieldhurst returned. Spying her ladyship's untouched teacup on the small table beside the bed, she picked it up and took an experimental sip. It was cold, which was unsurprising, but of a better quality than Lucy was accustomed to, as the tea leaves typically found at the house where she lived with several other females of the same profession had generally seen more than one use before they came into the women's possession. As a result, Lady Fieldhurst's tea was rather stronger than that to which Lucy was accustomed, and the more pungent brew made her sneeze.

Having no handkerchief, she opened the top drawer of Pickett's bureau and searched for one amongst the stockings and cravats. She found one, but she also found something else — something that drove such petty concerns as handkerchiefs from her mind.

"Gorblimey!" she breathed, withdrawing a necklace of white stones the size of wrens' eggs.

Granted, Lucy was no expert on gemstones (her clientele not being made up of the class of men who might shower such riches on their paramours), but it was obvious even to her untrained eye that these stones could not possibly be real. In fact, she was not sure that diamonds of such a size existed at all; but even if they did, she was quite certain that John Pickett could not afford them. The gems, therefore, must be imitations. And since Lady Fieldhurst was not the sort of woman upon whom a man might bestow fake jewels, they were obviously never meant to adorn her ladyship's person.

If not her ladyship, then, for whom was the necklace intended? There could be only one answer, concluded Lucy, grinning in delight. He must have planned on giving it to her. After all, he did occasionally request her assistance in his investigations (although in recent months, these requests had not come as frequently as they once did), and he never failed to reward her for her efforts on his behalf, even if these rewards did not take the form she might have preferred. While it was true that she had not done anything for him lately which might merit such lavish compensation, her withers were unwrung. Clearly, he had intended to ask for her help, and had been injured before he could make the request. She had a sudden and horrible vision of him dying before he could present the gems to her, and the necklace being claimed by one of those vultures who always seemed to come from out of nowhere following the death of anyone who lacked obvious heirs.

"You've got my help whenever you need it," she promised Pickett's recumbent form, "but I'm not about to leave this thing here for no one else to find."

She opened the clasp and draped the necklace about her own neck, then admired the effect in the spotted mirror over the washstand. Her smile faded as she considered a new and terrible possibility. She had nowhere to wear such a showy piece, barring the occasional visit to the theatre with Pickett, and so it would of necessity spend a great deal of time lying at the bottom of her own bureau drawer. She had no very great faith in the honesty of any of the women with whom she shared lodgings; money was hard to come by in their shared profession, and money that did not entail spending time on one's back was especially rare. It was highly likely, then, that the necklace would be stolen from her and taken to the nearest pawnshop. Why, it might fetch as much as a guinea or more! No, Lucy decided, if anyone was going to profit from the sale of the jewels, it was going to be herself.

"I'm sure you won't mind, ducks," she told Pickett. "But I've no place to wear it, not really. Mayhap I'll take the money and buy a new gown — something that'll be less of a temptation to those harpies I live with — and I'll wear it next time you take me to the theatre. You'd like that, wouldn't you?"

Taking Pickett's silence for assent, she removed the necklace and stuffed it into her bodice.

Mr. Colquhoun, arriving at Bow Street shortly after leaving Pickett's lodgings, was met with the unsurprising information that no word had yet been heard from Mr. Pickett.

"No, I don't suppose it would have," he informed Mr. Dixon, the bearer of this bad news. "In fact, I've just come from Mr. Pickett's flat."

"He's alive, then?" asked another Runner, overhearing the discussion.

"Barely, but yes. He's unconscious — it appears he was struck in the head as he was escaping the theatre — but he is alive, at least for the nonce."

William Foote nodded. "That's good to know, sir."

Unfortunately, it was the only bright spot in Mr. Colquhoun's day. Within an hour of his return to Bow Street, he had a most unwelcome visitor in the form of a member of the Russian contingent, a tall, stout man with a thick black beard and a thicker accent.

"You tell me this will not happen, *nyet*?" this worthy accused him in menacing tones. "You say Princess Olga's jewels be safe, *da*?"

"Your Excellency, no one regrets the theft of Princess Olga's diamonds more than I do," Mr. Colquhoun said in what he hoped translated as a soothing voice. "But I'm sure I need not remind you that the theatre caught fire last night and, well, you know what the poet said about the best-laid plans of mice and men."

"*Ba!* I spit me on your English poets!"

Under different circumstances, Mr. Colquhoun might have pointed out that Robert Burns, like himself, was Scots, not English. But he reminded himself of his own words to John Pickett regarding the provocation of an international incident, and kept a firm grip on his rapidly fraying temper. "Be that as it may, Your Excellency, I'm sure you will be pleased to know that in every case, the stolen gems have eventually been recovered."

" 'Eventually'? I care nothing — *nichego,* do you hear? — for your 'eventually'! I spit me on 'eventually'!" In proof of this statement, he spat on the floor. "It is clear to me, *ser,* that you have, how do you say, a department of imbeciles!"

Mr. Colquhoun was willing to do a certain amount of boot-licking for the sake of diplomacy, but this blatantly unfair criticism of his men he would not permit. "Now see here, Your Excellency," he said, his face darkening ominously, "there's no cause to be insulting! If you'll look about you, you'll see that my men have already made a considerable sacrifice for Her Royal Highness's sake. Several of them sustained injuries in last night's fire and one, a young man not yet twenty-five years old, is even now lying at death's door. The fact that the jewels were stolen in spite of them in no way negates their efforts. But in all honesty I must tell you that if I had to make a choice between Her Royal Highness's diamonds and the lives of my men, the diamonds would lose every time."

While His Excellency sputtered over this home truth, Mr. Colquhoun glanced about the room and located William Foote among a knot of Runners, no doubt all of them discussing the fire.

"Now, Your Excellency," continued the magistrate, "one of my men has had considerable success in recovering stolen jewels. I am assigning Mr. William Foote to this case in the expectation that he will be no less successful where Her Royal Highness's diamonds are concerned. Mr. Foote!"

William Foote detached himself from the group of Runners and joined the magistrate at the bench. "You wanted me, sir?"

"This is His Excellency, Vladimir Gregorovich Dombrowsky, part of the Princess Olga Fyodorovna's entourage. He tells me the princess's diamonds were stolen last night in spite of all our precautions. You seem to be the best man where these jewel theft cases are concerned, so I'm putting you in charge. Your Excellency, you may make your complaints to Mr. Foote. I have nothing more to say to you!"

Having delivered himself of this speech, he left the bench hastily lest he say something to his noble client that he might later have cause to regret.

Alas, Mr. Colquhoun's troubles were far from over. He had to endure a most unpleasant meeting with his tailor, who was only slightly placated by the placing of a very expensive order of clothing that Mr. Colquhoun neither needed nor particularly wanted. Obeying a sudden impulse, he instructed the tailor to make up another tailcoat of Bath superfine in the same blue cloth as the one he had hired for his young protégé, and according to the same measurements, and add it to his order. He told himself that Lady Fieldhurst might yet give John Pickett occasion to wear such a garment; he rejected the half-formed idea that, should Pickett succumb to his injuries, he might be buried in it.

Mr. Colquhoun was only too glad to escape Bow Street at the end of the day, and gladder still when he called at Pickett's lodgings in Drury Lane to be met at the door by Lady Fieldhurst, no longer wearing

Pickett's brown coat over her undergarments, but clad in a morning gown of primrose yellow along with a radiant smile.

"He spoke!" she exclaimed by way of greeting. "Mr. Colquhoun, he spoke!"

"He's awake, then?" the magistrate asked eagerly, stripping off his hat and gloves as he entered the modest flat.

"No." Her smile faltered. "I'm not sure he was ever awake, at least not fully, but he did speak, and quite coherently, too."

"That's the best news I've had all day," said Mr. Colquhoun, his brow clearing. "What did he say?"

She led the way into the small bedroom, where Mr. Colquhoun was somewhat disappointed to see John Pickett lying very much as he had been when the magistrate had left him that morning.

"He complained that his feet were hurting," Lady Fieldhurst answered. "One of his feet, anyway. He didn't say which, but his left ankle appears to be slightly swollen, so I daresay that is the one. I rather think I landed on it, although he denied it at the time."

"You landed on it? My lady, I wish you will tell me exactly how the pair of you contrived to escape the fire. Having seen the theatre for myself, or what little is left of it, I am at a loss to account for it."

She gestured for him to take the single chair beside the bed while she sat on the edge of the mattress, as if her natural place were at Pickett's side. "You will find it hard to believe, I fear. The door to the box was locked from the outside, or jammed, or something, and by the time Jo — Mr. Pickett was able to get it open, the fire had reached the corridor, so going down the stairs was out of the question."

"Yes?" prompted the magistrate, tactfully ignoring her hastily corrected use of John Pickett's given name. "So what did he do?"

"He pulled down the curtain and tore it into strips, then knotted them together to make a rope for us to climb down."

Mr. Colquhoun's bushy eyebrows drew together over his nose. "You climbed down a makeshift rope in an evening gown?"

"Pray do not credit me with a courage I do not possess," she objected, raising a hand in protest. "In fact, it was Mr. Pickett who climbed down, carrying me on his back."

"Good God!" uttered the magistrate in failing accents.

"But the rope caught fire and burned through before we reached the ground, so we fell the last few feet. And I fear I may have landed on Mr. Pickett's ankle, for he was limping rather heavily when he stood up."

"And this blow on the head?"

"It happened outside, just after we had made our escape." She hesitated, wondering how much to tell him of the doctor's theory.

"And all for nothing," muttered the magistrate.

"I beg your pardon?"

"The Princess Olga's diamonds were stolen anyway, in spite of all our efforts." He looked down at the still figure in the bed. "I put him in danger for nothing. Mr. Pickett's sacrifice was in vain."

Lady Fieldhurst saw the pain in his eyes, and came to a decision. "Perhaps not, Mr. Colquhoun. There is something I must tell you."

She crossed the room to the bureau and pulled open the top drawer, then reached beneath the pile of stockings. Her hand met nothing but knitted stockinette. Surely she had put the necklace right here? Perhaps it had shifted when the drawer had been closed and opened again. She pushed aside stockings, cravats, and handkerchiefs, groping into the farthest corners of the drawer. The diamonds were gone. But who could have — her eyes narrowed as she identified the only person besides herself who had been alone with Pickett in the room. *Lucy Higgins,* she thought, *when I get my hands on you, I'm going to —*

"Yes?" prompted Mr. Colquhoun, still seated in the chair next to Pickett's bed. "What is it?"

She could hardly tell him about the diamonds now, not when she had no proof that they had ever been here. She was surprised to find herself relieved; she had dreaded seeing the look on his face when confronted with the possibility that his former pickpocket was perhaps not so reformed after all. Not, she reminded herself hastily, that she considered for one moment that John Pickett was capable of such a thing; still, unlike herself, Mr. Colquhoun had known him in his earlier, more criminal days, and might find it all too easy to believe. But now the magistrate clearly expected some revelation and, having committed herself this far, she had to tell him something.

"The doctor," she began, pausing to take a deep, steadying breath. "Your personal physician, I mean, not that dreadful surgeon! When the doctor was here, he gave it as his opinion that Mr. Pickett was deliberately struck down."

Mr. Colquhoun scowled rather fiercely. "I

see. And what evidence, if any, did he offer in support of this claim?"

"He did not think the collapse of the theatre roof would throw burning timbers outward in such a manner, and I confess I cannot recall seeing anything lying about that might have dealt Mr. Pickett such a blow. Besides that, Mr. Gilroy removed a few tiny splinters of black wood from the wound on Mr. Pickett's scalp. The black color was not from charring, he said, but from paint."

Mr. Colquhoun removed a small notebook from the inside pocket of his coat and began to make notes in just the same way she had seen Mr. Pickett do a dozen times before. "It appears I will need to have a word with my good friend Mr. Gilroy."

"In the meantime, Mr. Colquhoun, would you care for tea?" she asked.

The magistrate nodded. "Thank you, my lady, I would."

Her heart sank. Not until after she'd already made the offer did she remember that here there was no ringing for a servant; if tea were to be made, she would have to make it herself. Thankfully, the fire was already alight, so she had only to put a kettle of water over it to boil. Surely she could manage that! She filled the kettle and hooked its handle over the horizontal arm of the hinged crane affixed to one side of the fireplace. Then, very gingerly lest she scorch her fingers, she pushed the arm of the crane into the fireplace and over the fire. Or that was her intention, at any rate. Alas, she was a bit too cautious, and the arm moved only a couple of inches before halting abruptly, sending the water inside sloshing and a few drops running down the outside of the kettle to fall sizzling into the flames. After another push, and then another, the kettle was at last far enough over the fire to heat the water, but once that was done, she had no idea of how to get it out again; after all, she could hardly reach into the flames and grab it.

When the water began to boil several minutes later, she still had not come up with a solution to this predicament. She hardly knew whether to be mortified or grateful when Mr. Colquhoun, seeing her dilemma, came to her rescue.

"Here, let me get that."

He grabbed a hooked rod propped against the fireplace next to the poker, then caught the handle of the kettle with this instrument and lifted it from the crane. Julia watched, feeling utterly useless, as he traded the rod for a towel and used this to protect his hands while he poured the hot water into the teapot.

"Not that difficult, once you know how," he said reassuringly as he measured the tea leaves and added them to the water.

"Thank you," she said, giving him a rueful smile. "As you can see, I am eminently unsuited to be Mrs. John Pickett."

"About that," he said, frowning thoughtfully. "If I may be so presumptuous as to inquire, what do you intend to do about the annulment?"

She leaped to her feet and became very busy about the fetching and preparation of teacups. "At the moment, Mr. Colquhoun," she said rather more tartly than she'd intended, "I am doing my best not to be widowed again."

He made no response beyond a little grunt, which she took for a sign of approval, and she was thankful he did not press the issue. He lingered for half an hour, obviously hoping for some further sign of life from Pickett. Alas, these hopes were in vain, and Lady Fieldhurst was torn between sympathy for the magistrate and impatience for his departure, so that she might turn the modest flat upside down searching for the missing diamonds. At last he took his leave, and no sooner had the door closed behind him than she turned the key in the lock and began her exploration.

She started with the bureau, turning out not only the top drawer, but the rest of the drawers as well. She made two interesting discoveries, neither of which had anything to do with the missing jewels. In the second drawer down, she found three letters, tied together with a ribbon and written on paper of such a superior quality that her curiosity was instantly aroused. She glanced back at Pickett and found him still unconscious. Berating herself for a Nosey Parker, she nevertheless untied the ribbon and unfolded the topmost letter. She recognized it at once. *Mr. Pickett,* it read, *I would be honored. You may call for me at eight. Julia Fieldhurst Pickett.* Although of a somewhat earlier date, the other two were in her handwriting as well, both setting a time and date for a meeting with her solicitor to discuss an annulment. He'd kept her letters, the dear man, even after learning exactly what the annulment would require of him. Tears filled her eyes, and she dashed them away with the back of her hand.

"You are turning into a veritable watering pot," she scolded herself.

She tucked the letters back into their hiding place and returned to her search. She saw no sign of the diamonds, but in the bottom drawer, pushed all the way to the back and covered with what was apparently a spare set of bed linens, she found a pistol. She did not know quite what to make of this discovery; she had never thought of her gentle Mr. Pickett with a gun. She wondered if, should circumstances ever require it of him, he would be able to shoot a man in cold blood; she wondered if he already had. Shuddering at the thought, she put the pistol back where she had found it.

As Pickett's flat was small, even the most thorough of searches did not take long. Still, the work was tiring, and by the time she had finished the fruitless task, she was very conscious of the fact that she had not slept in almost forty-eight hours. She supposed she would have to confront Lucy, but even if she were willing to leave Pickett alone, she was not about to go capering about this less savory section of London alone in search of the girl. Setting aside the problem of the diamonds until she was well rested enough to approach it logically, she searched through Smithers's parcel and located a white linen night rail and her silver-backed hairbrush, part of a toilette set that had been a wedding gift from her parents. She removed her yellow gown and hung it from a peg beside Pickett's coats, then stripped off her undergarments and pulled the night rail over her head. Lastly, she took down her hair and brushed it out.

She fetched a thin blanket from the bottom drawer of the bureau (trying not to think about the pistol it concealed), then sat down on the wooden straight chair beside the bed, blew out the candle on the bedside table, and pulled the blanket up to her chin. Unfortunately, five minutes of squirming from side to side were sufficient to inform her that she was unlikely to get any sleep here, and the same search that had not yielded up the diamonds had been sufficient to inform her that the flat housed inadequate bedding for making up a pallet on the floor. If she was to sleep at all, it would have to be on the bed.

She cast the blanket aside, then tiptoed over to Pickett's bed, lifted the edge of the covers, and slid beneath, lying as near the edge of the mattress as she could without falling off. It occurred to her that, although she had been married for six years, she had never slept beside the late Lord Fieldhurst; like most aristocratic couples, they had maintained separate bedchambers with an adjoining door. At the end of her husband's conjugal visits, he had always bade her a good night and then returned to his own room. As the years passed with no sign of the hoped-for heir, these visits had become more and more sporadic, until at last the adjoining door might have ceased to exist and neither of them would have noticed its absence.

Now, lying stiffly beside John Pickett, she reflected that someday, after the annulment was granted, he would have a real wife — a real Mrs. Pickett who would know how to build a fire and be able to boil water for tea over it, and who would be entitled, if she so desired, to roll over into the center of the mattress and curl up against her sleeping husband's side . . .

Sleep, so near only moments ago, had fled. She threw off the covers and left the bed, looking about the darkened room for some way to pass the empty hours. She remembered the stockings in the top drawer of the bureau and fetched a pile of these, along with her work basket, then picked up the flint and relit the candle on the bedside table. She wrinkled her nose at the hole in the toe. If she were really his wife, she would throw them all out and buy him new ones. No, she thought, smiling a little, if she were really his wife, she would outfit him from head to toe just as he had been at the

162

theatre. Not in evening clothes, of course, at least not all the time, but she had rather liked him in blue. She drew the chair nearer to the feeble light, threaded her needle, and set to work, singing softly to herself the duet from Handel's *Esther*.

" 'Who calls my parting soul from death? Awake my soul, my life, my breath . . .' "

Dimly, through the pain in his head, Pickett heard a female voice singing, and gingerly opened his eyes. An angel in white sat beside the bed, golden hair spilling over her shoulders as she plied her needle by the light of a single candle.

"Am I . . ." His voice came out as a croak. "Am I dead?"

The angel cast aside her sewing and came to sit on the edge of the bed. "Why, no, you're not dead!" She stroked the matted brown curls away from his face with gentle fingers. "You have been injured, my love, but I intend to take very good care of you."

She had not meant to call him that. It had slipped out all on its own, but his brain was too cloudy to notice.

"My lady? What . . . what are you doing here?"

"At the moment, I am darning your stockings," she said, gesturing toward her work

163

basket. "They really are in appalling condition, you know. Can I get you some water, or perhaps laudanum for the pain?"

He frowned. "You shouldn't . . . shouldn't be here."

"And where else should I be, but beside my husband in his hour of need?"

She wasn't sure he was capable of understanding a jest. His gaze was growing cloudier by the second, and he seemed to be slipping away before her eyes. He did smile, though, however feebly, and she knew he had heard and understood.

"I wish . . . I . . . wish . . ."

And then he was gone, returned to whatever twilight world held him captive. "I know," she whispered, blinking back tears. "So do I."

CHAPTER 10

IN WHICH LADY FIELDHURST COMES TO A DECISION

A firm knock on the door awakened Julia the following morning, and she was surprised to discover that she had contrived to fall asleep on her chair after all. She rose stiffly and fumbled for her dressing gown in the parcel of clothing packed by Smithers. In fact, she had been more than a little surprised to find her pink satin wrapper folded neatly and tucked in amongst the black mourning gowns; she could only suppose the lady's maid had found the prospect of her mistress wearing such a fanciful garment less objectionable than the thought that she might appear before a man — even an unconscious one — in nothing but her night rail. She shoved her arms into the sleeves of her wrapper, tied the belt about her waist, and opened the door, fully expecting to see Mrs. Catchpole with a fresh supply of water and a scuttle full of coal. But it was not the landlady who stood there on the other side of the door.

"Why, Mr. Colquhoun!" she exclaimed, surprised to see the magistrate at so early an hour. "I should have thought you would be at the Bow Street office."

"It's Sunday," he pointed out. "Even magistrates have an occasional day off, you know."

"Is it Sunday already?" She put a hand to her forehead, blinking in confusion. "Time seems to have stood still for me, I'm afraid."

"I don't doubt it," he said, striding past her into the room, "which is why I'm going to stay here while you return to your own house and get some sleep."

"Oh, but I couldn't possibly —"

"Of course you can." He brushed aside her objections as easily as he might have a frivolous claim brought before the magistrate's bench. "My coachman is waiting below with instructions to take you home. I regret I could not furnish him with the street and number, so you will have to do so yourself."

She shook her head. "This is very thoughtful of you, Mr. Colquhoun, but quite unnecessary. If it is indeed Sunday — and I suppose it must be — then you will want to be in church."

"I happen to believe my Christian duty

lies elsewhere this morning. I implore you, my lady," he added coaxingly, "if you will not do it for your own sake, pray do it for mine. Mr. Pickett will never forgive me if he wakes up and discovers that I've let you wear yourself out with nursing him."

She suspected he was probably right, and felt herself weakening. Still, she could not like the idea of leaving Mr. Pickett, even in such capable hands as his magistrate's. "He did awaken last night, very briefly," she confessed, glancing toward the bedroom. "If he should wake up again and find me gone —"

"I shall promise him you will return later." Seeing her beginning to waver, he added, "Come, my lady, you can be no good to him if you are asleep on your feet."

"Very well," she said with obvious reluctance. "Only give me a chance to get dressed."

She allowed Mr. Colquhoun to look in on Pickett while she changed clothes in the outer room, although this reluctance to disrobe in the presence of the unconscious Pickett had less to do with modesty than with a reluctance to suggest to the magistrate a degree of intimacy between herself and his most junior Runner that she was only just beginning to admit, even to herself.

As she fastened the bodice of her peach-colored kerseymere morning gown, she recalled several instructions for Mr. Colquhoun. She could not in good conscience leave Pickett to his magistrate's care without first unburdening herself.

"If he should awaken again, Mr. Colquhoun, pray do not worry him with questions about the jewel theft, for he is still far from well," she cautioned him as she took her leave.

"I promise," he said, walking with her as far as the door.

"And try to persuade him to drink something," she continued. "I should have done so last night, but I was so surprised to see him awake that I did not think of it until he had slipped away again, and it was too late."

"I shall do my best," promised Mr. Colquhoun, pushing her gently but firmly out the door.

"And if he is in pain, you may give him a dose of laudanum. You will find the bottle on the table beside the bed."

"Very well," said Mr. Colquhoun, and prepared to shut the door in her face.

"Oh, and Mr. Colquhoun —"

He heaved a very pointed sigh. "Yes, my lady?"

"If — if there is any — any change — will

you please send for me?"

He did not pretend to misunderstand her. "If he should take a sudden turn for the worse, I shall send for you at once," he said, more gently this time.

"Thank you," she whispered, and allowed him, finally, to close the door.

He turned the key in the lock lest she recall any further instructions, and blew out a long breath. "If ever two young people needed their heads knocked together!" Shaking his head over the folly of youth, the magistrate went into the bedroom where his young protégé slept.

His vigil was long and tedious, being interrupted only once, by Mrs. Catchpole with the water and coal she had promised. He answered her probing questions with the curtest of replies, and she soon returned to her shop, torn between annoyance at being so soundly rebuffed and pleasure in the presence under her roof of so forceful and distinguished a gentleman.

And then, about four hours into Mr. Colquhoun's watch, Pickett stirred and opened his eyes.

"My lady?" he muttered.

"No, I'm afraid you'll have to settle for your magistrate," said Mr. Colquhoun, shifting his chair so that Pickett might see him

169

without being obliged to turn his head.

"There was — there was a fire," Pickett said, his voice somewhat stronger. "Lady Fieldhurst —"

"Lady Fieldhurst is quite all right — which is more than I can say for you," he added with a sternness that did not quite disguise his concern.

Pickett smiled wistfully. "I thought she was here. Dreaming, I guess."

"That was no dream. Her ladyship has been nursing you ever since your heroics at the theatre."

"This is no place for her," Pickett protested, frowning. "She shouldn't have to do such a thing."

"I should like to see you try and stop her! I did insist she go home and sleep, however."

"Thank you, sir. That was good of you."

"Nonsense! Least I could do, since you might say I'm responsible for the whole thing."

"No sir, how could you be?" Startled, Pickett turned his head toward the magistrate, and instantly regretted it. "God, my head hurts!"

"I don't doubt it. The doctor left a bottle of laudanum to ease the pain. I can give you some, if you'd like."

"I would, sir, thank you."

Mr. Colquhoun measured out the dose, and Pickett raised himself onto one elbow to swallow it down.

"Nasty-tasting stuff, as I recall," observed the magistrate. "Perhaps some water to chase it down?"

Pickett nodded, and drank deeply from the glass the magistrate held to his lips. Then he collapsed back onto the pillows, exhausted from even these minor accomplishments. "What about the princess's diamonds?" he asked. "Were they stolen?"

"Never mind that now," Mr. Colquhoun said, rearranging the blankets that had slipped down.

"They were stolen, weren't they?" Pickett persisted.

Mr. Colquhoun hesitated. He remembered Lady Fieldhurst's warning against badgering the young Runner with questions; in fact, he quite agreed with her ladyship on the matter. But he suspected Pickett would fret himself more over what he didn't know than he would over an abbreviated account of the truth. "Yes, they were stolen," he admitted.

Pickett nodded, and grimaced at the pain in his head. "I thought they must have been." His voice was weaker, although whether this was the result of his exertions or of the laudanum he'd been given, Mr. Colquhoun did not know. "The fire —"

"You're not to worry your head over it, do you understand?" the magistrate added hastily. "I've got a man on it, and I have no doubt the diamonds will be recovered very shortly."

"But — no arrest?"

Mr. Colquhoun sighed. "No, no arrest, I'm afraid."

Pickett shifted suddenly in the bed and grabbed the magistrate's arm. "Something strange . . ." he said, his eyes beginning to glaze over. "At the theatre . . . meant to tell you . . ."

Even as he spoke, his grip on Mr. Colquhoun's sleeve slackened and his hand fell away.

"You can tell me later, John. Try to rest now —"The magistrate patted his shoulder. " — son."

Lady Fieldhurst did not realize how weary she was until she lay down on her own bed. She fell asleep almost the instant her head hit the pillow, and slept soundly for the next six hours. She awoke with her head thick and stupid, and could not at first recall why she was asleep in what must be, to judge by the light spilling through the bedroom

172

windows, the middle of the day. Then it all came rushing back: the fire, the theft of the diamonds, and worst of all, Mr. Pickett lying insensible in a small flat in Drury Lane.

It was this last that spurred her to action. She threw back the covers, splashed water over her face to banish the last of the cobwebs, and dressed quickly, anxious to return to him with all possible speed. She had almost finished her hasty toilette when she heard a light scratching at the door.

"Come in," she called.

The door opened, and Thomas the footman stuck his head in. "Begging your pardon, ma'am, but Lady Dunnington is below."

Julia sighed. At any other time she would have been delighted to see her friend, whom she had believed to be wintering with her husband at the Dunnington country estate. But now all her thoughts were for John Pickett, who might be waking up at any moment and wondering at her absence.

"Very well, Thomas, I shall see her. You may show her into the drawing room, and tell her I shall be down directly."

Thomas hurried away to carry out these instructions, and a few minutes later Julia joined her friend in the drawing room.

"Julia, my dear, where in the world have

you been keeping yourself?" demanded Emily Dunnington, greeting her with air kisses on either side of her face. "I have been trying to see you since yesterday, and your servants have steadfastly denied me with the most cryptic of excuses!"

"I beg your pardon, Emily, but it has been a rather difficult few days," said Julia, marveling at her own previously unsuspected talent for understatement. "I suppose you have heard about the fire at Drury Lane Theatre on Friday night?"

"Oh, yes," said Emily with a wave of one white hand. "All of London is abuzz. From what I hear, it brought Handel's *Esther* to a screeching halt. It must have been quite dreadful."

Lady Fieldhurst shuddered at the memory. "It was. I was there."

"Julia! I trust you are all right. But what of the rest of your party? Much as I dislike the new Lord Fieldhurst, I should not wish to see him burned to a cinder."

"Nor should I, but I was not in the Fieldhurst box." She took a deep breath, bracing herself for the recriminations that were sure to follow. "In fact, I was accompanying Mr. Pickett."

"*What?* My dear Julia, never say you sat in the pit!"

"Of course not! Mr. Pickett was on an assignment, and was stationed in one of the boxes. He needed a — a female companion to render him less conspicuous, and so he invited me to accompany him. And I accepted."

"*Less conspicuous?* A lady whose husband has been dead for less than a year, and who was herself suspected of murdering him? I can see how your Mr. Pickett might be unfamiliar enough with the ways of the *ton* to persuade himself that such a scheme might work, but not you. Surely you must have known better!"

"Perhaps, but it is all water under the bridge now. In any case, the fire must have driven all else from the *ton*'s collective mind."

"Yes, the fire," said Lady Dunnington, her eyes narrowing in concern. "How did you contrive to escape?"

"Oh, Emily, I wish you might have been there!" exclaimed Lady Fieldhurst, raising glowing eyes to hers.

"In a burning theatre? I am very glad I was not!"

Julia continued as if she had not spoken. "He was quite magnificent. The fire had already reached the corridor just outside the box, cutting off all hope of escape for us that way. So Mr. Pickett tore down the curtains and fashioned them into a rope, then climbed down while carrying me on his back."

Lady Dunnington listened to this recital in wide-eyed amazement, but her response, when it came, was not what Julia could have wished.

"Poor, *poor* Lord Rupert!" she exclaimed, invoking the name of the man who had almost been Julia's lover. "He never stood a chance against such a figure of romance!"

Julia frowned at her friend's levity. "It isn't funny, Emily. Mr. Pickett suffered an injury just after we escaped the theatre, and is even now unconscious in his flat in Drury Lane. I have been there since the night of the fire, nursing him. But enough about me," she added hastily, lest Lady Dunnington start asking uncomfortable questions. "You said you had been trying to see me. For what, pray?"

As a strategy, it worked beautifully. Lady Dunnington grabbed her hand and gave it a squeeze. "My dear Julia, you will never credit it! Dunnington has brought me to London to consult with an *accoucheur*. It appears we are anticipating a blessed event late this summer."

"Emily, how wonderful!" exclaimed Julia,

recalling that it was Mr. Pickett who was indirectly responsible for the reconciliation of Emily and her long-estranged husband.

"I hope it may be a girl this time, since we already have the two boys. How I should enjoy launching a daughter into Society! Only think, Julia, if you and Fieldhurst had had a son, they might have made a match!" Her smile disappeared abruptly. "What a stupid thing to say! Forgive me, Julia, I did not mean —"

"No, no, it is quite all right. It does not hurt so much as it once did," Julia assured her, and was surprised to discover that it was true. While a part of her would always regret her childless state, she had recently discovered that there were other endeavors to which she could turn her mind, other causes to which she could devote herself. And for this, she knew, she had John Pickett to thank.

"I am glad of that, for I have something particular to ask you, but *not* if it would cause you pain! I should like it very much if you would agree to be the child's godmother."

"Why, Emily, I would be delighted! Only," she added, her smile fading, "are you quite certain? It seems to me that a godmother should be someone in a position to do something to help establish the child in some way, and — well, I am not quite sure if you — that is —"

"Julia, you cannot still be thinking of Fieldhurst's death, can you? It is not as if you ever had to stand trial, you know. By the time any daughter of mine makes her curtsey in Society, all of that will be long forgotten."

"It isn't that, at least, not exactly." Her gaze faltered, and her hands plucked at the folds of her skirt. "It is only that — Emily, if I were to — to stay with Mr. Pickett, would you stand my friend?"

Lady Dunnington looked utterly bewildered. "I'm still here, aren't I?"

"No, I mean if I were to *stay* with him. Forever. As his wife."

"His wife?" Lady Dunnington echoed incredulously. "Julia, my dear, you cannot have thought!"

Lady Fieldhurst shook her head. "On the contrary, I have spent hours upon hours with nothing to do *but* think."

"You would be ostracized from Society," pointed out Lady Dunnington. "Most of your friends would no longer receive you."

This argument failed to impress. "Would these be the same 'friends' who once suspected me of murdering Frederick? Remind me, if you will, why their opinions should matter to me."

"You will not be invited anywhere," Lady Dunnington insisted, determined to make her friend reconsider taking so drastic a step.

"No, but I have not been invited anywhere this year past, being in mourning, and I have been surprised at how little I have missed it. Besides, there are many amusements that require no invitation beyond the ability to pay a fee for admission — the theatre for one, or the gardens at Vauxhall, or any number of concerts or lectures. Although I cannot understand why I would wish to go gadding about Town in any case, when I might have Mr. Pickett waiting for me at home; indeed, my greatest pleasures over the last ten months have been those moments spent in his arm — er, company," she finished feebly.

Lady Dunnington's eyebrows rose at this near slip, but she gave no other indication she had noticed it. "You would be poor, or near enough as makes no odds," she reminded Julia.

But this argument, too, carried no weight. "According to the terms of the marriage contract, I will continue to receive my jointure even if I choose to remarry. I cannot imagine how Papa persuaded Frederick to agree to such a thing — no doubt Frederick thought he would live forever — but I am eternally grateful to Papa for doing so." She gave a rueful smile. "Much as I adore Mr. Pickett, I fear I should be hard pressed to live on his wages."

Lady Dunnington was silent for a long moment. "It appears you have thought this through quite thoroughly."

"As I said, I have had a great deal of time on my hands over the last few days. I am fully aware of what it would mean. And yet when I weigh the thought of giving him up against even the most crushing retributions Society could mete out — oh Emily, there is no comparison!"

In spite of her misgivings, Lady Dunnington was moved. "My poor Julia!" She laid her hand over Lady Fieldhurst's and gave it a little squeeze. "You really do love this man, don't you?"

Julia nodded. "More than anything."

"I cannot like it — you know I cannot! But if this is truly what you want, then yes, I will stand your friend, and I will still want you to be my daughter's godmother. Although —" she added with mock severity, " — if she should elope with her dancing master or some such thing, I shall know whom to blame!"

"I shall do my best to discourage any inclination to follow my example and make a *mésalliance*," Julia promised, smiling.

"I shall even treat your Mr. Pickett with civility when we meet, although I cannot promise not to tease him just a little. Good heavens! Do you realize your husband is half the age of mine? What will they find to talk about, I wonder?"

"Us, I should guess," Lady Fieldhurst predicted.

"Very likely. But tell me about the fire! How was Mr. Pickett injured?"

Julia's brow puckered. "In truth, I cannot say. He had his arm about me — no amorous intent on his part, Emily, only a desire to get me out of the building safely, so you need not look at me in that knowing fashion! — so I was slightly ahead of him and did not see what happened. He fell forward when the roof collapsed — in fact, he landed on top of me. I assumed he must have been knocked off his feet by the blast, but when the doctor examined him, he saw evidence of a blow to the head. He even —" She was suddenly reluctant to say it, as if speaking the words aloud somehow made them true. "He even suggested the blow might have been deliberately inflicted."

"Do you mean to say that someone may

181

have attacked him on purpose? Whatever could he have done to make such an enemy?"

Julia shrugged. "I wish I knew. He was at the theatre that night to investigate a series of jewel thefts. Perhaps he found out something that someone didn't want known." She remembered his reaction as he observed the royal party through her opera glasses. "Or saw something — or someone — he was not supposed to see."

Emily rolled her eyes toward the ceiling, making mental calculations. "And over thirty-five hundred people had just evacuated the theatre, in addition to any number of curiosity seekers milling about in the street — Julia, it seems to me that any assailant must have been taking a terrible risk of being seen."

"Perhaps you're right," Julia said slowly. "Granted, it was dark outside, and the flickering light of the flames would have made it difficult to identify details — facial features, for instance — but surely out of so many people someone must have noticed something." Coming to a decision, she rose abruptly to her feet. "At any rate, it is worth a try."

"What is worth a try?" asked Lady Dunnington, unaware of any plan of action having been suggested.

Julia set her jaw. "I intend to find out who did this to Mr. Pickett, and I am going to bring him to justice."

CHAPTER 11

IN WHICH LADY FIELDHURST TAKES MATTERS INTO HER OWN HANDS

After Lady Dunnington had gone (still not entirely convinced that her friend was not making a rash decision that she must eventually come to regret), Julia sat down at her writing desk and applied herself to the task of composing a suitable advertisement. After several abortive attempts, she finally produced one that she felt was capable of eliciting the desired response. *Reward offered for Information concerning Attack on Unarmed Man in Russell Street on the Night of the Drury Lane Theatre Fire. Call in person, Number 84 Drury Lane. Inquire of Mrs. P.* She folded the paper and sealed it, then directed it to the *Times* in Printing House Square, Blackfriars. Then she rang for Thomas the footman, and while she waited for him to answer her summons, she dashed off another missive, this one to Mr. Walter Crumpton, Esquire, of Crumpton and Crumpton, Solicitors, Lincoln's Inn Fields.

"You rang, my lady?" asked Thomas, hovering in the doorway.

"Yes, I have a few errands for you," she said, shaking sand over the last of her letters. "A couple of letters to deliver, and then I need you to try to find that girl, Lucy, who came to Mr. Pickett's lodgings yesterday."

"Yes, ma'am!" said Thomas, brightening.

"Tell her I must see her as soon as possible. I realize she may be — busy — this evening, but tomorrow will suffice. Have her call on me at Mr. Pickett's rooms." As Thomas contemplated this command with every appearance of eager anticipation, she added firmly, "I realize it may present quite a challenge for you to find her again, and I shall see that you are well recompensed for your efforts, but whatever additional wages I pay you are *not* to end up in Lucy's purse, if you take my meaning."

"Yes, ma'am," said Thomas again, crestfallen.

Not long after she sent Thomas on his way, Rogers appeared in the drawing room to inquire, as he said, into her young man's health. Upon discovering that she was preparing to fly once more to Mr. Pickett's side, the butler urged her to allow him to fetch a cold collation for her to eat before her return to that insalubrious part of Town.

It did not take her long to discover that she could spend much more time arguing the point than she would if she were simply to agree to it. Given these combined distractions, she was much later in returning to Drury Lane than she had anticipated. In fact, by the time the carriage set her down in front of the chandler's shop below Pickett's lodgings, the sun was already beginning to set. She climbed the stairs to the flat above and rapped on the door. A moment later, the magistrate opened it.

"I am so sorry, Mr. Colquhoun," she said breathlessly, sweeping past him into the room. "I had intended to be back long before now."

"Never mind, my lady, you needed the rest."

"How is he?" she asked urgently. "Has he — ?"

"He awakened once, earlier this afternoon. He asked after you —"

"Oh, and I wasn't here!" she exclaimed in dismay.

"I told him I'd sent you home to get some sleep, and assured him that you would return later," said Mr. Colquhoun.

"You did well." Without taking the time to remove her pelisse and bonnet, she hurried into the small bedroom where Pickett lay, apparently oblivious. She sat down quietly on the edge of the bed and took his hand in both of hers.

"John?" she called softly. "John, I've come back."

"I doubt he will awaken again for some time," opined the magistrate. "He complained of his head aching, so I dosed him with laudanum."

"His head? Not his feet?"

"No." And this was something that had puzzled him. "I must say, my lady, it seems to me rather peculiar that, having sustained a blow to his head, he would complain of a relatively minor injury to his feet. Is it possible you might have misunderstood?"

"No, for he spoke quite plainly," she said, then turned her attention back to her patient. "John? I'm sorry I had to leave you. I had not meant to be gone for so long."

In spite of Mr. Colquhoun's predictions to the contrary, Pickett's eyes fluttered open. "My lady?"

"Yes, love, how do you feel?"

"Drunk," he said groggily.

"It's the laudanum," said the magistrate, tactfully ignoring the endearment she had let slip. "I daresay it will wear off soon, John — at which time you will probably wish it had not," he prophesied grimly.

He received no reply. Mr. Colquhoun had never thought of himself as being particularly invisible — in fact, he had put on flesh in recent years — but as he watched the pair of them conversing in hushed voices, he was struck with the thought that he might have disappeared, for all the notice they took of him; as far as the two young people were concerned, they might have been the only ones in the room. And perhaps that was as it should be.

"I'll be back tomorrow," he said aloud to no one in particular, then backed away from Pickett's bedside and quietly showed himself out.

It could not be said that they took any more notice of the magistrate's leave-taking than they had of his presence. Lady Fieldhurst stood up just long enough to divest herself of pelisse and bonnet, hanging them both on the peg beside the door before returning to her perch on the edge of the mattress.

"Would you like something to drink, John?" she asked. "Water, perhaps, or tea?" She was not entirely confident of her ability to boil water without scorching her fingers — or worse — but if he wanted tea, then no sacrifice was too great.

"Just water, please."

He pushed himself up to a sitting position to drink, and although she was almost a foot shorter than he, she supported him with one arm about his shoulders while she steadied the cup he held to his lips. He took a few sips, then allowed her to set the cup on the table beside the bed.

"You shouldn't be here, my lady, but I'm glad you are." It was the most he had spoken since he'd been injured, and she could tell the effort it cost him. "I can't thank you — I can never thank you enough —"

"Hush," she scolded gently, laying her finger on his lips. "The only thanks I need is for you to make a full recovery." Actually, there was something else as well, but although she flattered herself that he would find it no very great burden, she knew him well enough to suspect he might worry; and since no mental distress must be allowed to interfere with his recovery, she would wait until a later time to broach that particular subject.

Pickett, of course, knew nothing of this, but for him, her presence was enough. He captured her hand and kissed it, then sank back down onto the pillow with a sigh.

"John," she began, disregarding her own advice to Mr. Colquhoun not to worry him with questions, "do you remember anything that happened before you were — before you went down? Did you perhaps see anyone, or hear anything?"

"I don't — I can't —" He grimaced with the effort of concentration. "It hurts to think."

"Then don't," she said quickly, regretting that she had brought it up. "Don't think, just rest. Shall I go into the other room so you can sleep?"

"No!" As she started to move away, he grabbed her wrist. "I want to see you."

She gave a self-conscious little laugh. "I fear I'm not much to look at, at present."

"You're beautiful," he said, looking up at her with his heart in his eyes.

In fact, he was not much to look at, either. His eyes appeared sunken, his brown curls were tangled and matted, and his chin sported three days' growth of fine dark whiskers. And she wanted nothing more than to be able to look at him every day for the rest of her life.

"If you're not ready to go back to sleep, perhaps I could read aloud to you," she suggested. "I noticed *The Vicar of Wakefield* on the shelf. It is a favorite of my mother's, so I know it well. Shall I fetch it?"

He nodded, and grimaced at the pain in

his head. She left the room and returned a moment later with the book, fully expecting to find him asleep. But no, he lay watching the door as if impatient for her return. She drew the chair as near to the bed as possible, then sat down, opened the book, and began to read.

" 'Chapter one,' " she said. " 'The description of the family of Wakefield, in which a kindred likeness prevails, as well of minds as of persons. I was ever of opinion, that the honest man who married and brought up a large family, did more service than he who continued single and only talked of population. From this motive, I had scarcely taken orders a year, before I began to think seriously of matrimony . . .' "

He was asleep before she finished the first chapter. She set the book aside, then kissed him on the forehead and set about the task of discovering everything she could about the case that he was investigating, and that had ended so disastrously. The logical place to start, she decided, was with the small notebook he always carried in the inside pocket of his coat. She had tucked it away in his top drawer along with the diamonds, and when she looked there, she was relieved to discover that it, at least, was still where she had left it. She took it from its hiding place and returned to the chair beside the bed, determined to learn everything she could from it.

Unfortunately, this was not much. She knew Pickett's handwriting well enough; in fact, the top drawer of her writing desk held a couple of letters written in this same hand and kept for reasons that at the time she had not fully understood, or perhaps had refused to acknowledge. The problem lay not in his penmanship, but rather in the fact that he employed a system of abbreviations that she could not begin to decipher. She examined one page after another with no more success, until she turned over a leaf and found herself looking at a crude rendering of the theatre's interior. Pickett lacked the advantage of a drawing-master such as she had enjoyed, but the horseshoe-shaped seating arrangement was instantly recognizable, and if she had harbored any doubts as to what the sketch represented, these would have been allayed by the "X" marking the location of the box where they had sat. A lopsided star shape marked the royal box, while an apparently random assortment of letters — a "D" here, an "M" there, and a "G" over there — apparently indicated the location of other members of the Bow Street force. It was an interesting glimpse into his work (let alone the methodical workings of his mind), but not very informative.

"My lady?"

At the sound of his voice, she dropped the little notebook onto the floor beside her chair, out of his range of vision. She was not prying, exactly — or if she was, it was at least in a worthy cause — but he would not like it if he knew she was doing a little investigating of her own, and nothing must be allowed to vex him in his current fragile state.

"Yes, darling, what is it?"

"Is it c-c-cold in here t-t-to you?"

"Well, it *is* February," she reminded him, rising to search the small flat for an extra blanket nevertheless.

But it would not be February much longer, for March was only a few days away. Soon spring would return, and with it another social Season, another crop of young ladies emancipated from the schoolroom and launched onto the *ton* in the hopes that they might make a brilliant match. Alas, she knew all too well that brilliant matches were not always what they were made out to be, and hard on the heels of this thought came the realization that spring would also bring the anniversary of her husband's death. It was strange to think that this time a year ago, she'd had no idea John Pickett even existed; now, at least in the eyes of the law, he was her husband. But that, too, was supposed to change with the coming of spring. Far from being impatient to put the episode behind her, as her solicitor seemed to think she must be, she did not like to think of what her future might be without John Pickett in it.

Pushing away an image too dreadful to contemplate, she pulled the covers up to his chin and brushed a drooping curl back from his brow — and was shocked to find his skin far warmer than the temperature in the room warranted.

"S-s-so c-c-cold," said Pickett through chattering teeth.

She pressed her palm to his forehead, and her worst fears were confirmed. This was the fever the doctor had spoken of. What had he said? Something about how the risk of infection was the greatest danger in injuries of this type. Now it appeared that the "greatest danger" had come to pass, and she hadn't the slightest idea of what to do. She must send for Mr. Gilroy, but how? A glance out the window revealed no one in the dark street below — no one whom she would trust to deliver a message, at any rate — and she had no intention of going for the doctor herself. Quite aside from the fact that she would not feel safe traipsing about London unescorted at such an hour, she had no intention of leaving Pickett alone.

No, it appeared the doctor would have to wait until morning. In the meantime, she could only try to keep Pickett as warm and comfortable as possible. She snatched up the poker beside the fireplace and stirred the banked coals back to life, then plundered the bureau drawers for every spare sheet and blanket she could find and spread them over the bed, topping them off with her own woolen pelisse. And finally, having done all she could, she put on her white cambric night rail and slid beneath the mountain of covers, pressing close to Pickett's side and wrapping her arms around his shivering form in an effort to warm him with her body and her love.

She awoke the next morning a bit embarrassed to find herself nestled closely against him. Edging away, she laid the back of her hand against his unshaven jaw and found it still unnaturally warm; clearly his fever had not abated in the night.

"John?" she called softly. "John, darling, wake up."

There was no response. Under happier

circumstances, she reflected, it might be rather lovely to begin each new day by waking up next to him; given the current state of affairs, however, she hadn't the luxury of savoring this novel experience. Mrs. Catchpole would be arriving soon with fresh supplies of water and coal, and Thomas (assuming he did not allow his search for Lucy to trump all other considerations) shortly thereafter with a hamper of food as well as clean clothes. This, too, was the day her advertisement was to appear in the *Times*, and since she did not know at what hour, if ever, it might begin to bear fruit, it behooved her to be prepared. With a sigh for what might have been, she rolled away from Pickett and left the warm cocoon of the bed for the frigid room beyond.

She made a rudimentary toilette and put on a fresh gown, and had just finished twisting her hair into a simple knot when she heard a thump on the door. She opened it to find Mrs. Catchpole with a scuttle full of coal in one hand and a pitcher of water in the other.

"Good morning, my lady," Pickett's landlady said cheerfully as she waddled into the room. She set the pitcher on the table, then bent over the fireplace and began arranging coals on the grate.

"No, not in here," Julia said quickly. "Save the coal for the fire in his bedroom. I can keep the door closed to retain the heat."

Something in the tone of her voice alerted Mrs. Catchpole. She stood up and regarded Julia keenly. "Aye, ma'am, but you'll want a fire here for boiling water, since it's the one what's got the crane to hang the kettle from." She glanced at the closed door to the bedroom. "Taken a turn for the worse, has he?"

"I'm afraid so," Julia confessed. "I fear the wound may have become infected, for he came down with a fever last night. I should like to have the doctor in to look at him again, but I dare not leave him alone. Do you know of someone who might be trusted to deliver a message?"

"Aye, my lady, that I do. Depend upon it, we'll have that doctor here within the hour. As for the fire, never you mind; there'll be more coal where that came from."

Mrs. Catchpole was as good as her word, for in addition to the landlady bearing an additional scuttle of coal, the doctor arrived far more promptly than Julia had any reason to expect.

"Thank you for coming so quickly, Mr. Gilroy," said Julia, opening the door to his knock.

"Not at all, Mrs. Pickett," he assured her. "In fact, I have been wondering how Mr. Pickett fared, and had thought to take a look at him today in any case."

"I fear the news is not good," she confessed. "He has awakened several times, and has even spoken, but last night he began running a fever."

Mr. Gilroy offered no opinion on these observations, but strode across the room and through the door into the bedroom where Pickett lay.

"Mr. Pickett?" called the doctor in carrying tones. "Mr. Pickett, I am Mr. Thomas Gilroy, your attending physician. Let's have a look at you, shall we?"

Receiving no response, he began deftly unwinding the bandages encompassing Pickett's head. "Hmm," he said, frowning.

"What is it?" Julia asked eagerly.

"The wound appears to be no worse, but the unnatural warmth of his skin indicates that infection has set in."

It was what she had feared, but somehow hearing it stated so baldly made it infinitely worse. She took a deep, steadying breath. "So what do we do now?"

The doctor shrugged. "I'm afraid there is very little we *can* do. There are no medicines that are effective against infection. I could

198

always attempt to draw out the infection by bleeding him —"

"Oh, must you?" Julia protested, remembering his blood-drenched coat. "He has lost so very much blood already."

Mr. Gilroy looked speculatively at his patient. "It is true that in some cases the body successfully fends off the infection on its own, while in others —" He shook his head, and Julia had no difficulty in interpreting what happened in those other cases. "Still, he is young and, I assume, otherwise healthy. We might wait a few more days and see what happens, if you would prefer it."

Julia nodded uncertainly. "Yes, thank you, Mr. Gilroy."

He reached into his bag and withdrew a small pouch. "Willow bark," he explained, spreading the pouch open to show her its contents of splintered and dried plant material. "Some physicians have reported success in reducing fever by having the patient drink a tea brewed with it. Unfortunately," he added, glancing at the unconscious Pickett, "the patient must be awake to ingest it. Still, if he has awakened before, he may well do so again. Should that be the case, I suggest that you brew some and try persuading him to drink it. Other than that, you appear to have done exactly as you ought, keeping him as warm and comfortable as possible."

"Thank you, doctor, but is there nothing else I might do?" asked Julia with a hint of desperation in her voice.

The doctor sighed. "Pray, Mrs. Pickett," he said. "Just pray."

CHAPTER 12

IN WHICH AN ADVERTISEMENT YIELDS UNEXPECTED RESULTS

The smell of smoke still hung heavily in the air when Mr. Colquhoun reached Bow Street on Monday morning. He'd had no word from Lady Fieldhurst since he'd left John Pickett in her care the previous evening. He told himself that this must be a good sign; surely she would have sent word to him if — well, if anything untoward had happened after he'd gone.

He had scarcely seated himself at the magistrate's bench before he was approached by Mr. Dixon, at fifty years of age the eldest of the Runners.

"Mr. Colquhoun," said this worthy, nodding his grizzled head. "Have you any news on Mr. Pickett?"

"I have at that," said the magistrate. "He has awakened several times, but only briefly. He appears to have no memory of the events of that night, and is in no condition to speak of them even if he did. Still, I am cautiously optimistic."

"That is good news, sir," said Mr. Dixon. "But as I recall, Mr. Pickett has no family. Surely he is not alone?"

"No, he has — someone — staying with him."

Something in the magistrate's expression must have given him away. "Someone? But who? If I may be so bold," added Mr. Dixon hastily.

Mr. Colquhoun was reluctant to betray the young couple who, he suspected, would *not* be getting an annulment anytime soon. And yet, he reasoned, anyone who called to inquire after Mr. Pickett would discover the truth quickly enough.

"In fact, her ladyship, the Viscountess Fieldhurst, has taken it upon herself to nurse him — not the wife of the present holder of the title, but the widow of the previous one."

"Well, if that don't beat the Dutch!" exclaimed Mr. Dixon, chuckling. "Leave it to our Mr. Pickett to land on his feet. I wonder, if I were to get myself coshed on the head, could I get a ladyship to look after me?"

"I'm sorry to disappoint you, Mr. Dixon," said Mr. Foote, joining them at the bench, "but youth has its advantages, you know.

You're neither as young nor as pretty as Mr. Pickett." A smattering of uncomfortable laughter greeted this sally, as all the men present recognized it as more of a gibe at the absent Pickett than at its apparent target.

"Too true, alas," noted Dixon with an exaggerated sigh. "But Mr. Colquhoun was just relaying good news about young Mr. Pickett. It seems he's waking up at last."

Mr. Foote looked to the magistrate for confirmation.

"Aye, although he's still a bit rattled in the head. Seems to have little or no memory of what befell him on the night of the fire."

"Good news, indeed," agreed Mr. Foote. "And I hope I may soon have more good news to report. In the meantime, I have something here that I think you'll find pleasing."

He reached inside his coat and withdrew a necklace of emeralds, the green stones winking in the morning sunlight streaming through the windows. Mr. Colquhoun's bushy white eyebrows rose.

"Lady Oversley's, I gather? Pleasing indeed! Well done, Mr. Foote. Where did you find them?"

"In a pawnshop in Feathers Court," he said.

Mr. Colquhoun frowned. "Feathers Court? Seems a rather unsavory address to be trading in jewels of this quality."

"I daresay it was chosen for just that reason," said Mr. Foote. "I suspect our thief already had a buyer waiting, and Mr. Baumgarten's shop was selected because it would be the last place we might be expected to look."

"Sounds like a reasonable conjecture. Tell me, Mr. Foote, what tipped you off?"

Mr. Foote shook his head. "Nothing in particular, but since the thefts all seemed to be taking place around the Drury Lane Theatre, it seemed wise to check the pawnshops in that area."

"But still no leads as to our thief's identity?"

Foote shook his head. "I'm afraid not, sir. In between protesting his innocence of any wrongdoing, Mr. Baumgarten refuses to name his supplier. I don't know, perhaps he doesn't know the man's name."

" 'Man'?" Mr. Colquhoun echoed sharply, bushy white brows drawing together over his nose. "You are sure the seller is a man?"

Mr. Foote looked rather nonplussed. "He didn't say, sir, but I assumed it must be so."

"Assumptions are dangerous in this business, Mr. Foote," the magistrate said. "I should have thought you had been around long enough to know that."

"Yes, sir," muttered Foote, flushing.

"Begging your pardon, sir." Mr. Maxwell, a man of almost forty who had recently joined the Bow Street force after a French ball put paid to his military career, came rushing up to the bench waving a newspaper. "I wondered what you made of this tidbit in the *Times.*"

"The part about an anonymous hero who hustled the royal party out of their box just before the fire broke out?" asked the magistrate, scowling. "Yes, I saw that. I would give a lot to know who the fellow was."

"So would the Russians, sir. They're offering a considerable reward for information."

Mr. Colquhoun jerked a thumb in the direction of his most senior Runner. "If they are looking to pay out a reward, perhaps they should talk to Mr. Foote," he suggested with tongue in cheek. "It appears he's just about to pocket a tidy sum for the recovery of the Oversley emeralds."

"Congratulations, Mr. Foote," said Dixon, then added jovially, "Couldn't you share the wealth with those of us who are looking toward retirement?"

Mr. Maxwell's mind, however, was on other things. "Congratulations, Mr. Foote," he said distractedly, then turned back to the magistrate. "But that wasn't what I meant. Have you seen this, sir? Or are you perhaps the one responsible for it?"

He handed the newspaper over the bench, pointing toward an advertisement not quite halfway down the page. *Reward offered for Information concerning Attack on Unarmed Man in Russell Street on the Night of the Drury Lane Theatre Fire. Call in person, Number 84 Drury Lane. Inquire of Mrs. P.*

The magistrate sat up abruptly. "What the devil — ?"

"So you didn't place the advertisement, sir?" asked Mr. Maxwell. "Then who did?"

"I detect the fine Italian hand of her well-meaning but meddlesome ladyship," grumbled Mr. Colquhoun.

"Who is Mrs. P.?" asked Dixon, receiving the newspaper from the magistrate and scanning the cryptic lines. "Mr. Pickett is not married, and I thought his mother had been dead this age."

"Aye, dead or deserted," confirmed Mr. Colquhoun. "I doubt the boy knows himself. No, I believe our mysterious Mrs. P. is none other than Lady Fieldhurst herself."

Mr. Maxwell goggled at the very idea. "A viscountess is pretending to be Mr. Pickett's wife?"

In fact, there was no pretense about it, but that was no one else's business. Quite aside from keeping the young couple's secret, Mr. Colquhoun found himself reluctant to give Mr. Foote any more ammunition with which to torment Mr. Pickett upon his return to Bow Street, or any more fodder with which to nurture the grudge the elder Runner had held against the younger for more than a decade.

"I suppose I shall have to call on 'Mrs. P.' myself and see what's toward," said the magistrate with a sigh. "Mr. Foote, I'll see about getting you that finder's fee as soon as I return."

The group about the magistrate's bench dispersed, all except Maxwell, who hung back.

"Yes, Mr. Maxwell? What is it?"

"It may well be none of my business, sir, but exactly what gives between Mr. Foote and Mr. Pickett?"

Mr. Colquhoun made a dismissive gesture. "Professional jealousy, no more and no less. You may be aware that Mr. Pickett first came to our attention as a juvenile pickpocket."

Maxwell nodded. "I had heard something to that effect, yes. But surely his work here has more than made up for any youthful crimes he may have committed."

"Aye, and committed at his father's instigation at that, for a more shiftless — but that is neither here nor there. In fact, Mr. Foote's resentment stems from an incident ten years ago, when he was still on the foot patrol. He arrested young John Pickett, who was scarcely fourteen years old at the time, for petty thievery. I dismissed the charges and sent the boy off with a flea in his ear. Mr. Foote took my leniency in the matter as a personal affront, and insisted I had made a mistake. In fact, he predicted the lad would be back to his thieving ways within a fortnight. And he was quite right; after all, what are the direst threats of a magistrate compared to the demands of a supposedly loving father?"

"It must have been quite a blow to Mr. Foote to find himself obliged to work side by side with the same man he'd once arrested," observed Mr. Maxwell, glancing over his shoulder toward the other side of the room, where Foote regaled the foot patrol with an account of his recovery of the Oversley emeralds.

"Aye, especially when young Mr. Pickett solved a case that had stymied Mr. Foote for weeks. He wasn't even with Bow Street at the time," added the magistrate with a reminiscent gleam in his eye. "After I sentenced his father to be transported to Botany Bay, I realized that the boy Mr. Foote had brought in was the man's son. I thought I could prevent him from following in his father's footsteps by offering him an opportunity to earn an honest living, so I arranged for him to be apprenticed to a coal merchant. Faugh! Coal merchant!" he echoed contemptuously, berating himself, not for the first time, for his lack of foresight. "I should have seen to the lad's education instead. I doubt Eton or Harrow would have taken a boy of his background, but Westminster might have, especially if I'd called in a few favors. But I had no idea of the boy's intelligence at that time, and so for the next five years, John Pickett delivered coal to the magistrate's court. On one such occasion, he was obliged to wait for payment until I'd finished hearing a case. By the time I brought him a bank draft, he'd picked up a copy of the *Hue and Cry* left lying about, and simply by reading about the case, picked up on the one clue that Mr. Foote had overlooked. To make a long story short, I bought out the remaining years of his apprenticeship from my own pocket and brought him to Bow Street as a member of the foot patrol. He was all of nineteen years old at the time, to Mr. Foote's thirty."

Mr. Maxwell chuckled, for in spite of his competence, Mr. Foote was not particularly well liked. "I'll wager that did not sit well with Mr. Foote."

"No, indeed! And while I can understand his sentiments on that occasion, perhaps even sympathize with them to some extent, I did not expect him to nurse a grudge for fully a decade after the fact. Ah well," he added with a shrug, "Mr. Foote is pocketing a tidy sum for himself in finders' fees these days, so perhaps it will soon be Mr. Pickett's turn to envy him."

But even as he said the words, Mr. Colquhoun knew he did not believe them. He suspected Pickett was incapable of the sort of festering resentment that Mr. Foote had harbored toward him for ten long years, largely because Pickett considered himself undeserving of his good fortune, while Foote felt himself entitled to more. Mr. Colquhoun wished he could grant Pickett just a bit of Foote's arrogance, while giving Foote a rather larger share of Pickett's humility.

Mr. Maxwell, recognizing that the confidential interview was at an end, thanked the magistrate for enlightening his ignorance, and returned to his work. As for Mr. Colquhoun, he had more important things to do than coddle the wounded vanity of a grown man — and the most pressing of these involved a visit to Drury Lane and "Mrs. P."

After seeing the doctor on his way and receiving the day's supplies of coal and water from Mrs. Catchpole, Lady Fieldhurst spent the rest of the morning fussing about Pickett's flat, folding his linen and putting his bureau drawers in some semblance of order, washing and drying his meager collection of plates and cups, and even arranging his small library in alphabetical order — a frenzy of housewifely activity that served to distract her from trekking back and forth to Pickett's bedside to feel his forehead in the desperate hope that his fever might have abated.

At last, having run out of things to set straight, she fetched *The Vicar of Wakefield* from its place on the mantel (under "G" for Goldsmith, between Fielding's notorious *Tom Jones* and Matthew Lewis's popular gothic novel, *The Monk*) and settled down beside Pickett's bed to read aloud in the hopes that he might hear and find her voice soothing.

" 'Chapter Two: Family Misfortunes —

The loss of fortune only serves to increase the pride of the worthy. The temporal concerns of our family were chiefly committed to my wife's management; as to the spiritual, I took them entirely under my own — ' "

She had not finished the first paragraph when a knock sounded on the door; Thomas, no doubt, come with her daily supplies and, she hoped, some news of the recalcitrant Lucy. She cast the book aside, the unfortunate vicar and his family's woes forgotten.

But it was not Thomas, much less Lucy, who stood leaning against the door frame. Instead, Julia found herself confronting a man she'd never seen before in her life, a tall, lean man in a shabby frock coat and frayed knitted cap pulled low on his head. His eyes were beady and black, and his face was pockmarked.

"Mrs. P.?" he asked, revealing a mouthful of blackened teeth.

"Yes," she said uncertainly.

"I'm 'ere about the bit in the newspaper."

"Oh! Oh yes, my advertisement. Won't you come in Mr. — ?"

He tugged at the hank of greasy dark hair sticking out below his cap. "Bartlesby, ma'am. Jem Bartlesby, at your service," he said, and although he bowed low, she could not think his grin anything but insolent.

He stepped into the room, and for the first time Julia began to question the wisdom of placing such an advertisement. Somehow she had expected any respondents to be of the aristocracy or perhaps the gentry, other theatre-goers who had escaped the conflagration ahead of herself and Mr. Pickett. She had not anticipated the possibility of being obliged to entertain such persons as Mr. Bartlesby, and the knowledge that she could not count on Mr. Pickett's coming to her rescue, should she stand in need of him, made her feel frighteningly vulnerable. She wished Mr. Colquhoun were here. Even Lucy's company would have been welcome; given that damsel's profession, Julia suspected Lucy would know how to deal with the likes of Mr. Bartlesby should the situation warrant it. She glanced toward Pickett's room, and was thankful she'd closed his bedroom door to contain the heat; at least Mr. Bartlesby need not know how very unprotected she was. Of course, two of the three chairs were in that room as well, but this presented no particular difficulty, as she was not inclined to encourage Mr. Bartlesby to linger.

"Am I to understand, Mr. Bartlesby, that

you have information for me?"

"I might 'ave," he said. "What's it worth to you?"

This was another issue she had not anticipated. What price did one put on such information? No cost was too great to make Mr. Pickett's attacker pay for his crime, but surely it would be unwise to tip her hand too soon.

"I shall give you a shilling to hear what you have to say," she answered, hoping she was being neither too generous nor too parsimonious. "More afterward, if I deem the information worth it."

Mr. Bartlesby was silent for such a long moment that Julia feared he refused to answer. As she debated the wisdom of increasing her offer, he finally spoke.

"In the street outside the theatre, it were. I seen a stout fellow with a cudgel. Black as a burnt stump, 'e were, from all the smoke, but 'e 'ad a 'ead full o' black 'air, and a thick beard to match."

Julia's eyes widened at this account. In the back row of the royal box, seated beside the incognito princess, had been a man who matched Mr. Bartlesby's description exactly. Her heart sank as well, for it would be a very delicate matter to prefer charges against a member of the Russian royal court.

"And you saw him strike Mr. — you saw him strike a man with this cudgel?"

"Oh, aye, 'e coshed this 'ere unarmed fellow, then took 'imself off."

"Where did he go?" Julia asked urgently.

"Now, that I can't tell you. I didn't know it would be important," he added apologetically.

Julia could not but wonder at a philosophy that would deem the attack of an unarmed man unimportant, and determined to remove Mr. Pickett to her own residence in a less unsavory part of Town as soon as he could be safely transported. "Thank you, Mr. Bartlesby, you've been most helpful. I believe you have earned your shilling and another besides." She picked up her reticule from the table and withdrew the two coins. "Will you furnish me with your direction, in case I should need to contact you again?"

He shook his head. "Nay, ma'am, that I won't do, for there's no love lost between me and Bow Street, if you take my meaning. Still, a message left at the Cock and Magpie will find me."

"Thank you, Mr. Bartlesby," Julia said again, moving toward the door to indicate that the interview was at an end. She was thankful she had not been so indiscreet as to mention Mr. Pickett's occupation, as the

215

revelation might have sealed Mr. Bartles-by's lips. "If you should think of anything else, I hope you will inform me."

"Aye, for a price," he assured her, biting each of the two coins in turn before slipping them into the pocket of his coat.

He tugged his forelock and took his leave, and she had hardly shut the door when Mr. Colquhoun arrived with a folded newspaper under his arm, his face dark with wrath.

"Do you mind telling me what this is all about?" He opened the newspaper with a snap of his wrists and jabbed a finger at the offending advertisement.

"I am seeking information from anyone who might be able to identify Jo — Mr. Pickett's attacker," she said defensively. "And I'm getting it, too. A man just left — you might have met him on the stairs — who was most obliging."

"Aye, I'll warrant he was — for a price," Mr. Colquhoun growled.

"Well, yes," confessed Lady Fieldhurst. "Two shillings, in fact, but it was money well spent."

"And how do you know he wasn't telling you a Banbury tale just to collect the proffered reward?"

"I see your point, Mr. Colquhoun, and perhaps I should have worded my advertisement differently — offering payment only if the information should lead to an arrest, perhaps. But I am persuaded Mr. Bartlesby's contribution was worth every farthing. You see, I believe I know the man he described."

The magistrate's eyebrows rose in skeptical surprise. "Indeed?"

"Well, I don't *know* him, precisely — that is, we have never been formally introduced. But I am quite certain I know who he is."

"Then who, pray, is he?"

"I do not know his name, but he was seated in the royal box, in the back row just beside Princess Olga. A large man with black hair and a thick black beard."

"Good God!" exclaimed Mr. Colquhoun in failing accents. "You've just described His Excellency, Vladimir Gregorovich. And this Bartlesby saw him attack Mr. Pickett? Small wonder His Excellency was so impatient to know how the investigation was progressing!"

"You have met him, then?"

"Unfortunately, yes. He came to Bow Street the day after the fire, the blackguard, demanding to know what I was doing about the theft of Princess Olga's diamonds. I'll wager I can guess who's got them now!"

And I'll *wager you can't,* thought Lady

Fieldhurst. Aloud, she merely said, "But I don't understand why he should attack Mr. Pickett."

"Perhaps he thought Mr. Pickett might have seen him do the deed from his vantage point across the theatre," suggested the magistrate. "If so, he must have a very high estimation of Mr. Pickett's eyesight."

"Oh, but I had brought my opera glasses and let Mr. Pickett use them!" Julia exclaimed. "So it is quite possible he might have seen something that His Excellency found threatening. In fact, now that I think of it, I am almost certain he did. To be sure, he saw something that struck him as odd — I cannot remember his exact words — but then he realized the theatre was on fire, and I fear the matter, whatever it was, was forgotten in the more immediate crisis."

"A pity, that," remarked Mr. Colquhoun. "We can only hope he will remember it when next he awakens."

Julia sighed. "As to that, I am afraid I have bad news to report. He began running a fever last night. The doctor has seen him this morning, and he says the wound has apparently become infected."

"I see." Mr. Colquhoun scowled, needing no further explanation to know that this diagnosis was not encouraging. "May I sit with him?"

"Of course. I am merely keeping the door closed to preserve the heat." She opened the door to the bedroom and preceded the magistrate inside. "In fact, I would be grateful if you could stay with him this afternoon while I pay a call upon Her Royal Highness, the Princess Olga Fyodorovna."

The magistrate's scowl grew fiercer. "Just what plan are you hatching, my lady?"

"I intend to find out all I can about His Excellency, Vladimir Gregorovich."

Mr. Colquhoun could not agree to this. "Don't think I'm not grateful to you for providing Bow Street with so promising a lead, my lady, but I believe you have done quite enough. It is time you left the investigation in the hands of those who have been professionally trained for it."

"This all sounds very well, Mr. Colquhoun, but can you name one person on your force who would have the entrée to the Russian court as well as I?"

"As soon as my Runner states his business, he will not be turned away," predicted the magistrate.

"I daresay he will not. But I flatter myself the Princess Olga would be much more forthcoming to a lady of the British aristocracy come to offer her sympathy on the loss of the diamonds — a lady, moreover, who is intimately acquainted" — she felt herself blushing at the unfortunate choice of words — "with a member of the Bow Street force, and can reassure her as to its competence. And if I should ask her, as one woman to another, to recount her experiences on the night of the fire, who knows what she might confide?"

"I see your point, my lady, but have you considered that His Excellency might learn of your visit, and connect you with Mr. Pickett? After all, you were sharing the same box. No, I cannot ask such a thing of you."

"You didn't ask," she pointed out. "I offered."

"Then I fear I must decline your very generous offer."

"But Mr. Colquhoun —"

"To be blunt, my lady, I am not thinking of your welfare, but of Mr. Pickett's. If any harm should come to you, and he should learn of it —"

"I do see your point, Mr. Colquhoun, and I must say your scruples are admirable. But I can't —" She glanced at the still figure in the bed. "I can't sit here day after day, seeing him like this, and do nothing!"

"On the contrary," the magistrate said, his tone surprisingly gentle, "I believe you have done a great deal already, probably more than you know. But — if you will forgive my asking — in two weeks' time, when the petition for annulment comes before the ecclesiastical court?"

She took a deep, steadying breath. "As far as I am concerned, there isn't going to be any annulment," she said. "If he wants one, of course, I will yield to his wishes in the matter, but I have already written to my solicitor instructing him to suspend his efforts on my behalf, and to surrender to me any relevant documents — including a certain physician's letter that Mr. Pickett will no doubt wish to place on the fire, where I suspect it belongs."

The magistrate was silent for a long moment as he pondered this revelation, which, if the truth were known, did not shock him nearly as much as Julia thought it might. "I see," he said at last. "I suppose that changes things. Very well, my la — er, Mrs. Pickett, if you wish to call upon the Princess Olga at her hotel, I will not stand in your way. But you are to report any findings directly to me, do you understand, and under no circumstances are you to even hint that His Excellency is under suspicion! Do I make myself clear?"

"Very clear," she said, smiling broadly at

him, now that she had won.

"As for my sitting with him, however, I wish I could, but I fear I have been absent from Bow Street too much already. Is there no one else who might oblige?"

She paused to consider the question. Her own staff was already being put to considerable inconvenience, but more to the purpose, she did not want Mr. Pickett waking up to a stranger, and her servants were unknown to him except for Rogers the butler, who had his own duties to attend to, and Thomas the footman, who was at that moment scouring the streets of Covent Garden in search of Lucy.

Lucy . . . As little as she liked the idea, she had to admit that Lucy would do nothing to harm him, at least not intentionally.

"There is a girl," she said without enthusiasm, "a prostitute, actually, who I suppose I can trust to look after him."

"Lucy Higgins," said the magistrate, nodding in understanding.

"You know her?" she asked, surprised.

"As you might guess, given her profession, she appears rather frequently before the bench. But if she is our only alternative, I think I had best stay with him after all, for my opinion of Miss Higgins is not high." He hesitated a moment, then added, "He once entertained the idea of marrying her, you know."

"He — he would have married — *Lucy*?" She sat down abruptly on the edge of the bed, her hand pressed to her abdomen as if she had just received a blow to that area.

"He did not love her, he was quite clear on that point," Mr. Colquhoun assured her. "In fact, he was convinced that, since he could not have the woman he wanted — I trust I need make no explanations on that head — he could give meaning to his blighted existence by rescuing Miss Higgins from the gutter. You will have noticed that our Mr. Pickett is a rare one for the grand romantic gesture," he added with a twinkle in his eye.

"I have indeed," she said, smiling wistfully down at Pickett and running her fingers through his disheveled curls. She had been the object of one of those grand gestures herself, for he had been willing to allow a doctor to falsely declare him impotent in order to release her from an accidental marriage he was sure she could not want. In fact, as much as she regretted what had befallen him at the theatre, she shuddered to think that the annulment would have been granted and they would have gone their separate ways, had the fire and its aftermath not forced her to recognize her own heart.

"In fact, it was to remove him from Lucy and try to talk some sense into him that I dragged him off to Scotland," the magistrate continued.

"Was it?" asked Julia in some surprise. "I confess, I thought you had taken him to Scotland to get him away from me."

"It is true that I was not best pleased to find you there," admitted Mr. Colquhoun. "Still, your presence did more to dissuade him from marrying Lucy than anything I might have said. And, given the way things have turned out, I cannot be sorry. I wonder, though, if you are aware of what you are letting yourself in for. His prospects, you must know, are no more than what he makes them. Mind you, if he were a decade older, I would not hesitate to put his name forward for a magistracy, but a lad not yet five-and-twenty? Any such suggestion would be laughed to scorn, and rightfully so."

"I am well aware of how Society must view such a match, and I assure you, it does not matter to me one whit. Any true friend will stand with me, and as for the others, they may think what they like. If it is a matter of money that concerns you, I must tell you that my widow's jointure was established in such a way that it will not end with my remarriage. In fact, Mr. Colquhoun," she concluded, lifting her chin and giving the magistrate a rather smug smile, "your protégé has married a fortune, albeit a modest one by Society's standards."

"Hmmm," was Mr. Colquhoun's only comment. He suspected Lady Fieldhurst's fortune would be anything but modest in John Pickett's eyes. He further suspected his youngest Runner was not the sort of man who would be content to live on his wife's largesse.

But surely the most urgent matter at present was to get the boy well. Anything else could wait for another day.

CHAPTER 13

THE FURTHER MISADVENTURES OF THE PRINCESS OLGA'S DIAMONDS

The disadvantages of placing such an advertisement as hers soon became all too apparent to Lady Fieldhurst. Scarcely a quarter-hour after Mr. Colquhoun had departed, there came another knock on the door. Opening it, Julia found a mousy-looking young woman clutching a squirming infant.

"Mrs. P.?" the visitor asked timidly.

"Yes. What can I do for you?" asked Julia, fairly certain she already knew.

"I come about the advertisement in the newspaper."

"Excellent! Do come in," urged Julia, harboring none of the misgivings she'd suffered upon inviting Mr. Bartlesby into the flat.

"Thankee, ma'am," murmured the woman, shuffling into the room.

"Am I to understand you have some information regarding the — the incident described in the advertisement?"

"Aye, ma'am, that I do."

She hitched the child higher on her hip, and Julia felt compelled to offer a hospitality that had been denied Mr. Bartlesby.

"Won't you sit down?" Julia gestured toward the only chair remaining beneath the table, the other two having been removed to the bedroom.

"Thankee, ma'am," the young mother said again, then sat down, settled the infant on her lap, and picked up her tale. "My man is a stagehand at the theatre, see, and when I heard it was on fire, I came running to make sure he was all right. I'd just got there and was searching for my Davy in the crowd when I heard this loud noise — it was the roof crashing in, but I didn't know that at the time, did I? — and I turned 'round to have a look-see when I seen this fellow up and cosh another fellow in the head with a sort of cudgel, and the second fellow go down like a load of bricks and land right on top of a lady — I suppose that would be you, wouldn't it, ma'am?"

"Yes, it would. But this first man, the one who struck the other — I should like to know more about him, if you please."

"Well, that's just what I can't tell you, more's the pity, for it was that dark, excepting for the fire, and that made it hard to see."

"But you must have noticed something," urged Julia.

"From what I could tell, he weren't the sort of fellow you'd be likely to notice," the woman insisted. "Neither short nor tall, neither young nor old, neither lean nor fat."

"What of his coloring?" asked Julia, thinking of the Russian. Surely a bushy black beard would have been hard to miss, even under the conditions the woman described.

The woman scrunched her face up, trying to remember. "Like I said, it was hard to tell what with the fire behind him, but I had the impression of light hair, worn long."

"I see," said Julia in a flat voice. This was what Mr. Colquhoun had tried to warn her about: persons coming and offering her a Banbury story in exchange for coin. Fortunately, there was one way to determine whether the woman was intentionally lying, or whether her memory — or her vision — was merely playing tricks on her. "What of facial hair? Did he have any?"

Her would-be informant shook her head. "No, ma'am, of that I'm certain. Leastways, if he had a beard, it weren't much of one." She brightened suddenly. "Wait a minute, ma'am, I've just remembered something else! I did get a side view of him, and he had a sort of pointy nose. I noticed that in particular, because it stood out so bold and black against the orange light from the fire."

"Yes, well, thank you for your assistance," Julia said with considerably less warmth. "Your story has been most — enlightening."

"I thought — it said in the advertisement that you would pay," the woman said hopefully.

Julia sighed. Yes, she had promised payment, no matter how useless the information. She reminded herself that the woman's husband — no, she'd never claimed to be married to her Davy — her *man* would be out of work for some time to come, and in the meantime there was a child to support by whatever limited means were available to her. Julia thought of Lucy and her sisterhood, and supposed this young mother thought lying *to* a woman for money less objectionable than lying *with* a man for the same reason. Telling herself she was doing it for the sake of the baby, Julia picked up her reticule from where it lay on the table and offered the woman a shilling.

"Thankee, ma'am." The woman bobbed a curtsey and scooted out of the room as if fearful Julia would change her mind and demand the return of her coin.

Alas, this call was the first of many. A steady stream of hopeful informants climbed the stairs to number eighty-four Drury Lane, each with a different story to tell. Some insisted Pickett's attacker was tall, others swore he was short. Some recalled his light hair, others claimed he was dark. Some described him as solid and muscular, while others maintained that his figure was willowy. Interestingly, not one had noticed the thick black beard so vividly described by Mr. Bartlesby. Julia was obliged to dole out coins, since her advertisement had promised she would do so, but she was forced to admit that she had never realized London was such a haven for liars.

During a lull in the steady parade of false informants, Julia decided a cup of tea would not go amiss. She put water over the fire to boil, priding herself on this newly acquired skill, and had hardly risen to her feet when there was yet another knock upon the door. Heaving a sigh at her own stupidity in placing such an unintentionally generous advertisement, she went to the door and jerked it open — and found herself confronting the larcenous Lucy Higgins, escorted by Thomas, Julia's own footman.

"Lucy!" she exclaimed in honeyed tones

belied by the kindling expression in her eye. "Do come in. Thank you, Thomas, you have done very well. That will be all," she added to the young man who entered the room in Lucy's wake.

"I thought perhaps I might escort Miss Higgins back home," Thomas said hopefully, regarding his fair charge with ill-concealed admiration.

"Miss Higgins is more familiar with Drury Lane and its environs than you are," pointed out his mistress. "I'm sure she can manage to find her way home with no difficulty."

"Yes, my lady," Thomas conceded, crestfallen. He sketched a bow in her direction, then made another for Lucy's benefit, and reluctantly took his leave.

"How is he?" asked Lucy, and her glance toward the closed bedroom door gave Julia to understand that Thomas was not the subject of her inquiry.

"Never mind that." Julia was perversely reluctant to share any part of John Pickett, even a report as to his health, with the young woman who, but for the intervention of the magistrate, might have been his wife. "I have a more urgent matter to discuss with you. The last time you were here, you took something from this flat. I should like it returned, if you please."

Lucy did not pretend to misunderstand her. "And why should I, my Lady High-and-Mighty?" she retorted, lifting her pointed chin.

"Because it doesn't belong to you!"

"No, but he was going to give it to me."

"Nonsense!" exclaimed Julia, although she felt a little unwell at the very idea. "Why should he?"

"He used to give me things from time to time for helping him with his investigations, didn't he? Like when you was accused of killing your husband. He give me this here bonnet." She patted the drooping plumes of the horrendous headwear with proprietary pride.

"He — *he* chose that?" asked Lady Field-hurst, making a mental note never to let her husband select her millinery.

"No, but he give me the money to buy it for myself, which is the same thing, ain't it?"

"I see," said Julia with unconcealed relief. Actually, she considered it to be not at all the same thing, but she was too concerned with the more pressing matter at hand to argue the point.

"You never thought he'd bought 'em for you!" exclaimed Lucy with a sneer. "He hasn't the money to buy the sort of things *you'd* expect from a gentleman friend, so it stands to reason he bought 'em for me."

"He didn't buy them."

Lucy's eyes grew round. "He *stole* 'em?"

"Of course not!" Julia answered a bit too emphatically.

"Whose are they, then?"

Julia sighed. "In fact, they belong to the Russian Princess Olga Fyodorovna."

"Ha!" scoffed Lucy. "As if a princess would hold any truck with fake diamonds!"

"But Lucy, they aren't fake! They are very much real, and worth more than I shall ever see in my lifetime! The Bow Street force was charged with the task of ensuring their safety, and it will look very bad for Mr. Pickett — indeed, for the entire Bow Street force — if they are lost. So you see why you must return them," she concluded in a more coaxing tone. After all, she reminded herself, it was she, and not Lucy, who was Mrs. John Pickett. At the very least, she could afford to be kind.

Alas, her good intentions were short-lived.

"But returning them is just what I can't do," Lucy insisted. "I — I don't have 'em anymore."

"You don't have them? Why not, pray?"

"I spouted 'em," Lucy confessed miserably.

" 'Spouted'?" echoed Julia in some confusion, being unfamiliar with the term.

"I sold 'em to a pawnshop."

"You sold them to a pawnshop?" Julia shrieked, then glanced guiltily toward Pickett's bedroom door and lowered her voice. "You sold them to a pawnshop? Lucy, how could you?"

"I had no place to wear 'em, and the other girls would've stolen 'em, anyway," Lucy said defensively. "Anyway, I needed the money worse than I needed gew-gaws, so I spouted 'em. How was I to know they were real?"

"You sold them to a pawnshop," Julia said dazedly, struggling to absorb the enormity of this fresh disaster.

Lucy dug in the pocket of her tattered gown and withdrew a handful of coins. "I got two bob and six for 'em," she said hopefully.

"Two shillings and sixpence." Julia collapsed onto the solitary chair and dropped her head into her hands, the picture of despair. "Lucy, you must buy them back at once!"

"But I've already spent part of the money, haven't I? A girl's got to pay her rent, you know."

"Very well, then, I shall make up the difference," declared Julia. She reached once again for her reticule, thankful that she'd had the foresight to fill it with coins in preparation for the appearance of her advertisement in the newspaper. "The pawnbroker will no doubt demand more than the two and six he gave you, so I shall double it; that should allow you to buy back the diamonds, and him to make a tidy profit as well. On no account, however, are you to so much as *hint* that they might be worth more than that!"

"All right, all right," Lucy grumbled. "D'you think I've never bartered before? More than you have, I'll be bound!"

Lady Fieldhurst could not deny it. After Lucy had set out for the pawnshop, Julia turned back to the fire, where the water had by this time come to a boil. She made herself a cup of tea and took it to Pickett's bedroom, where she sat down in the chair beside the bed and picked up the book where she had left off.

" 'Chapter 3: A migration. The fortunate circumstances of our lives are generally found at last to be of our own procuring. The only hope of our family now was, that the report of our misfortunes might be malicious or premature . . .' "

If only they were, thought Julia. If only

they were.

Pickett heard the soothing feminine voice long before he was able to identify it. When he realized it was none other than her ladyship speaking, he made the colossal effort to open his eyes. Sure enough, she sat beside his bed with a book in her hand. She was wearing a peach-colored dress he'd never seen before, and he was struck anew by her beauty, evident even in funereal black of mourning but all the more so in the elegant and expensive gowns she'd been born to wear. She was as far above him as the stars in the heavens; he'd known it all along, even as he'd fallen ever more deeply in love with her.

She turned the page, and the leaf broke free from its well-worn binding and fluttered to the floor. She paused in her reading and bent to pick it up, and although Pickett could not see the floor from his vantage point on the bed, he could picture in his mind's eye the frayed rag rug and the bare wooden boards beneath, their varnish nothing more than a distant memory. He had always thought himself fortunate in his lodgings, having two whole rooms to himself while no more than a stone's throw away, whole families crowded together in a single room. Now, however, seeing her ladyship here only served to remind him how mean his flat — no, his *life* — must appear in her eyes. Never had he been more conscious of the gulf that separated them.

She didn't belong here, he thought, watching as she took a sip from a chipped teacup before resuming her reading. Her lips were slightly pursed, and he found himself staring at her mouth. Had he really kissed those lips, or had he merely dreamed it? No, it had been real, he was sure of it. She'd even kissed him back. It was more, so much more, than he had any right to expect. He could die content, and she could go back to Mayfair, back to her own kind. He would be all right on his own, with his landlady — what was her name? — to look in on him from time to time. He opened his mouth to tell her so, but something entirely different came out.

"Don't go."

She looked up at the sound of his voice, the vicar and his family's troubles forgotten.

"Good morning, John," she said, although the hour was well past noon. "So you've decided to wake up at last, have you?"

She laid the book aside and moved to sit on the edge of the bed, then placed the back of her hand against his flushed cheek. It was still much too warm.

"The doctor left something to bring your fever down," she said, remembering the water she'd just heated for tea. It should still be hot enough to steep the willow bark in, if she could persuade him to drink it. "If I make it up for you, do you think you could drink some?"

He nodded, and winced at the pain in his head. "I'll try."

She rose to fetch another teacup from the other room.

"Don't go," Pickett said again, catching at the skirt of her gown like a child fearful of being left alone.

She sat down on the edge of the bed and detached his hand from her skirt so that she might clasp it in both of her own. "I'm not going far, only into the next room. I'll be right back, I promise."

Forgetting for the moment her determination to keep the bedroom warm, she left the door open so that he might watch as she took a cup down from its hook and filled it with hot water from the kettle. She returned to the bedroom, shutting the door behind her, and added the doctor's dried willow bark mixture to the water in the cup. She allowed it to steep for several minutes, during which she kept up a generally one-sided conversation of cheerful trivialities in an effort to keep Pickett awake.

"Here we are," she declared at last, having deemed the tea ready.

He raised himself up on one elbow, and she lifted the cup to his lips.

"Yes, I daresay it tastes quite dreadful," she said when he grimaced, "but the doctor says it might bring the fever down."

He could not manage more than a few sips before collapsing back against the pillow, exhausted from the effort. She wasn't sure he had ingested enough of the concoction to do any good, but she dared not press him further. She had set the cup aside and was going to suggest that she read some more when he spoke again.

"What day is it?"

What day? She had no idea. Time had ceased to exist since the night of the fire. Mr. Colquhoun had been here on Sunday, and sent her home to rest. Had that been yesterday, or the day before?

"Tuesday, the twenty-eighth of February," she said with less than perfect accuracy, for in fact it was still Monday, the twenty-seventh. "Spring will be here before we know it," she added brightly.

239

"The annulment," Pickett said. "Has it — ?"

"Pray do not vex yourself over the annulment," she beseeched him, running loving fingers through his tousled curls.

"Are you still my wife?"

"Yes, love, I'm still your wife," she assured him, blinking back tears.

"Good," he said with a sigh, and drifted back off to sleep.

Julia was thankful that he was still asleep when Lucy returned some time later, for she did not want him distressed by the loss of the diamonds. Still less did she want the task of explaining their presence in his possession in the first place. After all, how did one explain the unexplainable?

"Lucy! Thank heaven you're back," she exclaimed softly, lest he hear and awaken again. "Did you get them?"

"No, your ladyship," she confessed miserably. "I couldn't."

"Why not? Would the pawnbroker not sell them to you? Is he demanding more money?"

"Worse," she said, wringing her hands in their fingerless gloves. "He's already sold them."

"*What?*" Even in her worst imaginings, Ju-

240

lia had not considered that the diamonds might be already beyond their reach.

"It's true, my lady. Somebody else has already bought them. I tried to get Mr. Baumgarten to tell me who — I figured you'd want to know — but he clamped his trap shut, and wouldn't open it again for no amount of money, even though I offered him the five bob you give me. I didn't think you'd mind," she added apologetically.

"No, Lucy, you did exactly right. But oh heavens, we are in the suds! If those diamonds should be discovered, if they should be traced back to the pawnshop and thence to Mr. Pickett's possession —"

"Pshaw!" Lucy dismissed this possibility out of hand. "How could they be?"

"They could certainly be traced back to you, and unless you have exalted associations of which I am unaware, the only connection between you and the Princess Olga Fyodorovna is Mr. Pickett."

"Oh," said Lucy, abashed. "What would happen, then, if they were traced back to him?"

Julia shook her head, wishing she had a better understanding of how the law operated. "I don't know. I suppose at the very least he could be charged with the theft and imprisoned. At worst —" She recalled what he had said that night about how the theft of the jewels, purely a theoretical speculation at that point, might spark an international incident. Just how far would the British government go to assuage any seeming offense to a much-needed ally? Surely justice would be swift and harsh, under such circumstances. "At worst," she said, her voice breaking on the words, "he could hang."

CHAPTER 14

IN WHICH LADY FIELDHURST QUITS DRURY LANE FOR MORE RARIFIED CIRCLES

What should one wear to a meeting with a Russian princess, Julia wondered as she surveyed the gowns hanging in the clothespress. She had left Mr. Pickett in his magistrate's care, and was preparing for her visit to the Princess Olga, the visit for which she had argued so vehemently.

Now that the hour was upon her, however, she realized there were difficulties she had not anticipated, the first of these being the question of what to wear. Every one of her gowns (with the exception of the blue one, which had died a gruesome death) was at least a year out of date, since she'd been in mourning for the past ten months. Still, she was less concerned with fashion than she was with protocol; it would not do to appear at Grillon's Hotel in an ordinary carriage dress or promenade gown. No, formality was the thing, and the most formal gown she owned, aside from her wedding dress, was the one she had worn for her presentation at court shortly after her marriage to the Viscount Fieldhurst. It was not here; for a moment she almost regretted dismissing Smithers, who would have known at once where to look for it.

After searching from room to room, she finally located it in the third-best bedroom. She dragged it out of the clothes-press and spread it over the bed to examine it. It was almost seven years old, much older than even the most ancient gown hanging in her own room. Fortunately for her, the royal court was resistant to change, particularly where fashion was concerned. At court, the styles of the last century still prevailed: knee breeches instead of pantaloons for the gentlemen and, worse, wide hoops for the ladies which, when combined with the high waist dictated by current tastes, had made her look as if she were emerging from the top of a birdcage.

If she were to leave off the hoop, she decided, the gown itself was not half bad. The bodice was made of white satin, with short puffed sleeves and a tiny ruff standing up at the back of the neck that grew narrower over the shoulders until it disappeared entirely into each side of the scooped neckline. The skirts, alas, were cut wider than current fashion dictated (a matter of necessity, if they were to accommodate the despised hoop) but the overskirt of light blue velvet was edged with wide gold braid and swept into a most imposing train. Of its more intimidating qualities, Julia had reason to know: As the newly married Viscountess Fieldhurst, she had spent hours practicing in front of a mirror in order to master the art of backing away from the royal presence without tripping over the voluminous velvet folds.

Yes, her presentation gown would do. She lifted it in her arms like a particularly unwieldy child, and carried it to her bedroom. It would be impossible for her to put it on unassisted, much less dress her hair in a style worthy of the occasion, so she rang for a housemaid to play the rôle recently vacated by Smithers.

"Thank you, your ladyship, I'd be that pleased to help," enthused the nineteen-year-old Betsy, combining gratification at her unexpected rise in the world with a young woman's inborn love of all matters pertaining to personal adornment. "Such a beautiful dress," she added, stroking the velvet overskirt with reverent fingers.

"Beautiful, yes — and heavy and uncomfortable, but the only thing I own that is even remotely suitable for the occasion," Julia said drily, unbuttoning the front of her peach-colored kerseymere and pulling it over her head.

With Betsy's assistance, Julia put on the formal presentation gown and soon stood before the looking glass, waiting patiently as her temporary lady's maid fastened up the back. She was pleased to note that it still fit as well as it had done seven years ago, and pushed aside the realization that this circumstance was largely due to the fact that she had been unable to conceive a child.

"Which of your jewels will you wear with it, your ladyship?"

This was another difficulty Lady Fieldhurst had not anticipated. The diamonds and sapphires she had worn with the gown at her presentation had not belonged to her, but to the Viscount Fieldhurst and, upon his death, had passed to George to bestow upon his wife. In fact, this was true of most of her jewels, and all of the best pieces. She did have a fine set of opals that had once belonged to her mother, which that lady had passed along to her daughter when her own health had failed, forcing her to withdraw from Society. Still, Julia feared the Russian court would be unimpressed with opals, no matter how fine.

Julia sighed. What she lacked in quality, she must attempt to compensate for with quantity.

"Fetch me my jewel case, Betsy," she said.

When the maid complied, Julia had the girl bedeck her with almost every piece she owned. After Betsy had finished, Julia surveyed her reflection in the glass, and thought she resembled nothing so much as a walking advertisement for Rundell and Bridge; still, from what she recalled of the bejeweled Russian ladies seated in the royal box at Drury Lane, she doubted they would see this excessive ornamentation as a disadvantage.

She then sat down at her dressing table so that Betsy might dress her hair, which the girl did by piling Julia's golden locks atop her head and coaxing tiny finger-curls to fall about her ears. In fact, so adept was she at this skill that Julia suspected Betsy's leisure hours were frequently occupied in performing similar operations upon her own head.

"What will you wear in your hair, your ladyship?" asked Betsy, stepping back to admire her handiwork. "Feathers, perhaps, or would you prefer flowers?"

Julia was prepared for this question, it having been uppermost in her mind while Betsy arranged her coiffure. Feathers, she felt, were too suggestive of court presentation, given the fact that no fewer than seven ostrich plumes were *de rigueur* for that occasion. Flowers, on the other hand, were surely better suited for a schoolroom miss than for a widow of seven-and-twenty.

There was another option, however, one to which she had never sought recourse and, if she were to be perfectly honest, to which she had thought she never would. A jeweled coronet resided in the floor of the jewel case, beneath a false bottom. In fact, it was a part of the Fieldhurst collection, but when Julia had tried to give it to the woman who should now possess it by right, George's unassuming wife had laughed at the very suggestion, assuring her predecessor that she would have nowhere to wear such an extravagant piece and begging her to keep it against the day when George's son and heir would take a wife. Julia had had nowhere to wear it, either, which was why it had languished, forgotten, in the bottom of her jewel case. Mrs. John Pickett would have even less occasion for such a display of opulence, but she would wear it now, while she had the chance, and in the worthiest of causes.

"Look in the bottom of the case, Betsy,"

she instructed the little maid. "No, it lifts up, you see? Yes, there."

"Ohhh!" breathed Betsy when she saw what lay beneath. "Oh, ma'am!"

In fact, Julia's response upon seeing her reflection in the looking-glass adorned with this diadem was much the same. She wondered fleetingly what Mr. Pickett would think were he to see her like this, and decided it would be much better if he did not; he would very likely decide that he was unworthy to kiss the hem of her garment, and insist upon releasing her from the marriage regardless of his own feelings in the matter. He was, as Mr. Colquhoun had noted, a rare one for the grand romantic gesture.

Her toilette complete, Julia caught the blue velvet train over her arm and descended the stairs with care, accompanied by Betsy following from behind and Rogers hovering solicitously in front, fully prepared to catch his mistress should she trip over her hem and fall. She reached the ground without mishap, however, and allowed Rogers to hand her into the carriage that was already waiting at the door. She was soon settled within, and it seemed no time at all before she was set down in front of Grillon's Hotel in Albemarle Street. Once inside, she asked for the Princess Olga Fyodorovna and was assured that, yes, the Russian aristocrat was indeed staying there, along with most of her retinue.

Lady Fieldhurst sent up her card, and was ushered to a chair where she might sit while she waited for a response. She hoped she had not been overly optimistic when she had assured Mr. Colquhoun of her entrée into such rarified circles; in truth (although she suspected her Mr. Pickett would fail to appreciate the distinction), viscounts were fairly low on the ladder of aristocracy: higher than barons and baronets, certainly, but beneath earls, marquesses, and dukes. And then there were the royal dukes, laws unto themselves, who were the Princess Olga's counterparts among the British aristocracy. Just as Julia would not have marched up to the door of St. James's Palace and demanded admittance, she hoped she was not overstepping in calling upon the Russian princess at her hotel.

She need not have worried. The seat of the chair had not yet grown warm beneath her when a servant with a starched apron and mob cap approached. "My Lady Fieldhurst?" she asked in charmingly accented English.

"Yes," Julia acknowledged, nodding her

head cautiously lest the coronet be dislodged.

"Her Royal Highness the Princess Olga Fyodorovna will see you," the woman continued. "If you will please to follow me?"

Julia did so, and was soon admitted to the most opulent hotel room she had ever seen. She wondered if Grillon's rooms were always so extravagantly outfitted, or if this room was furnished with the princess's own belongings. Either way, she had not long to consider the question, for the Princess Olga Fyodorovna sat in a chair before the fire, her gnarled, be-ringed hands resting atop the elaborately carved head of an ebony cane.

"Your Royal Highness," said Julia, sinking into the deep curtsey reserved for royalty. "Thank you for your willingness to receive me."

"Lady Fieldhurst." The princess acknowledged Julia with a nod, then gestured toward the vacant chair adjacent to her own. "Pray be seated. I suppose you are here to talk about the theft of my jewels?"

"I — why, yes, I am," said Julia, somewhat taken aback by the forthright manner in which the princess raised a subject that Julia had feared might take some exercise of diplomacy to approach. "I was at the theatre that night, as well."

"I remember seeing you there," stated the princess in excellent, if slightly accented, English. "You were sitting in the box opposite, with a remarkably good-looking young man. The Prince of Wales told me your identity — I was a little acquainted with your husband, having met him once or twice over the years through his connection with the Foreign Office — but of your companion, the Prince admitted he knew nothing."

"No, His Royal Highness would not have known Mr. Pickett. In fact, my escort that evening was one of the Bow Street Runners assigned to your protection."

"I see. Well then, it is a good thing he is handsome, is it not? No, don't fire up at me, girl," she added, seeing Julia's kindling eye and flushed cheeks. "In all fairness, I suppose it would not have mattered how many of your Bow Street Runners were assigned to keep watch over the diamonds. If even the fire was not enough to prevent the theft, what could a mere thief-taker have done?"

"You may be right," Julia conceded, "but I must protest that Mr. Pickett is anything but a 'mere thief-taker.' "

"Oh?" The princess's carefully plucked

eyebrows arched toward her hairline. "And what is your handsome Bow Street Runner's opinion of the theft?"

Julia sighed. "Whatever he thinks, he is unable to tell us at present. He was gravely injured in escaping the fire, and although he has moments of lucidity, he is in no condition to speak of anything he may have seen."

"A pity," remarked the princess. She glanced at a small table in one corner of the room, where tall white candles flanked a painted icon of a melancholy Madonna and oddly proportioned Christ child. "I shall light a candle for him, yes?"

"I — yes, thank you," said Julia, touched by the Russian lady's thoughtfulness. "I should appreciate that very much."

The princess scowled fiercely at her. "I believe your regard for this young man goes beyond the professional, does it not? Take him as a lover if you must, but it will not do for a woman of your station to appear publicly, as you did that night, with such a person. We must hope the fire will drive from the *ton*'s collective memory your indiscretion at the theatre."

Julia felt herself blushing beneath the woman's too-perceptive gaze. She was not ashamed to own Mr. Pickett as her husband before the world, but she had learned her lesson. The last time she had claimed to be Mrs. Pickett, she had discovered after the fact that she had embroiled them both in a legal Scottish marriage by declaration; she would not do so again without his knowledge, much less his permission.

"I thank you for your concern, Your Royal Highness, but it is misplaced. I have committed no indiscretion. In fact, Mr. Pickett's escort was part of the plan for safeguarding your diamonds. My presence was merely to make him appear less conspicuous in a box than he might have been alone and, if necessary, to prevent him from making any glaring errors of etiquette that might have betrayed his incognito."

"Ah! I see," said the princess, and her ready acceptance of this explanation made Julia perversely determined to see that Mr. Pickett was not slighted.

"On a personal level, however, I must own that I consider Mr. Pickett a very dear friend, and one to whom I owe a great debt. Besides rescuing me from the burning theatre, he once kept me from hanging for my husband's murder." Seeing her opportunity to steer the conversation away from so intimate a subject — and back to the purpose for which she had called upon the princess in the first place — she added, "That is why I have every confidence in his ability to recover your diamonds, once he is sufficiently recuperated."

"Then we must pray his recovery is swift," Princess Olga said with a rasping laugh, "for I fear poor Vladimir Gregorovich has no such confidence where your Bow Street men are concerned."

"Vladimir Gregorovich," echoed Julia, weighing the name against the one mentioned by Mr. Colquhoun, and finding them the same. "Would that be the large, bearded gentleman in your box that evening?"

"Yes, and his wife Natasha was there also. She was the one wearing the diamonds on that occasion. I suppose Vladimir fears it looks bad for him, the diamonds being stolen while they were in his wife's possession. A venerable old family, you know — he is related to the Tsarina on his mother's side — but no money at all, more's the pity."

Julia made suitable regretful noises, but her brain was awhirl. Here was motive indeed! She had some idea of how expensive continued association with the royals could be; several of her late husband's acquaintances had made up part of the Prince of Wales's profligate Carlton House set, and were deeply in debt as a result. If this was

255

the case with Vladimir Gregorovich and his wife, then the recent rash of jewel thefts plaguing London must have appeared as a godsend. What better way to recoup one's finances than by stealing the very jewels one was supposed to be safeguarding, especially when everyone from Princess Olga to Mr. Colquhoun and his Bow Street force expected some such attempt to be made? The fire could only have made the task easier, as it would have been easy to claim they must have been stolen during the chaos surrounding the royal party's evacuation from the burning theatre. Alas, there was still the question of how they came to end up in the pocket of Mr. Pickett's coat.

"It must be most distressing to his wife, the fact that the jewels were stolen while in her care," Julia observed.

The Princess Olga inclined her gray head. "Yes, she was quite, what do you say, hysterical when she realized they were missing. Of course, all our nerves were on edge, on account of the fire. Thank heaven that young man warned us in time!"

" 'Young man'?" Julia echoed. "What young man was that?"

Even as she asked the question, she reminded herself that it could not possibly have been Mr. Pickett, as he had never left their box. In fact, given Her Royal Highness's advanced age, the Princess Olga might have referred to any male under the age of fifty as a "young man."

"I regret I never heard the fellow's name mentioned," the princess answered. "A great pity, for I should have liked to see that he was rewarded for his efforts on our behalf. I shall certainly speak to your Prince of Wales on the subject."

"What did this young man look like, your Royal Highness? What did he do that you consider deserving of a reward?"

"He entered our box — quite uninvited, in fact, but in light of what followed, we were not inclined to stand upon ceremony — and told us the theatre was burning, and we must get out with all due haste. Which we did," she added emphatically. "As for his appearance, it was rather, what is the word, undescript?"

"Nondescript," said Julia, nodding in understanding. "Unremarkable."

"Yes, that is so. He was somewhere between thirty and forty in years, and his hair was neither dark nor fair."

A rather unhelpful description, thought Julia, and one that might apply to hundreds, if not thousands, of London's male inhabitants. Still, she had to wonder if, while he was being so helpful, the "young man" had not also helped himself to the Princess Olga's diamonds, perhaps with their wearer's cooperation. It would certainly be safer to enlist an outsider's assistance than for Natasha or her husband, Vladimir, to be discovered with the stolen diamonds on their persons. Of course, in that event they could always claim to have found them. She shook her head in bewilderment. There were so many possibilities to consider! If this was the sort of thing John Pickett dealt with every day, then he earned every one of his twenty-five shillings a week, and a great deal more besides.

"And it was after this, er, young man bade you leave the theatre that you realized the diamonds were missing?"

"It was after we were outside, as we were being hurried into the prince's carriage." The princess gripped the head of her cane so tightly her knuckles turned white — reliving, no doubt, the fear and distress of that night.

"Is it possible, then, that the diamonds were stolen while you were evacuating the theatre?"

The princess shrugged her frail shoulders. "I suppose so. In all the confusion, any number of gems might have been stolen without our taking the slightest notice. I fear our flight from the theatre was hardly conducted in a manner befitting our rank, but dignity tends to go out the window when one's life is in danger."

Julia, recalling her own skirts hitched above her knees and her legs locked tightly around Mr. Pickett's waist, could not deny it.

Too late, she realized she had allowed herself to be distracted by Princess Olga's anonymous "young man," and tried to steer the conversation back toward Vladimir Gregorovich and his wife. Alas, the princess appeared to have nothing more to say on that particular subject, and Julia was powerless to press the matter without asking questions that could only be seen as impertinent. They exchanged fruitless speculations as to the cause of the fire, the damage to the theatre and the likelihood of its being rebuilt, and as soon as she could tactfully do so, Julia took her leave. Before she returned to Pickett's lodgings and reported her findings to Mr. Colquhoun, however, there was one more thing she wanted to do. She might not have a better opportunity, and she was not at all certain she could persuade Mr. Colquhoun to agree in any case. She inquired at the hotel desk and sent her card up to Vladimir Gregorovich's wife, Natasha.

Lady Fieldhurst had been gone for perhaps an hour when Pickett began to stir, muttering incoherently and thrashing to and fro beneath the blankets.

"John?" called Mr. Colquhoun, laying aside the copy of the *Times* he'd brought and moving his chair nearer to the bed. "John, can you hear me?"

Pickett's brown eyes fluttered open. "Sir?" He turned his head from side to side, searching. "Where is — ?"

"Her ladyship will return shortly. Until then, I'm afraid you'll have to make do with me. How do you feel?"

Pickett gave a shaky laugh. "I've been better."

"You've looked better, too, if I may say so," observed the magistrate. "Does your head hurt? I can give you some laudanum, if you have need of it, and I've been instructed to brew you a willow bark tea for the fever, if you feel you can drink it."

Pickett made a moue at the memory of the bitter tea, but nodded.

"Very well, then, I'll start some water boiling." Mr. Colquhoun left the room long enough to put the kettle over the fire, then returned to the bedroom and administered the promised laudanum.

"What day is it?" asked Pickett, leaning back against the pillows once the medicine was down.

"It's Tuesday, the last day of February."

"Then — the annulment —"

"Don't fret yourself over the annulment, lad," counseled the magistrate, patting him on the shoulder. He believed her ladyship had been quite serious when she'd declared there was to be no annulment, but, as much as he would have liked to set Pickett's mind at ease, that was a conversation for the two of them, and one in which he would play no part. More in the hope of diverting the boy's mind than in the expectation of getting any new information, he asked, "Do you remember anything about the theatre? Anything before the fire, I mean. Did you notice anything suspicious, anyone acting strangely?"

Pickett grimaced with the effort of remembering. "Before the fire — the royal box —"

"Hold on, I believe the water for your tea is boiling," said the magistrate, heaving himself up from his chair.

But by the time he'd removed the kettle, added the dried willow bark, and carried the brew back to Pickett's room, the lauda-

261

num had begun to take hold, clouding Pickett's mind and slurring his speech.

"Yes, John, you were saying about the theatre?" prompted Mr. Colquhoun, in between trying to coax sips of willow bark tea down his throat.

" — The box — shouldn't have been there —"

"No, you shouldn't have been there," the magistrate said with a sigh, setting aside the willow bark tea as a lost cause. "None of you should have been there. I hold myself entirely to blame."

Pickett, lapsing once more into unconsciousness, made no reply.

Lady Fieldhurst had not long to wait before she was summoned to the Russian lady's presence.

"*Madame* Gregorovich?" she asked, recalling from some long-ago lesson with her governess that Russian aristocrats used the honorifics of the French tongue, French being, she supposed, the language of diplomacy.

"*Nyet,*" the woman said with raised brows. "I am Natasha Ivanova."

"I — I beg your pardon," stammered Lady Fieldhurst. "I was given to understand that you were the wife of Vladimir Gregorovich."

"*Da,* I am *Madame* Dombrowskaya."

Lady Fieldhurst shook her head in bewilderment. "I — I'm afraid I don't understand, *Madame.*" The *madame* part, at least, she seemed to have got right.

The Russian lady, whatever her name was, bestowed upon her a rather condescending smile. "Our Russian names are not like your English ones. We have the patronymic, what you call the surname, *da,* but it is different for men and women. My husband, he is Vladimir Gregorovich Dombrowsky because he is the son of Gregor Dombrowsky. Me, I am Natasha Ivanova Dombrowskaya. Ivanova because I am the daughter of Ivan, and Dombrowskaya because I am the wife of Monsieur Dombrowsky."

"I see," murmured Lady Fieldhurst, although in fact she was thoroughly confused. She supposed it must be easier for the Russians, as they would have been taught these distinctions from childhood. She wondered if the unspoken rules governing the British aristocracy were equally baffling to Mr. Pickett, who would have had no governess or tutor to instruct him as a youth; she decided they must be, recalling his small yet undeniable missteps at the theatre. And while there was no one to know of her own errors except for *Madame* Dombrowskaya

263

(or whatever her name was), he had been obliged to enact his rôle as a gentleman in full view of over three thousand people — and save for one or two minor miscues, had carried it off as one to the manner born. The realization made her admire him all the more. It could not have been easy for him to navigate such unfamiliar waters, and for the first time she realized she was asking a great deal of him, to give up the familiar in favor of a more privileged yet alien way of life. She made a private vow that she would never give him cause to regret it.

"Now that we have established, what do you say, my identity," said Madame Dombrowskaya, gesturing toward a sofa upholstered in straw-colored brocade, "how may I be of service to you?"

Julia took the proffered seat, and her voluminous train formed a puddle of blue velvet about her feet. "Actually, I had hoped to be of service to you," she confessed. "I understand you were wearing the Princess Olga's diamonds when they were stolen during your escape from the theatre."

"*Da,* what of it?" Natasha Ivanova's friendly demeanor cooled considerably. A guilty conscience, Julia wondered, or was she merely weary of answering questions? Thinking back to the dark days when she had been the primary suspect in the murder of her husband, Julia supposed that many of her own actions, born of shock and fear, could have been interpreted as evidence of guilt. She was fortunate in that Mr. Pickett had not subscribed to the popular assumption; surely she must show Madame Dombrowskaya the same consideration.

"It must be most awkward, losing something of value that belonged to someone else," said Julia in sympathetic accents. "I remember once losing my mother's pearls during my first Season in Bath. I felt quite dreadful about it, particularly since they had been my father's wedding gift to her."

Madame Dombrowskaya looked down her aristocratic nose. "There is a great deal of difference between your mother's pearls and the Princess Olga's diamonds."

"Yes, I suppose so," acknowledged Julia, trying hard to extend the benefit of the doubt to a woman toward whom she felt a growing dislike. "Still, Mama's pearls eventually turned up, and I have no doubt Princess Olga's diamonds will do the same."

The Russian lady gave a disdainful sniff. "Perhaps. But these pearls, you were so foolish as to lose through your own carelessness. Her Royal Highness's diamonds were stolen. It is not at all the same thing, *nyet*?"

265

"Er, *nyet,*" agreed Julia. "I suppose they are worth a great deal?"

"More than any English viscountess would have reason to know," retorted Madam Dombrowskaya.

"I don't doubt it," Julia said with a rather forced smile, accepting the insult at face value. "Still, one must wonder what the thief thinks he — or she — may do with them. Surely they would be recognized if they were worn, would they not?"

"*Da.* What of it?"

"Perhaps the thief did not consider this until after he — or she — had done the deed," suggested Julia. "Perhaps, having stolen the diamonds, the thief realized he could not hope to profit by them, and attempted to dispose of them before they were found in his — or her — possession."

The haughty Russian scowled. "What are you saying?"

"I am merely suggesting that the thief, fearing disgrace, may have decided to dispose of them by, say, slipping them into the pocket of some innocent and unsuspecting person."

"*Ba!* Why should anyone do such a thing? It makes no sense!" She rose from her chair, stiff with offended dignity. "I believe you speak in riddles, Lady Fieldhurst, and I am in no mood for riddles. I shall bid you good day."

Thus dismissed, Julia had no choice but to take her leave with what dignity she could muster. She rose from her seat on the sofa, but before she could make good her escape, the door separating the sitting room from the bedchamber opened, and *Madame* Dombrowskaya's husband, Vladimir, entered the room, his sinister-looking countenance rendered all the more formidable by a fierce scowl.

"This Englishwoman, does she trouble you, *golubka*?" he demanded of his wife.

"It was certainly not my intention to trouble *Madame* Gregor, er, Ivanov, er, Dombrowskaya," Julia put in as hastily as the language barrier would allow. "I only wished to commiserate with her on the loss — er, theft, that is — of the Princess Olga's diamonds. As I was telling *Madame,* er, your wife, Your Excellency, I believe I may understand a little of how she must feel, as I once had the misfortune to misplace jewels that did not belong to me."

"Pearls," put in *Madame* Dombrowskaya with a disdainful sniff.

Julia had thought it best not to offer any reassurances as to the ability of the Bow Street force to recover the diamonds since, if the Russian couple had indeed stolen the diamonds themselves, such reassurances were the last thing they would wish to hear. But as her tactful attempt at discovering how the diamonds had come to be in Mr. Pickett's possession had been firmly rebuffed — and as it appeared she was about to make a hasty exit in any case — she might as well set the cat amongst the pigeons and see what, if anything, might be determined by their reaction.

"I have had dealings with the Bow Street force myself, and found them to be both competent and resourceful. I have no doubt the diamonds will be returned to the princess very shortly, and the culprit punished for his crimes."

Vladimir Gregorovich muttered something incomprehensible yet apparently highly unflattering about Mr. Colquhoun, but showed no sign of being disturbed by the prospect of retribution for the criminal. The mention of the magistrate, however, served to remind Julia that he was waiting in Mr. Pickett's flat for her to relieve him.

She was suddenly impatient to return to Drury Lane. She could not decide if Madame Dombrowskaya's indignation or her husband's belligerence was genuine, or merely the manifestation of a guilty conscience. In fact, she was more than ready to dump the entire affair in Mr. Colquhoun's lap — provided she could do so in a manner that would not betray her own knowledge of the diamonds. She sighed. Perhaps the magistrate was right: perhaps she was not suited for this sort of work, after all.

No, she reminded herself, her efforts had not been entirely wasted, for she had learned that the Russian couple had a motive for stealing the diamonds. And if she had momentarily deviated from her original intention and gone chasing briefly after mares' nests, well, she had known Mr. Pickett to do so on occasion. But the truth was out there somewhere, and she would not give up. Not as long as Mr. Pickett needed her.

CHAPTER 15

IN WHICH JULIA FACES DOWN
THE FIELDHURSTS

Julia took her leave of the Russian aristocrats with what dignity she could muster, then instructed the coachman to convey her directly to Pickett's flat in Drury Lane. As he was prepared to hand her into the carriage, however, she recalled that the restaurant at Grillon's Hotel was second to none. She was, she admitted, growing a bit weary of the cold collations prepared by her cook and delivered faithfully by Thomas every day, and she suspected Mr. Colquhoun would not say no to sirloin of beef and all its accoutrements, either. She commanded the coachman to wait, and went back inside to procure luncheon. When she entered Pickett's flat a short time later, it was with her train over her arm and a wicker basket in her hand.

"Well, well, my lady, don't you look fine?" exclaimed the magistrate. "Perhaps it's a good thing Mr. Pickett is asleep, as the sight of you in full regalia would likely be enough to frighten the poor lad to death."

Julia shook her head. "No, not fine, merely ostentatious. Still, it served not to disgrace me utterly before Princess Olga and her entourage." She turned the subject to one who was, in her opinion, infinitely more important than any number of Russian princesses. "Has he slept the entire time, then?"

"No, he awoke briefly, about an hour after you had gone."

"That is good news," said Julia, aware of a pang of disappointment nevertheless at having missed one of his all too infrequent bouts of consciousness.

"I fear I make a poor nurse, however," continued Mr. Colquhoun. "I boiled water and brewed willow bark tea, as you instructed, but I made the tactical error of giving him laudanum first. By the time the tea was ready, the laudanum had taken hold, and I could not persuade him to stay awake long enough to drink it. I am sorry, my lady. I confess, my only thought was giving him relief from any pain."

"I don't blame you, Mr. Colquhoun. I should not have wanted him to suffer." She sighed. "I am discovering that this nursing business is largely a matter of trial and error

271

— and I confess to having made more than my share of errors. If he recovers, I fear it will be in spite of me, rather than because of anything I have done."

Privately, Mr. Colquhoun suspected it was the continued presence of Lady Fieldhurst that kept Pickett clinging to life at all. Aloud, however, he merely said, "What is that smell, my lady? If that is your perfume, you must tell me where you got it, so that I may buy my Janet a barrel of it."

Julia laughed. "It is luncheon from Grillon's. Have you eaten? I thought you would know what to do with sirloin of beef and roasted potatoes."

"Indeed, I do," said the magistrate with enthusiasm. "Thank you, my lady. It was well done of you to think of it."

While Mr. Colquhoun unpacked the basket, Julia fetched the bottle of wine included in Thomas's most recent delivery. Finding no wineglasses, she was obliged to decant it into teacups, whereupon Mr. Colquhoun, far from being offended by this breach of etiquette, assured her of his willingness to drink directly from the bottle, should the need arise. Julia then selected two chipped earthenware plates from Pickett's modest collection and filled them with beef, potatoes, and thick slices of bread spread with butter. As neither she nor the magistrate wanted to leave Pickett alone, they carried their feast into the bedroom, Mr. Colquhoun bringing the third and last chair into the room to serve as a makeshift table.

"I wish he would awaken so that we might offer him something to eat," she fretted, surveying Pickett's slumbering form. "It appears to me that he is growing shockingly thin."

"He'll fatten up soon enough once he's recovered," predicted the magistrate.

Julia opened her mouth to scold him for being so glib, then noticed the creases marring his forehead as he regarded his protégé, and realized his optimism concealed a concern every bit as great as her own.

"I shall see to it that he does," she answered, adopting his own cheerful manner. "I have no desire to be married to a scarecrow."

"So tell me, my lady," said the magistrate around a mouthful of sirloin, "how was your visit to the Princess Olga?"

"Her Royal Highness was most obliging," Julia recalled as she refilled his wine. "She told me something about Vladimir Gregorovich Dombrowsky that I think you will find interesting."

Mr. Colquhoun, remembering his own

less than friendly exchange with the Russian, was eager to listen. "Did she, indeed?"

"It seems Vladimir and his wife Natasha are in need of money."

"Are they, now? That is interesting! Pray continue, my lady."

"She didn't say much more than that, only that his is a very old family, related to the Tsarina on his mother's side, and that they have no money." She paused. "I could not help thinking that it would be much easier to steal diamonds if one were already wearing them about one's neck."

"A very valid point, especially in view of the fact that he has been badgering me for a quick arrest."

Julia frowned thoughtfully. "Has he? Forgive me, but why should he do so, if he and his wife are the thieves?"

"Hasty arrests frequently lead to the wrong persons being convicted, as I am sure you, of all people, must be aware." He cleared his throat and continued haltingly. "And there, too, I owe you an apology. I was too ready to believe you guilty of your husband's murder. Had anyone but Mr. Pickett been assigned to the case, you might well have stood trial for it."

"Believe me, Mr. Colquhoun, I am fully aware of how damning the evidence against me must have looked. Indeed, I owe Mr. Pickett a debt I can never repay. But you were speaking of Vladimir Gregorovich."

"Yes, he's been making rather a nuisance of himself. It appears Vladimir is eager to see some hapless Englishman pay for his own crimes."

Julia, knowing exactly which hapless Englishman had been selected as the sacrificial lamb, found her gaze straying to Pickett.

"So what happens now?" she asked the magistrate.

"I'll pass the information along to the Runner assigned to the case. He will need to question both Vladimir and his wife — Natasha, did you say her name was? — and then begin making inquiries at pawnshops in the area."

Julia was about to mention her own visit with Natasha, but at the mention of pawnshops her hand jerked convulsively, sending her wine sloshing over the edge of the cup. "P — pawnshops, did you say?" She became very busy mopping up the spill, hiding her expressive countenance from the magistrate in the process. "Why pawnshops?"

"The thief — let us assume for the moment that it is Natasha — cannot possibly wear the diamonds, for they would be

275

recognized at once," explained Mr. Colquhoun, putting forth the same argument that she herself had made to Natasha Ivanova Dombrowskaya. "The logical assumption, therefore, is that she — or her husband — will attempt to sell them."

"But — but surely the thief, assuming him or her to be Russian, would wait until his return to Russia to sell the diamonds," argued Julia rather desperately.

"Do you think so?" asked Mr. Colquhoun, scowling as if this possibility had not occurred to him. "Why, if I may ask?"

"If they were sold while still in England, the payment would be made in British pounds," she pointed out. "Surely it would be better to wait and be paid in rubles, or whatever they use in Russia."

"Hmm, I see your point," acknowledged the magistrate. "Still, gold is welcome in any country, and our thief will doubtless want to dispose of the diamonds as quickly as possible. And then there is the fact that the other stolen jewels have been recovered at pawnshops. If Vladimir and his wife are the thieves, then we must assume this theft has nothing to do with the others except perhaps providing the inspiration. But if it was perpetrated by the same person and in the same manner as the others, then it stands to reason that the diamonds will most likely be disposed of in the same way."

"I see," said Julia in faltering tones, realizing that to belabor the point would only raise the magistrate's suspicions. She told herself that even if the Runner should discover the pawnshop where Lucy had sold the diamonds, his first concern would most likely be recovering the jewels. Surely, she thought desperately, any pawnbroker dealing in stolen goods would be extremely reluctant to reveal his sources, thus killing the goose that laid the golden eggs. Unfortunately, she could not quite make herself believe it. She feared the pawnbroker would be only too eager to offer up his supplier in order to divert Bow Street's attention from himself. She could only hope that the Runner assigned to the case would limit his search to pawnshops in the main thoroughfares, and leave unexplored the more obscure streets such as Lucy frequented.

The thought of the diamonds being traced back to Mr. Pickett was enough to deprive her of any appetite, and she let Mr. Colquhoun finish off the last of the feast, which he did with enthusiasm. He insisted upon cleaning up the dishes, since she had provided the meal, and she allowed herself to be persuaded; she remembered the tea fiasco all too clearly, and had no desire to reveal her ignorance of domestic tasks any further than she had done already.

Scarcely had the magistrate completed this chore and begun to take his leave when a pounding on the door shook the very walls, and a voice from without called, "Open this door, Cousin Julia! I know you're in there!"

"Oh, no!" exclaimed Lady Fieldhurst in failing accents. "George!"

" 'George'?" echoed Mr. Colquhoun.

"Lord Fieldhurst, I should say," she explained, regarding the door with distaste. "My husband's — my *late* husband's — cousin and heir."

"How did he know where to find you?"

"He has known of my whereabouts since the day after the fire."

His brow cleared. "Well, then! If he had any objections to your presence here, surely he must have voiced them before now."

"Oh, he has done so, I assure you! But I fear what has brought him down upon my head was a certain letter I sent to my solicitor, thanking him for his efforts on my behalf regarding the annulment of my marriage to Mr. Pickett, and informing him that further action on his part will not be necessary."

"I see." Mr. Colquhoun scowled fiercely as a fresh volley of blows resounded on the other side of the door.

"I shall have to face him sooner or later," said her ladyship with a sigh. "I suppose I might as well have done with it."

She moved toward the door, but the magistrate's voice held her back. "My lady, do you want me to stay? Perhaps I could reassure him as to the boy's prospects."

She had to smile at that. "I seem to recall your telling me that his prospects were no more than what he made them. Thank you, Mr. Colquhoun, but no. Mr. Pickett needs no one to defend him, and I" — she took a deep, steadying breath — "I must do this for myself."

And so saying, she grasped the knob and opened the door.

The viscount blinked at the sight of her in what Mr. Colquhoun had termed full regalia, and Julia was doubly glad that she had not taken the time to return home and change clothes.

"About time, too, Cousin Julia," scolded George, recovering himself quickly. He brushed past her into the flat, carrying in his wake two females: one an elderly lady clad in mourning draperies of unrelieved black, the other a woman of middle age wearing a russet pelisse and an apologetic smile.

Julia held her coronet-crowned head high. "Good afternoon, George," she said with crushing civility. "Mother Fieldhurst, and — my lady." She was never quite sure how to address George's wife, since they both bore the title of Lady Fieldhurst. Fortunately, it was a dilemma that arose but rarely, since she made a point of avoiding the current viscount as much as possible. "May I present Mr. Patrick Colquhoun, magistrate of the Bow Street Public Office? Mr. Colquhoun, Lord Fieldhurst, the dowager Lady Fieldhurst, and the current viscountess."

Bows and curtsies were exchanged, as even the barest courtesy required, and then Mr. Colquhoun turned to her and took her hands in his.

"I'll be leaving you now, my lady. Unless," he lowered his voice, "you are quite certain you do not want me to stay?"

"Thank you, Mr. Colquhoun, but I am quite certain."

"Very well, then. Good luck to you." He gave her hands a reassuring little squeeze, and left her alone to confront her late husband's disapproving relations.

"Won't you come in?" Julia urged the trio,

gesturing toward the bedroom door. "I have been closing this room off in order to keep it as warm as possible."

"I have come to put a stop to this nonsense once and for all," the viscount informed her roundly, following her into the bedroom where Pickett lay. "Gather whatever things you may have brought here, and we shall go. The carriage is waiting below."

She sat on the edge of Pickett's bed and gestured for her unwelcome visitors to take a seat. "I have already explained to you, George, why that is quite impossible."

He plopped down onto the middle one of the three straight chairs, then waited until his ladies had taken their seats on either side of him before announcing, "You are making yourself ridiculous, Cousin Julia!"

"Am I? But I suspect it is not *my* appearing ridiculous, but *yours* that is your primary concern."

"Never mind that! It is your responsibility as a Fieldhurst to —"

The moment had come. She took Pickett's unresponsive hand in both of hers and clutched it tightly, drawing strength from his weakness. "But I am not a Fieldhurst, not anymore. I am Mrs. John Pickett."

"My smelling salts!" The dowager viscountess fumbled in her reticule for her vinaigrette, then raised the tiny silver filigree box to her nose and sniffed its aromatic contents.

"Yes, so Mr. Crumpton informs me." Lord Fieldhurst reached into his coat and extracted a folded paper. "I have here a letter to Mr. Crumpton —"

Julia sighed. "I rather thought you might."

"It is purportedly from you, although I find it almost impossible to believe that even you would take so foolhardy a step. It says you intend to drop the annulment proceedings and remain married to this — this —" Words failed him.

"This *man,* George. I realize the concept might be foreign to you, but Mr. Pickett is a *man.*"

The viscount shot to his feet and began to pace. "Damn it, Julia, I'll not have it! Frederick must be spinning in his grave!"

At the mention of her murdered son, the dowager Lady Fieldhurst blew her nose loudly into a black-bordered handkerchief. Still, the beady eyes glaring at Julia over the delicate folds of cambric were sufficient to inform her that the gesture was less indicative of grief than an attempt to bring her errant daughter-in-law to a sense of her own guilt. Julia lifted her chin, refusing to be intimidated.

"What you will or will not have, George, has very little to say to the matter. And since Frederick is dead, his thoughts on the subject, if indeed he has any at all, need not concern me."

George turned quite purple in the face. "For God's sake, Julia, take a good look at yourself, and then look about you!" The sweep of his arm encompassed everything from the coronet on her head to the small, shabby room in which they sat. "You were once mistress of Fieldhurst Hall! Is *this* what you want?"

"No." Julia's gaze shifted to the sleeping form of the man whose hand she still held. "*This* is what I want."

"By God, Julia, I'll not —"

"Sit down, George."

George's wife never raised her voice, but when she spoke it had the effect of a gunshot.

"I beg your pardon, Henrietta?" demanded George, his expression that of a man whose favorite spaniel had suddenly turned and bitten his hand.

"It is not my pardon you should be begging, but Julia's. It is obvious that she is very devoted to this young man and, well, one has only to consider his actions on her behalf over the last ten months to guess his feelings for her."

"But — but —" George sputtered. "A Fieldhurst and a *Bow Street Runner,* of all people? I should feel as if I were failing in my duty to poor Frederick if I did not make some attempt to bring his widow to a consciousness of her own folly!"

"Julia was a good wife to your cousin while he was alive, George, but Frederick is dead. Neither he, nor you, nor any of the Fieldhursts have any further claim on her." As George wavered, his wife delivered her home thrust, with the gentlest of smiles on her face. "Let her alone, my dear. Perhaps if we had been as strong as she when we were first wed, a great many people would have been spared a lot of unnecessary pain."

She meant, of course, that *he* should have been as strong, and everyone in the room knew it. For it was not Henrietta but George who had made a bigamous marriage and sired three illegitimate sons by a woman who had every reason to believe herself legally wed, while his true wife, married earlier and in secret, lived as a fallen woman with her own two sons — the legitimate Fieldhurst heir and his younger brother.

"Very well," muttered George, giving up the battle he realized he could not win. "But know this, Cousin Julia: I will never receive

Mrs. John Pickett, and if I should chance to meet her in public, I shall refuse to acknowledge her!"

"Oh, George!" exclaimed Julia. "Do you *promise*?"

George merely glared at her, then swept from the room with the tattered remains of his dignity drawn tightly about him. The dowager trailed behind him, as did his wife, who turned back at the door to address Julia.

"May I be the first to wish you very happy, my dear?"

"Thank you. And — what you said in there — I am very much obliged to you, my lady."

She laughed at that. "Oh, please call me Henrietta. We should sound utterly ridiculous 'my ladying' one another."

"George assures me that will never be an issue," Julia reminded her ruefully.

"As to that, well, try not to mind George too much, my dear. He has never felt himself competent to succeed your husband, and he attempts to compensate for his inadequacy with bluster. Once one understands that, much can be forgiven him."

"You are very generous, my la — Henrietta," Julia observed. "I wonder if his other wife would agree."

"I said 'much' not 'all,' " the viscountess pointed out with a twinkle in her eye. "As far as your own marriage is concerned, George must of course do as he thinks best, but I confess I should very much like to meet your Mr. Pickett — to meet him socially, that is. I spoke to him once, very briefly, while he was investigating Lord Fieldhurst's murder. While I think we had best not inflict poor George on your husband until he has had a little time to grow accustomed to the match, I hope you will bring Mr. Pickett to tea one day. George usually takes tea at his club on Monday and Wednesday. If you should care to call, you and your husband may both be certain of a welcome."

"Thank you — Henrietta," Julia said again, wondering, not for the first time, what this lovely woman had ever seen in George. "I may well do that."

"Henrietta!" bellowed George from somewhere beyond the door.

"I'm coming, dear," called the viscountess, rolling her eyes at Julia in a droll expression before taking her leave.

After they had gone, Julia closed the door, let out a long breath, and returned to Pickett's room.

"We did it!" she crowed, taking up her usual place on the edge of the bed and clasping his hand in both of hers. "Oh my dear, I wish you could have heard."

Her smile faded at his utter lack of response. She freed one of her hands so that she might stroke her fingers through his tangled curls. "I never could have done it without you, you know. I have allowed myself to be ruled by the Fieldhursts for seven years. Until I met you, it had never occurred to me that I might do otherwise. I don't know how I came to be so — so *spineless*! I was not always so; I suppose Frederick must have worn me down. But those days are over, and it is all because of you."

Liberally dosed with laudanum, Pickett nevertheless heard his lady's voice and opened his heavy eyes. Lady Fieldhurst sat on the edge of his bed, smiling radiantly and wearing — was that really a crown on her head? He squeezed his eyes shut and opened them again with an effort. Lady Fieldhurst was still there, and yes, she wore a jeweled crown on her head.

His foggy brain could supply only one explanation. The annulment had been granted, and she had married one of the royals. Which one? The Prince of Wales was already married, as was the Duke of York; she'd pointed out his duchess in the royal box. How many royal dukes were there, anyway? He hoped she hadn't married the Duke of Cumberland; she'd said she didn't like dancing with the Duke of Cumberland. He'd danced with her himself, once, on a dark terrace in Scotland. And to think that they'd been married at the time, and hadn't even known it. He wondered if she'd liked dancing with him better than dancing with the Duke of Cumberland. Still, there was something wrong — she ought to be somewhere else, St. James's Palace, maybe . . .

"Shouldn't be here," he said, his voice slurred from laudanum. "Husband won't like it."

"*You* are my husband, John," she said, laughing as if the whole thing were a great joke. Which he supposed it must be to her, a thief-taker thinking that a viscountess would ever want to be his wife . . .

"No," he insisted. "Royal duke. Best go back . . . back to the palace."

The effort was too much. She was no longer his. She never really had been. She was married to someone else, so there was no reason not to surrender to the blackness that was always lurking in the corners of his consciousness, waiting to reclaim him. He gave in to the darkness. There was no reason not to, now.

" 'Royal duke'?" echoed Julia in bewilderment, struggling to make sense of his fevered mutterings. It seemed strange to think that he still labored under the belief that their marriage would soon be annulled, when in her own imagination she had already borne him off to her residence in Curzon Street and installed him there as the master of the house. "I would love to know what thoughts are stirring in that usually clever brain of yours. Oh well, never mind. Just rest now, darling."

She leaned forward to drop a kiss onto his brow, and the jeweled coronet that she had all but forgotten escaped the pins that anchored it to her hair. It slid off her head and landed at a crazy angle on his. Enlightenment dawned.

"Ah! I suppose that makes a certain sort of sense." She straightened the coronet on his head, and sat upright to study the result. "John Pickett, Duke of Drury Lane. And your Duchess loves you very much."

CHAPTER 16

A CONSUMMATION DEVOUTLY
TO BE WISHED

It was with some misgivings that Mr. Colquhoun left Lady Fieldhurst to the tender mercies of her late husband's family. He hoped she would not allow them to browbeat her. It was true that at one time he'd had no very high opinion of her ladyship, when he'd believed her to be amusing herself at John Pickett's expense by encouraging affections she had no intention of returning. Since then, however, he'd come to the realization that she was not at all the frivolous Society lady he'd once thought; in fact, he had been surprised to discover that she was a woman of hidden depths, and that her affection for his protégé was as sincere as his own. He only hoped her strength of character was sufficient to withstand the pressures brought to bear by the Fieldhurst cabal; he would hate to see the boy lose his lady this late in the game.

Such were the magistrate's reflections as

he made his way to the Bow Street Public Office. Once there, however, he was obliged to set these thoughts aside and turn his attention to the more pressing issue of the missing diamonds. He took his usual place at the bench and summoned William Foote.

"I have a job for you, Mr. Foote, and frankly, I don't envy you the task," he began. "It has come to my attention that our friend Vladimir Gregorovich Dombrowsky and his wife may have had reason to steal the diamonds themselves."

"The Russians?" Mr. Foote's eyebrows drew together in a thoughtful frown. "But surely they haven't been in England long enough. The first thefts took place just before Christmas, did they not?"

The magistrate nodded. "Yes, and the Princess Olga and her entourage arrived in this country only six weeks ago, in mid-January. I don't mean to suggest that they have been behind all the thefts. But they will certainly have heard of the others, and who knows what ideas the knowledge may have put into their heads? We have it on excellent authority, the Princess Olga herself, that the Dombrowskys are in need of funds. Perhaps they saw an opportunity to steal the Princess Olga's diamonds, knowing that their crime would be mistaken for one of a string that began while they were still in Russia."

Mr. Foote shook his head. "I don't know. It seems unlikely, if I may say so. To my mind, it's more probable that all the thefts were committed by the same person."

"Aye, and you may be right, but the possibility bears looking into, nonetheless. You'll have to question the fellow, and his wife, too. You'll find them at Grillon's Hotel in Albemarle Street. And try to use a little diplomacy, mind you! It won't do to set his back up, and if you can contrive to accomplish the thing without letting him realize he's under suspicion, so much the better."

"I'll do my best," promised Mr. Foote.

Mr. Colquhoun gave a grunt of acknowledgment. He didn't doubt Foote's sincerity, but he did have his reservations as to just how good Mr. Foote's best would be. Although the man was efficient enough at his work, and there was no denying the fact that he'd enjoyed a prodigious run of luck in recovering most of the other stolen jewels, Mr. Foote was not particularly well liked among the Bow Street force, and Mr. Colquhoun found it unlikely that the upper classes would take to him any more readily than the middling ones had done.

No, his choice for the task, had that young man been available, would have been John Pickett. Not that he would have wished the temperamental Russian on the boy, precisely, but Pickett had a gift for mimicry that allowed him to imitate the speech of his betters without even being aware that he was doing so. Then, too, there was his association with Lady Fieldhurst; not the least benefit of that unusual pairing was the fact that the lad had become at least somewhat accustomed to rubbing elbows with the aristocracy. It occurred to Mr. Colquhoun that their marriage, though not without its own unique challenges, might well prove to be the making of both parties — provided, of course, that her ladyship had the gumption to stick to her guns against her late husband's family.

Well, he would certainly be curious to know how that interview had come out, but he doubted he would have an opportunity to find out before morning; having given Mr. Foote his orders, he felt himself duty bound to be present in Bow Street to hear the results of the senior Runner's inquiries.

"While you are about it, Mr. Foote," he added, "I shall also expect you to comb the pawnshops, just in case Dombrowsky — if in fact he is the thief — should attempt to convert the diamonds to ready money before returning to Russia, where the jewels would be much more likely to be recognized."

"Begging your pardon, sir, but I've already begun to do so."

"Good man! I'm sure I need not tell you that, should they turn up, you are to try and find out anything you can about who brought them in."

"Of course," said Foote, scrawling in his notebook. "Mind you, I've tried to do so with all the other jewels, but with no success. Up to this point, our thief — or thieves, whichever the case may be — has hidden his tracks well."

"Ah well, he may slip up yet," said Mr. Colquhoun with a sigh. "Then we'll have him. In the meantime, learn what you can, and keep me informed of your findings."

Mr. Foote, correctly interpreting this as a dismissal, took his leave and set out on his assigned task.

That night, having divested herself of her preponderance of jewelry as well as her cumbersome presentation gown (although this last was not accomplished without difficulty), Julia pulled her pink wrapper on over her petticoat and stays, then settled down once more with *The Vicar of Wakefield.*

" 'Chapter Four'," she read aloud, " 'a proof that even the humblest fortune may grant happiness, which depends not on circumstances, but on — ' "

"My lady?"

"Yes, John?" At the sound of his voice, she laid the book aside and moved to sit on the edge of the bed. "How do you feel?" She laid her hand on his forehead, and while it was still far from cool, she thought it not quite so warm as it had been.

"My lady, tell me the truth." His eyes were bright with fever, but his gaze was sharper, more focused than it had been a few hours earlier, when he'd been babbling about royal dukes. "Am I going to die?"

"Why, no, my darling, of course you're not going to die!" she insisted with a vehemence quite unsuited to the sickroom. "You're getting better every day."

His brow puckered in bewilderment. "What — what did you say?"

"I said you're not going to die."

"No — something else. What did you call me?"

The moment of reckoning, it seemed, was at hand. "I called you my darling," she said, blushing a little.

"Thought so." He let out a sigh, and his eyes fluttered closed. "Dreaming again."

"No, you are not dreaming," she insisted. "I do love you, John. I didn't know how much, until I thought —"

"Not dreaming," muttered Pickett, turning away. "Delirious."

The time for talking was past. She cupped his face in her hands and, very gently lest she aggravate his injury, turned his head toward her and kissed him slowly and thoroughly on his parched lips.

"Are there any more questions, Mr. Pickett?" she asked when at last she broke the kiss.

He blinked in confusion. "You — you love me?"

She nodded. "Very, very much."

"Thank you — thank you for telling me," he said. "It's enough, just knowing. At least — at least it wasn't just me."

Julia listened to this disjointed speech in growing dismay. "Surely you cannot think I intend to let you go — not now, not after I came so close to losing you! No, my dear, I will not have it! The Fieldhursts may do their worst, but I will not give you up!"

"You mean — you're going to be my wife?"

"I'm already your wife, my darling, and I

intend to remain so."

"Really my wife?" he asked urgently, clutching at her sleeve.

"If you want me."

"*If* I want you?" He squeezed his eyes shut, then opened them again. "I don't doubt I'll leave you a widow again soon enough, but until then — my lady, if you're really going to be my wife, can we — can I — I don't want to die without making love to you, just once."

"You're not going to die, my darling, I won't let you," she insisted, but shrugged out of her pink wrapper and let it fall, then leaned down to kiss him again.

He was a rather more active participant this time, burying his fingers in her coiffure and returning her kiss with all the fervor of which he was capable.

"My lady," he murmured against her mouth, "may I take down your hair?"

"If you like," she answered softly, her words almost lost in their kiss.

"Oh, I like," he groaned, plucking out pins until the long curls spilled over her shoulders and onto his pillow, enclosing them both within a golden curtain.

With a strength that surprised her (and an exertion for which he would certainly pay the next morning), he tightened his arm about her waist and rolled over in the bed, bearing her with him until she was pinned beneath his weight. The movement dislodged a square of folded cambric from her stays, and it fell out onto the mattress.

"What — ?" Pickett began, recognizing one of his own handkerchiefs.

"A lock of your hair," she explained, moving it out of harm's way. "The doctor had to cut it, and I asked him if I might have it. Oh, John, I was so afraid it was all I would have left of you!"

"My lady —" He had to ask, even though he might not like the answer. " — are you absolutely certain you want to do this? The annulment — there'll be no turning back —"

She silenced him by putting her fingers to his lips. "There has been no turning back for me for some time now."

It was all the reassurance he needed. "My lady," he breathed. "My only love — *my lady* —"

As the candle on the bedside table burned lower, he explored with reverence and wonder all the secret places to which it was his right as her husband to have access. And by the time the candle finally guttered in its socket, the thief-taker and the viscountess had become man and wife indeed.

■ ■ ■ ■

His fever rose in the night, and Julia castigated herself roundly for allowing him —
no, *encouraging* him! — to exert himself.
Reluctantly slipping out of the bed and away
from the warmth of her sleeping husband,
she scurried across the room to the bureau,
snatched her night rail from the drawer, and
pulled it over her head. She padded barefoot
to the fireplace, then picked up the poker
and set about effecting repairs to the fire. It
flared back to life as she stirred the coals,
and she turned to regard John Pickett —
who was no longer a virgin — in the flickering light.

It had been too hasty a coupling to be
truly satisfying; apparently his fears of dying
before consummating the marriage had not
been exaggerated. Still, if this should prove
to be his only opportunity, then he deserved
the chance to conduct the exercise exactly
as he wished; she would treasure it all the
more, knowing it might be all they would
ever have. On the other hand, if he were to
recover . . .

Her lips curved in a little smile of womanly
wisdom. If he were to recover, they would
have the rest of their lives to do the thing

properly. She set aside the poker, slipped back into bed, and curled up against his side. She was still smiling when she fell asleep.

Mr. Colquhoun reached the Bow Street Public Office the next morning to find William Foote pacing back and forth before the magistrate's bench.

"Good morning, Mr. Foote. Have you been waiting for me? Dare I hope for news on the theft of the Princess Olga's diamonds?"

The senior Runner inclined his head in acknowledgment. "Yes, sir. In fact, I am in need of an arrest warrant."

The magistrate's eyebrows arched toward his hairline. "Excellent work! I confess, I had not hoped for success so soon." He took his place at the bench and reached for parchment and quill. "Your meeting with His Excellency Vladimir Gregorovich must have been most productive. Who are we arresting? Is it he, or someone else?"

"Someone else entirely, I'm afraid," Mr. Foote confessed, his gaze sliding away from that of the magistrate.

"Who, then?"

"You won't like it, sir," cautioned Mr. Foote.

"Faugh! I'm not here to administer justice only when it suits me," Mr. Colquhoun growled. "Let's have it with no roundaboutation, Mr. Foote. For whose arrest am I to issue a warrant?"

"I should like you to write out a warrant for the arrest of Mr. John Pickett of Drury Lane."

Mr. Colquhoun's face grew quite purple, and he threw down his quill. "You, sir, may go to the devil!"

"I assure you, I would not make such a request without sufficient evidence to back it up," said Mr. Foote, reaching into the pocket of his coat. He withdrew a necklace of sparkling white stones the size of wrens' eggs, and laid it on the bench. "I discovered this in a pawnshop in Feathers Court, and took the liberty of redeeming it for the sum of two shillings and six pence. I trust the department will reimburse me for expenses?"

"Never mind that," said the magistrate impatiently. "I should like to know what the devil made you think Mr. Pickett was the one doing the pawning!"

"May I remind you, sir, that Feathers Court opens onto Drury Lane only a stone's throw from Mr. Pickett's hired lodgings?"

"And may *I* remind *you*, Mr. Foote, that

Mr. Pickett has been lying insensible in his bed ever since the night of the fire? He is at present in no condition to pawn anything, stolen or no!"

"He must have had a confederate, of course. No doubt the plans were in place long before the fire." Seeing Mr. Colquhoun fairly quivering with fury, he added, "You must admit, sir, the proximity of the pawnshop to Mr. Pickett's residence cannot be ignored."

"I'll admit no such thing, sirrah! Mr. Pickett is far from the only person living in Drury Lane. Furthermore, one is not obliged to live in a particular street to avail oneself of its pawnshops. Oh, and perhaps you will explain why the devil Mr. Pickett should go to the trouble of stealing jewels worth a king's ransom only to pawn them for such a paltry sum. Pray tell me that, since you appear to have thought it all out."

Mr. Foote nodded in sympathetic understanding. "You are upset, sir, and I'm sure I don't wonder at it. But I spoke to the proprietor of the pawnshop, a fellow called Baumgarten, and he was able to identify the person who brought the jewels in." He paused a moment. "The seller was a young prostitute well known in the area, one Lucy Higgins by name."

Mr. Colquhoun groped behind him for his chair, and sat down heavily. Mr. Foote's so-called evidence was purely circumstantial, he told himself with more than a trace of desperation. It would never stand up in court. And yet . . . and yet he knew himself that John Pickett occasionally enlisted Lucy Higgins's aid, and he would be compelled to admit as much in court, should he be called upon to testify. He also knew of the boy's disreputable past, and that, too, would certainly come to light during any trial.

If it were anyone else, he would say it was his duty to write out the arrest warrant and let the truth, whatever it was, come out in court. He could do no less now. The cause of Justice, to which he had devoted so many years of his life, now demanded that he sacrifice a young man who stood in the place of a son to him. Strange how Justice did not seem nearly as noble a mistress as she had only half an hour ago. Well, he would hire the boy's defense counsel himself, he determined, and if his own testimony was requested as a character witness, then by God he would be eager to take the stand.

"Sir?" prompted Mr. Foote, clearly waiting.

Mr. Colquhoun snatched up parchment

303

and quill, then wrote out the warrant and signed his name with a flourish.

"There is your warrant, Mr. Foote," he said, thrusting the still-wet paper at him. "And may you rot in hell with it!"

"I realize how hard this is for you —" the senior Runner began, and although his tone was conciliating, it seemed to Mr. Colquhoun that there was something smug, even gloating, in his expression.

"Aye, you're enjoying this, aren't you? You wanted a warrant, you've got it, damn you!" bellowed the magistrate. "Now, get out of my sight!"

"Yes, sir." Mr. Foote rolled up the paper and tucked it into the hollow end of his black tipstaff, then made an apologetic little bow before turning and leaving the Bow Street Public Office with his tipstaff tucked beneath his arm.

His tipstaff, thought Mr. Colquhoun, watching him go. His tipstaff, made of wood and painted black . . .

No, it wasn't possible. Mr. Foote made no secret of his dislike for John Pickett, and he was certainly envious of the younger man's success. Still, from professional jealousy to attempted murder required quite a leap, and surely one no officer of the King's peace would be capable of making.

He complained of his feet hurting, Lady Fieldhurst had said. *One of his feet, anyway, although he didn't say which . . .* And one of his feet, the magistrate realized with growing conviction, would have been "foot." Was it possible that John Pickett, barely conscious, had not been complaining of pain as her ladyship had thought, but had been attempting to identify his attacker?

"Excuse me, Mr. Colquhoun, may I have a moment —"

"Later, Mr. Marshall," said the magistrate, brushing off another Runner who had approached the bench requesting his attention. "There's something I must do now."

He left the bench without a backward glance and set out for Drury Lane.

CHAPTER 17

AN END, AND A BEGINNING

A knock on the door awakened Julia the next morning, and she realized that the sheets beneath her were clammy. Almost afraid to hope, she laid her hand against Pickett's forehead, and found it cool and beaded with sweat; the fever had apparently broken while he slept.

She had no time to ponder the significance of this discovery, however. The knock sounded again, more urgently this time, and she scrambled out of bed, eager to impart the good news to Mr. Colquhoun. She shrugged on her pink wrapper and tied its belt about her waist, then turned to regard her oblivious husband, still sunk in what she hoped was nothing more than a deep and satiated sleep.

"That will be your magistrate," she predicted, then added mischievously, "You needn't be embarrassed, darling. He won't be able to tell the difference by looking at you."

She dropped a light kiss on his forehead — which still didn't wake him — and went to answer the door.

"Good news, Mr. Colquhoun —"

The words died a-borning. The man standing just outside was not the magistrate but a stranger who somehow looked vaguely familiar, a man in his mid-thirties with straw-colored hair, a beaky nose, and rather cold blue eyes.

"I — I beg your pardon," stammered Julia, although there was nothing in the visitor's appearance to render her uncomfortable — unless, perhaps, it was his appearance at Mr. Pickett's door while she was still in her wrapper with her hair trailing down her back. "I'm sorry, I was — expecting someone else."

The stranger nodded. "Mr. Colquhoun."

"You know him?" Even as she asked the question, Julia realized why he seemed familiar. This was one of Mr. Pickett's colleagues, the Runner who had been summoned to the theatre at Drury Lane to investigate the theft of Lady Oversley's emeralds. There was no reason, then, for her nagging sense of unease, much less her quite unreasonable urge to shut the door in his face.

"Yes, I know Mr. Colquhoun very well. In fact, I've come on his orders."

"Of course." To her disquiet was added disappointment. She had hoped to tell the magistrate the good news herself. "You may tell him that Mr. Pickett's fever broke in the night, and although his physician has not yet confirmed it, there is every reason to believe he will make a full recovery."

"That is good to know. I trust Mr. Pickett is in?"

Julia was not quite sure how it had happened, for she had not invited him in, but suddenly the stranger was inside the room, with the open door behind him. "He is, but he is sleeping, and I should not like to wake him. He has been very ill, you know."

"So I understand," said the stranger, slapping his tipstaff against his open palm in a manner Julia found vaguely threatening.

"I shall tell him you called, Mr. — ?"

"Foote. William Foote."

She recalled with sudden clarity Mr. Pickett's first brush with consciousness. *Foot . . .* he'd muttered, tossing to and fro in the bed. *Foot . . .* Perhaps, thought Julia with mounting apprehension, she had not landed on his ankle, after all.

"Yes, well, thank you for calling, Mr.

Foote," she said briskly, preparing to show him the door. "When Mr. Pickett awakens, I shall tell him you stopped by —"

The visitor fumbled in the pocket of his greatcoat. "That won't be necessary, my lady."

She heard a click, and was suddenly staring into the barrel of a pistol.

"I'll be seeing him now, if you please."

Every instinct urged her to shield her slumbering husband, for it was obvious that he, and not she herself, was Mr. Foote's real target. She was frantically trying to think how she might accomplish this without getting them both shot when a noise from the direction of the bedroom drew her attention as well as the unwelcome visitor's.

John Pickett stood framed in the doorway, looking thoroughly disreputable. Beneath the bandage wrapped around his head, his curly brown hair hung in tangles to his shoulders, and his jaw bore almost a week's worth of fine dark beard. He was clad in nothing but his smallclothes, and he held a pistol, which dipped and swayed in his shaky hand. But there was steel in his eye, and Julia wondered how she had ever doubted his ability to kill a man.

"Ah, there you are, Mr. Pickett. I'm pleased to see you up and about." Foote's sidelong glance took in Julia's unbound tresses and *déshabillé*. "It looks like you've been making good use of your time away from Bow Street, but I'm afraid the jig is up. I have a warrant for your arrest for the theft of the Princess Olga Fyodorovna's diamonds, signed by Mr. Colquhoun himself."

Stunned silence greeted this announcement, broken almost at once by Julia.

"Liar!"

"My lady, no —!"

Heedless of Pickett's half-formed protest, she kicked Mr. Foote sharply in the shin. He threw down his tipstaff and seized her wrist, wrenching her arm as he twisted it behind her back and pulled her to himself, holding her before him as a human shield.

"That was a stupid thing to do, your ladyship, but then I suppose our Mr. Pickett's interest in you doesn't involve your brains." He pressed the muzzle of the pistol to the side of her head. "It's a pity I won't be able to see you hang for your crimes, Mr. Pickett, as you should have done ten years ago, but I'm afraid I'll have to shoot you instead. How much easier it would have been for us all if you had died in the fire as you were supposed to, or from the blow I dealt you immediately afterward! It seems you have a hard head."

"Your quarrel is with me, Foote, not her ladyship," said Pickett, and although he could not hold the pistol steady, his gaze, at least, never wavered. "Let her go, and we'll settle this between the two of us."

Foote gave a snort of derision. "And allow her to go running for Colquhoun? Oh yes, he had to sign the warrant after I presented him with the evidence, but he didn't like it one bit. I'll wager it wouldn't take much persuasion to bring him running to rescue his darling."

"Wait," objected Pickett. "What 'evidence'?"

"Why, the Princess Olga's diamonds, of course, discovered at a shop in Feathers Court, where they'd been pawned by Miss Lucy Higgins, who is known to be a friend of yours."

"Lucy?"

"She took them from your bureau drawer," Julia explained. "I'd hidden them there after finding them in your coat pocket."

"But they weren't in my coat pocket," Pickett insisted. "I never had them."

Julia dared not move her head, but she bent a scathing look at her captor out of the corner of her eye. "*You* put them there, didn't you?" It was an accusation, not a question. "That was you outside the theatre, supposedly offering to help!" And he matched in every particular the description given by the young mother who had come in response to her advertisement, but she had been so enthralled with the idea of Vladimir Gregorovich as the guilty party that she had never considered the possibility that the woman's account, and not Mr. Bartlesby's, was the accurate one. Had Mr. Bartlesby seen the Russian leaving the theatre and decided that Monsieur Dombrowsky, as an obvious foreigner, would be a likely scapegoat, or had he invented a description out of whole cloth, only to have it fit a real person by the merest mischance? She supposed it hardly mattered now.

Foote chuckled. "You're finally catching on, aren't you? Yes, I sent you off to fetch a sedan chair while I stayed with Mr. Pickett. It would have been very awkward for me if a certain diamond necklace was discovered on my person, you see. And when I reached inside your coat to plant the diamonds, Mr. Pickett, I could feel your heart still beating and realized I hadn't killed you after all."

"I wonder you didn't finish the job while you had the chance," Pickett said bitterly.

"Oh, I intended to. But a crowd of well-meaning busybodies interrupted, and I was obliged to give up the plan and trust that the blow I'd already struck would eventually do for you. I was reasonably certain that someone would discover the diamonds in your pocket and leap to the obvious conclusion. I never expected her ladyship to interfere, much less Lucy Higgins. Of course, Miss Higgins had no way of knowing that Mr. Baumgarten, the proprietor of that particular pawnshop, has been working hand in glove with me since Christmas. She was hardly out the door before he sent a message to me, informing me that the diamonds had come into his possession after all, just as we'd intended from the first."

"Do you mean to tell me," demanded Pickett, "that all this time you've been pocketing finders' fees, *you've* been the one stealing those jewels?"

"Not doing the actual deed, no," the elder Runner was quick to demur. "I lack your particular gifts in that area. But mine was certainly the brain that devised the scheme. I had a — let's say a friend — working at the Theatre Royal in Drury Lane, whose task it was to relieve those ladies burdened down with baubles. This friend delivered the goods to Mr. Baumgarten's establishment, where I redeemed them for a fraction of their worth, brought them to Bow Street, and saw that they were returned to their rightful owners. The ladies had their trinkets back, I collected a finder's fee — from which I was able to reward my associates and still pocket a tidy profit — and everyone was happy."

"Everyone but Mr. Colquhoun," Pickett said.

It seemed to Julia that he was growing weaker before her eyes. He was swaying on his feet, his pistol arm drooping lower and lower. As she watched, he edged sideways away from the doorway to stand with his back against the wall — leaning against it to support himself, she was certain. And if she recognized the reason for that subtle movement, she had no doubt Mr. Foote did as well.

"As you say, everyone but Mr. Colquhoun." Foote's huff of annoyance was hot and fetid against her ear. "The old man wasn't content with merely returning the valuables to their rightful owners. He wanted an arrest, and when he conceived of his grand scheme, I knew the game was up. I couldn't stop the theft that night — the plans were already in place, and I had no chance to warn my associate — so the best

I could do was to steal them myself before he could do it, and make sure someone else took the blame. Fortunately for me, I knew just the person — someone whose own neck should have been stretched years ago."

"But all this has nothing to do with her ladyship," Pickett pointed out. "Let her go. You have my word that she will go straight back to her own home — no, my lady, I insist," he added, when she made a small sound of protest.

"The word of a pickpocket and a thief," Foote sneered. "Forgive me for not leaping at such a suggestion, Mr. Pickett, but aside from the likelihood that she would run straight to Bow Street in spite of any promises you might make, I have a certain grudge against her ladyship as well. Those damned opera glasses," he explained, seeing his quarry's puzzled expression. "I knew that if I stayed to the rear of the box, I would be invisible to all the Bow Street force except you, and you were stationed all the way across the theatre — able to see a man at the back of the box, but not to identify him, given the width of the building and the distance between us. And then I saw you peering at the royals through a pair of opera glasses. Knowing you for the thorn you've been in my side over the last decade, I knew it was too much to hope that you would fail to recognize me, or to realize what my presence meant."

"I knew you shouldn't have been there," Pickett said. "I remembered Mr. Colquhoun leaving the Bow Street office in your charge."

"Mr. Foote, was it you who urged the royal party to leave the theatre?" asked Julia in coaxing tones. "You must know that the Russians consider you quite a hero. In fact, the Princess Olga has the fixed intention of asking the Prince of Wales to reward you for your efforts on their behalf. Surely you would not wish to do anything now that might compromise their good opinion of you."

"Thank you for the warning, your ladyship, but I am convinced that eradicating vermin will always be seen in a positive light. Besides, the princess might be less impressed with my heroic efforts if she knew that it was I who started the fire in the first place."

"You put almost four thousand people's lives at risk, all for the sake of a diamond necklace?" demanded Pickett, indignation lending a temporary burst of strength.

Foote gave a short bark of laughter. "No, something far more valuable than that — I put almost four thousand people's lives at risk for the sake of saving my own skin. I'll admit it was a rough-and-ready plan, but keep in mind that my original and much neater scheme had already been shot to perdition. I had no doubt that if my associate was caught with the diamonds in his possession, he wouldn't hesitate to name me, so I did what I had to do. To my mind, you were the weak link, the one most likely to be able to identify me, and since I couldn't afford to leave any witnesses, you had to be eliminated. I made sure you would be trapped in your box — and a good thing, too, as I discovered when I saw you with those opera glasses — and then set the fire on my way back to warn the royals. It took hold quickly enough, given the number of candles and the abundance of velvet curtains and varnished woodwork, and in the confusion of their exit, no one noticed when I plucked the diamonds right off the lady's neck."

Pickett's lips twisted in a travesty of a smile. "Welcome to the brotherhood of pickpockets and thieves, Mr. Foote. But you've far surpassed me, you know. Even at my worst, I never tried to kill anyone."

"Believe me, I took no particular pleasure in the thought that other people might have to die — except, of course, where you were concerned. But then, you'd had it coming to you for a decade or more."

"And her ladyship? She was in the box when you locked me in, you know."

"Not 'locked,' Mr. Pickett. I merely wedged a small piece of wood in the door, and the heat from the fire did the rest. As for putting her ladyship in danger, well, her sins may have been minor compared to yours, but such is the price of keeping low company."

Julia's eyes met Pickett's, and she gave him a reassuring little smile. "He sounds so very much like George, doesn't he? What a pity we can't introduce them! They should have got along — if you will pardon the expression! — like a house on fire."

"My lady," breathed Pickett, "you are a marvel."

"Very touching, I'm sure," said Foote, perhaps justifiably annoyed at being reduced to a mere spectator in this scene of his own orchestration. "But it's time now to say goodbye to your high-born whore."

Pickett's nostrils flared at this insult to his lady's honor, and he raised his left hand to help support the pistol in his right.

Foote had the effrontery to laugh. "By all means, shoot, Mr. Pickett, if you are sure you can hit me and not her ladyship."

They stood there at an impasse, Pickett struggling to keep his pistol trained on Foote, while Foote held his own weapon to Julia's head.

"I — I can't — I'm sorry — my lady —"

"Do what you must, John," she said softly. "If you should happen to shoot me by mistake, know that you are already forgiven." She gave him a rather tremulous smile. "If I am going to be killed in any case, I had much rather die at your hand than his."

"And you will not be left to mourn for long," put in Foote, "for you will follow her ladyship very shortly afterward. So shortly, in fact, that it seems almost a pity I can't prolong your suffering, but I dare not delay."

"You'll still have to answer for it, you know," Pickett said. "My landlady is downstairs. At the first sound of a gunshot, she'll be pounding on the door."

"And what will she find? Why, that you became violent when confronted with your crimes. I was obliged to shoot you in self-defense, while your own shot went wide and tragically struck her ladyship, who had been pleading with you to go quietly. So, Mr. Pickett, which is it to be? Will you shoot first, or shall I?"

Suddenly there was a loud report, and Julia felt Mr. Foote jerk convulsively at her back. In the next instant she found herself freed, while her erstwhile captor lay twitching upon the floor in a pool of blood. She whirled about and saw Mr. Colquhoun framed in the doorway, a curl of white smoke rising from the barrel of the pistol in his hand.

"Thank you, sir," rasped Pickett, and slid slowly down the wall, to land in a heap on the floor.

"I can't let you do this, my lady," Pickett insisted.

Almost three hours had passed since Mr. Colquhoun's timely arrival, during which interval the coroner had been sent for and had borne Foote's body away; Mrs. Catchpole had cleaned the bloodstains from the bare wooden floor, complaining all the while (having come running up the stairs at the sound of gunfire, just as Pickett had predicted she would); and Mr. Colquhoun had lifted Pickett bodily off the floor where he had fallen and put him back in bed. He was awake again now, and was seated at the small scarred table between his magistrate and the lady who was his wife.

"Tell her, Mr. Colquhoun," he appealed

to the magistrate. "Tell her she can't throw her life away like this." Clad in shirtsleeves and breeches, he was painfully thin, but looked rather the better for having washed, shaved, and tied his hair back with a ribbon.

Julia, too, looked more presentable after dressing her hair and trading her blood-spattered wrapper for a morning gown of primrose yellow. She now presided over Pickett's table, dispensing tea into chipped and mismatched cups with a grace and elegance that would not have shamed the hundred-year-old Fieldhurst silver tea service.

Mr. Colquhoun, receiving his cup from her hand, shook his head. "I'm sorry, John, but I'm afraid I can't tell her anything of the kind. In fact, I dare not. As I understand it, the last man to cross her was driven from the premises at the point of a knife."

"I beg your pardon?" said Pickett, baffled.

"I shall explain later," Julia promised, chiding the magistrate with a reproachful look. "Will you not have another scone, John? You have had nothing to eat in days, and I refuse to have anyone say that marriage to me has caused you to waste away."

"It seems to me," put in the magistrate, picking up the thread of the conversation that Pickett's protests had interrupted, "that Lord Fieldhurst might well attempt to challenge the marriage in court. Since there have been cases where irregular marriages such as yours were overturned, I would suggest the pair of you circumvent any such legal action by doing the thing properly in church."

"An excellent notion," agreed Julia.

"The annulment comes before the ecclesiastical court in less than two weeks," Pickett objected. "It would take three weeks just to post the banns."

"Precisely," said Mr. Colquhoun, nodding. "That is why I strongly urge you to purchase a special license, so you may have the ceremony whenever and wherever you please. What do you think of a se'ennight hence? My Janet will have returned by that time, and she and I would be delighted to host the wedding breakfast."

"I can't afford a special license," Pickett protested. "And I refuse to let my wife buy her own marriage license. That is," he added hastily, "I *would* refuse, *if* I were really marrying her ladyship." The fact that they were even discussing such a thing, let alone the fact that the two people he loved most in all the world had apparently set aside their differences and were now allied against him, only proved that the world had turned upside-down while he'd lain unconscious.

"I'm sure your scruples do you credit, John," the magistrate said. "That is why I intend to pay for the special license myself. You may consider it a wedding gift. I would do no less for my own son," he added, anticipating Pickett's objections.

"But, sir, I'm not your son," said Pickett, pointing out the obvious.

"No, but by God you should have been, so let's have no more argufication, if you please!"

"Thank you, Mr. Colquhoun, that is very kind of you," said Julia, reaching across the table to give his hand a squeeze. "And I hope you will let us entertain you and Mrs. Colquhoun to dinner, once we are settled. After all, sharing a basket from Grillon's while John slept through the meal can hardly be said to count."

"My lady," said Pickett, interrupting these rosy plans for his future, "I am overwhelmed by the honor you do me, but it will not serve. All the plans are in place for the annulment, even the letter from the physician. I think we should — I *know* we should — we must go through with it," he concluded miserably.

"There will be no annulment, John." Julia

blushed scarlet, but she spoke in a voice that brooked no argument. "There can't be."

Pickett stared at her with an arrested expression. It was Mr. Colquhoun who broke the uncomfortable silence by pushing back his chair and heaving himself to his feet. "Well, well, look at the time," he said, even though there was no clock, or indeed any timepiece, in evidence. "I'd best be going. If you will accompany me as far as the door, John?"

Pickett, correctly interpreting this as a command instead of a request, rose and followed his magistrate rather numbly to the landing just outside the door. Once outside, Mr. Colquhoun shook him warmly by the hand.

"My boy, back in Scotland, when I informed you that you and Lady Fieldhurst had unwittingly contracted a valid marriage, I wished you happy with tongue planted firmly in cheek. I do so again now, but with the utmost sincerity. God's richest blessings upon you both."

"Thank you, sir, but — but we're not married, not really."

"Oho!" exclaimed the magistrate, chuckling. "If her ladyship meant what I think she meant, then you are very much married indeed!"

Pickett flushed crimson. "But I didn't — we haven't — at least, I don't *think* —"

"If you will heed a word of advice, John, every married man learns that there is a time to put one's foot down, and a time to nod and say 'yes, dear.' " He patted Pickett's shoulder. "I think it's time for you to start nodding."

"But sir, she's a viscountess!" protested the befuddled bridegroom, his voice rising on a note of panic. "She could have had anyone!"

"Yes, and she chose you." Seeing his protégé was not convinced, he added, "Don't take it so much to heart, son. I daresay most happily married men feel unworthy of their wives at one time or another. Let yourself be happy. You've earned the right as much as any man I know."

Pickett sighed. "Thank you, sir."

"And now," said Mr. Colquhoun, glancing at the door, "unless I miss my guess, you and your lady wife will have a great deal to say to one another, so I shall leave you to it. Oh, and don't hurry back to Bow Street, mind you! Aside from being a long way from fully recovered, you are, after all, on your honeymoon."

With this Parthian shot the magistrate

turned and headed down the stairs, leaving Pickett to face the woman he'd managed to trap in an accidental marriage in spite of all his good intentions. He found her still sitting at the table, regarding him with a quizzical little smile.

"Well, John?"

"What did you mean, there can't be an annulment?" demanded Pickett, taking the bull by the horns. "Do you mean to say that I — that you — that we —"

"Do you truly not remember?" asked Julia. "Really, I hardly know whether to be amused or insulted."

Pickett frowned thoughtfully, recalling the particularly vivid dream he'd had the previous night. "I remember a little. I thought I must have dreamed it. It wouldn't have been the first time," he confessed sheepishly.

"No, my dear, it was quite real."

He collapsed onto his chair, planted his elbows on the table, and dropped his head into his hands. "Oh, my lady," he groaned. "I am so sorry!"

Her smile faltered. "Are you, indeed? And here I flattered myself that you were pleased."

"I'm not sorry on my own account," he said hastily. "How could I regret the best thing that ever happened to me? But I thought I was going to die. I knew only what I wanted; I had no thought for what I knew I had to do. My lady, why didn't you stop me?" A new and horrifying possibility occurred to him. "I didn't — I never forced myself on you?"

"Not at all," she assured him. "In fact, you were quite gallant, and gave me every opportunity to change my mind. As for your forcing yourself on me, why, you are incapable of such a thing."

Her choice of words was perhaps unfortunate, given the doubts recently cast upon his manhood by the annulment proceedings.

" 'Incapable,' my lady?"

His earlier horror gave way to an almost comical dismay, and she realized the demands of the annulment, combined with his own lack of experience, had left him with a profound lack of confidence where conjugal relations were concerned. It would be her duty and privilege to reassure him on that head.

"I only meant that you are incapable of the sort of brutality that would force itself upon any woman against her will. As for the mechanics, I can assure you that all your parts are in good working order, and will no doubt perform quite delightfully with practice." As he considered the implications of this revelation, she added in a more serious tone, "Unless — John, have your sentiments undergone a change?"

"No!" he exclaimed, appalled at the very suggestion. "How can you think such a thing? You must know that life could hold no greater happiness for me than to have you for my wife! But from the moment I was informed of our marriage, I was determined not to hold you to a union that you could not — *cannot* possibly want!"

"Can I not? You do yourself less than justice, my dear."

He took a deep breath. "My lady, there are things you don't know about me — things quite aside from the obvious difference in our stations. Foote called me a pickpocket and a thief, and he spoke no less than the truth."

"Oh, I know all about that," said her ladyship, dismissing Pickett's disreputable history with a wave of her hand.

"You do?"

"I've watched you pick locks with a hairpin," she reminded him. "I thought it unlikely that you should have learned such a skill from Mr. Colquhoun. In fact, it was he who told me, oh, months ago, while we were in Scotland. I must confess, however, that I am less interested in your past than I am in your future."

"My lady, are you sure this is what you want?" Determined to bring her to some understanding of his own inadequacy, he stood up and spread his empty hands. "I can't give you any of the things you're accustomed to."

"I've had 'things' in abundance, John," she said with a trace of the old bitterness. "In general, I find them vastly overrated."

"I have nothing to offer you," he insisted.

"Nothing except yourself, perhaps, but that is all I want."

How in the world, he wondered, was one to remain noble and self-sacrificing with such a woman? "My lady —" He shook his head in bewilderment. "What did I ever do, to deserve that you should love me?"

"It isn't what you *did,* John, it's what you *are.*"

"A pickpocket and a thief?" he asked ruefully.

She smiled tenderly at him. "Among other things."

"You may feel that way now, but sooner or later you will regret the loss of your friends, your place in Society. If I believed you could really be happy with me —"

"When I was first married to Frederick,"

she said with great deliberation, "if anyone had asked me, I would have sworn we would be blissfully happy for the rest of our lives. You know how that turned out. I am older and wiser now, and I know there are no guarantees. I cannot promise you that I will always be happy, that I will never know a moment's regret. But if the past few months have taught me anything — indeed, the past week alone would have been sufficient to inform me, had I not already made the discovery! — if there is one thing of which I am absolutely certain, it is that I should be utterly miserable without you."

It was an unanswerable argument, for he had endured those same months of misery. There was one more question he had to ask, however, one detail from the dream that had been no dream, which in the harsh light of day seemed even more unbelievable than all the rest. "My lady, did you really keep a lock of my hair in your — in your —" He made a vague gesture in the direction of her bosom.

She stood and laid her hand on his chest. "I kept a lock of your hair against my heart, John. As I told you last night, I was afraid it might be all I would have left of you."

The world might have run mad, but this, at least, he knew how to answer. With the relieved sigh of one abandoning an unequal struggle, he took her in his arms and kissed her quite thoroughly, and suddenly the idea of a marriage between them seemed not only possible, but the most natural thing in the world. At the conclusion of this pleasant exercise, he lifted his head and straightened himself to his full height.

" 'Delightfully,' you said?" A smug little smile played about his mouth.

"With practice," she reminded him. Confidence was one thing, but it would not do to let him grow complacent too soon.

"I see." He stroked his chin, considering this implied criticism. "And does her ladyship have any suggestions as to where I am to get this practice?"

She smiled archly up at him. "Her ladyship does not, but Mrs. Pickett is just full of ideas."

"In that case," he said, bowing deeply from the waist and offering his arm, "Mrs. Pickett, will you do me the honor?"

"Why, Mr. Pickett, I thought you would never ask!"

She laid her hand on his arm with great ceremony, and together they entered the tiny bedroom and shut the door.

AUTHOR'S NOTE

The Theatre Royal in Drury Lane really did burn down on the night of February 24, 1809. The cause of the fire was never discovered, but from the incident we get the charming account of Richard Brimsley Sheridan — playwright, Member of Parliament, and manager of the Drury Lane Theatre — watching the blaze from a nearby coffeehouse. When urged by his friends to go home, he is reported to have said, "Can a man not enjoy a glass of wine by his own fireside?"

While researching the fire for this book, I made a most unwelcome discovery: the theatre was completely empty at the time. Few performances were staged during Lent, and no play, not even a rehearsal, had taken place on that particular night. Now, I'm sure this must have been very good news for all the people who would normally have been in the theatre and thus at risk, but it makes for dull fiction. So, for the purposes of this story, I took it upon myself to fill the theatre to capacity and mount a production of Handel's oratorio *Esther*. Aside from the fact that this particular piece was frequently performed during the Lenten season, the romantic duet between Esther and the king made it an easy choice.

And now, I have a confession to make. When I first began writing this series, I assumed it would end once the romantic relationship between John Pickett and Lady Fieldhurst was resolved. But now, having reached that point, I decided a marriage as unequal as theirs deserved to be explored further. By the time you read these words, I will have completed the sixth book in the series, titled *For Deader or Worse*, in which Pickett faces his greatest challenge yet: meeting his in-laws.

ABOUT THE AUTHOR

Sheri Cobb South is the award-winning author of more than twenty novels, including five titles in the John Pickett mystery series as well as several Regency romances, among them the critically acclaimed *The Weaver Takes a Wife*. A native and longtime resident of Alabama, Sheri recently moved to Loveland, Colorado, with her husband, and now has a stunning view of Long's Peak from her office window. When she is not writing, she enjoys reading, doing needlework, and singing in her church choir. She is also a sucker for old movie musicals and BBC costume dramas. Sheri loves to hear from readers, and invites them to email her at Cobbsouth@aol.com, "Like" her author page on Facebook, and/or visit her website at www.shericobbsouth.com.